Feeling Lucky?

Stunned by the ranger's pitching the gun at his feet, Quinn eyed the weapon lying in the dirt. He considered his odds while a drum pounded hard, sharp beats inside his forehead, inside his swollen chin. He looked up and caught the cold, killing look in the ranger's eyes and heard Maria say quietly, "Sam, don't do this. Don't kill him."

"See what he's doing?" Quinn said over his shoulder to the other two. "He *wants* me to make a move for my shooting iron. He wants me to grab it and come up fighting. But I see through his plan." Staring at the ranger, he gave a tense, knowing grin. "He took all the bullets out of my gun. Didn't you, Ranger? My gun's not loaded, is it?"

Sam stood staring calmly, at ease, yet with his gun hand poised at his side. "There's only one way you'll ever know for sure, Quinn."

RIDERS FROM LONG PINES

Ralph Cotton

A SIGNET BOOK

SIGNET
Published by New American Library, a division of
Penguin Group (USA) Inc., 375 Hudson Street,
New York, New York 10014, USA
Penguin Group (Canada), 90 Eglinton Avenue East, Suite 700, Toronto,
Ontario M4P 2Y3, Canada (a division of Pearson Penguin Canada Inc.)
Penguin Books Ltd., 80 Strand, London WC2R 0RL, England
Penguin Ireland, 25 St. Stephen's Green, Dublin 2,
Ireland (a division of Penguin Books Ltd.)
Penguin Group (Australia), 250 Camberwell Road, Camberwell, Victoria 3124,
Australia (a division of Pearson Australia Group Pty. Ltd.)
Penguin Books India Pvt. Ltd., 11 Community Centre, Panchsheel Park,
New Delhi - 110 017, India
Penguin Group (NZ), 67 Apollo Drive, Rosedale, North Shore 0632,
New Zealand (a division of Pearson New Zealand Ltd.)
Penguin Books (South Africa) (Pty.) Ltd., 24 Sturdee Avenue,
Rosebank, Johannesburg 2196, South Africa

Penguin Books Ltd., Registered Offices:
80 Strand, London WC2R 0RL, England

First published by Signet, an imprint of New American Library,
a division of Penguin Group (USA) Inc.

First Printing, May 2009
10 9 8 7 6 5 4 3 2 1

For Mary Lynn . . . of course

PART 1

Chapter 1

Arizona Ranger Sam Burrack stood at the front corner of an adobe apothecary building, staring up the wide dirt street toward the Wycliffe Bank and Trust Company. A few minutes earlier he'd watched three of four men walk into the bank, each of them wearing riding dusters much like the one he himself wore. The fourth man had stooped down between two of the horses, the reins to all the animals in hand. He appeared to inspect one of the horse's forelegs.

Each of the three who'd walked inside carried saddlebags over their shoulders—empty of course, Sam noted. Each wore his hat pulled low on his forehead. As they had entered the bank, Sam had seen them pull their bandannas up to cover their faces. Any minute now they would come running out, guns blazing, as always, he told himself. He was ready.

A block past the bank, he saw Maria standing at

the corner of an alleyway, also wearing a riding duster, hers concealing the double-barrel she held against her thigh. Sam didn't have to wonder if she was ready. Maria was always ready. He smiled slightly to himself, realizing that to anyone absently watching she would look like any other teamster or trail hand milling about on the boardwalk. He hoped so anyway.

The four robbers were known as the Stockton Gang, gunmen out of New Mexico. They were bank robbers, killers and rogues to the man. There was once six members in the gang, but Sam had put two of them out of business. He had killed one, Ned Bramlet, four months earlier when he trapped Bramlet and "Curly" Lee Krebs in a brothel outside Templeton.

Seeing his saddle pal Bramlet die with his chest blown open had taken an immediate toll on Curly Lee's courage. He'd given up without a fight. Sam had watched him draw a ten-year sentence in Yuma Penitentiary only six weeks ago. It had been Curly Lee who had tipped him about the upcoming bank robbery in Wycliffe.

How had Curly known?

Not only had he *known,* Sam reminded himself, but he'd actually called this job right down to the day, almost to the hour. *Interesting.* Sam considered it, realizing that no robbers he'd ever come upon in his years as a lawman ever knew this far in advance where their next job would be. These kinds of men were never that well organized. The fact that Curly had called this job so closely meant only one thing. There was someone higher-up calling the shots. *But who?* He'd have to give the matter more thought when he had time.

Up the street, out in front of the bank, Stanton "Buckshot" Parks stood up from the pretense of inspecting the horse's foreleg. He looked back and forth, then across the street, where he caught a glimpse of a familiar face before its owner ducked out of sight behind a tall saguaro cactus. "Damn it to hell," Parks growled under his breath. The face he'd seen had been that of Clayton Longworth, chief detective of the Midwest Detective Agency. Clayton Longworth never went anywhere alone, Parks thought.

He looked all around again, then toward the door of the bank, then toward the corner of an alley running alongside the new stone and adobe bank building. Any minute now, Charley Stockton and the Dolan brothers, Cap and Erry, would come out, right into a trap, he told himself. His job was to keep watch and hold the horses. He'd done that well enough. But now that he saw what was awaiting them, he couldn't think of any reason for him to stay there, other than loyalty.

Well . . . loyalty had its place, he thought, but this wasn't it. Crouching down, laying the reins to all of the horses over the hitch rail, he slipped out from among the animals, around the edge of the boardwalk and into a dusty alleyway. As soon as he felt the shadow of the alley engulf him, he broke into a hard run and didn't stop until he reached a corral full of horses behind the town livery barn.

No sooner had Parks slipped away into the alley than the ranger had also caught sight of Detective Chief Longworth. As soon as he saw the detective, he shot a look toward Maria. Had she seen Longworth? He wasn't sure, and he needed to know before the fight started and Maria stepped forward and Longworth mistook her for one of the Stockton Gang and—

It was too late. The door of the bank burst open. The three robbers ran out, guns in the air, firing wildly, creating panic in order to make their getaway. But now Sam's main concern was Maria. He watched her step forward from her position and swing the shotgun up from under her duster. He saw Longworth turn toward her; he saw the detective raise his Colt in her direction.

Maria saw Longworth now, but she also saw the three robbers race across the boardwalk toward their spooked horses. They looked all around for Parks as the animals reared and nickered. "Damn Parks to hell!" Stockton shouted, seeing the unhitched horses turn and race away along the wide dirt street.

Maria had no time to swing her shotgun toward Longworth, and the ranger was not going to stand by and let her get shot, accident or no accident. Facing Longworth while the robbers fired wildly and ran toward any horse in sight, Maria saw the detective fly forward and hit the dirt facedown as the ranger's rifle shot nailed him from behind, high in the left shoulder.

But she had no time to wonder about what she had just seen the ranger do. Cap Dolan, letting out a war whoop, came running toward her from across the street, firing two Colts at once. She braced herself against the waist-high shotgun and pulled the trigger. The impact picked Cap Dolan up and hurled him backward in a spray of blood.

In the street, Erry Dolan saw his brother fall. He turned, standing in the seat of the topless buggy where he'd just jumped up into and thrown its driver to the ground. "Brother Cap!" he shouted, firing at Maria as he spun the buggy quickly and raced straight toward her.

Sam's second rifle shot hit the robber in his chest, picked him up and flung him backward over the rear of the buggy, leaving him facedown, moaning in the dirt. The buggy raced another twenty yards before slowing to a halt in the middle of the dirt street.

Charley Stockton had managed to make it halfway down the boardwalk while the ranger had been busy shooting the detective and Erry Dolan. While he ran, Stockton had reloaded his Colt. Now, as the ranger turned the rifle toward him, Stockton fired repeatedly and shouted at the ranger as he ran, "You won't take me alive, you dirty son of—"

The ranger's shot cut his threat short. The slug hit him in the rib cage just beneath his right arm and sent him crashing through a large glass window and pummeling into a display of sharp farm implements. Barely before the sound of glass breaking and metal implements clanking had settled, the ranger hurried up the street toward Maria. She had walked over to the detective who was lying on the ground and had stood over him.

"Are you all right?" Sam asked her.

"*Sí,* I am all right," Maria assured him. She gestured toward Longworth, who lay clutching the front of his bleeding shoulder. "He is going to need a doctor."

"And here I am," said the man who had been thrown from his buggy. Dusting himself off from his fall into the dirt, he walked toward the downed detective. "I take it this man is not one of the robbers?"

"No," Sam said, "He's a detective with Midwest Detective Agency. His name is Clayton Longworth."

Longworth looked up at the ranger with a strange expression. "You—you shot me, Ranger? Didn't you . . . recognize me?"

"A lot was going on, Chief Longworth," Sam said. "Be glad I didn't hit you dead center." He paused, avoiding Maria's eyes, then asked the wounded detective, "What are you doing working alone anyway, with as many men as you've got?"

"I wanted . . . the Stockton Gang myself," Longworth said in a pained voice as the doctor attended to him. "The fact is . . . most of my detectives have gone over to the Pinkertons. It's hard keeping good help . . . these days. Some of them have turned to outlawing, themselves."

Sam shook his head and looked at Maria, who stood staring at him. "You shot him knowing who he was," she said quietly just between the two of them.

Sam didn't answer.

"I would have taken care of it," Maria said.

"I know you would have," he replied flatly.

When she saw he would offer nothing more on the matter, she said in an even quieter voice, "I cannot have you shooting an innocent man to protect me."

"I didn't kill him," Sam offered.

"You could have," she said.

The ranger just looked at her.

She eased up. "All right, you didn't kill him. But I would have taken care of it."

"I know you would have," he repeated in an unyielding tone.

Before either of them could say any more on the matter, a townsman ran up and said to the doctor, "The one in the street is shot something awful, Doc Wilson! The one in the mercantile is cut to pieces and got a pitchfork through his belly!"

"Tell them I'll be along directly," the doctor said calmly.

"Directly . . . ? But they'll be bled to death, Doc!" the man said excitedly.

"That would certainly save us all some time and

trouble, then, wouldn't it, Willard?" he said over his shoulder.

"What about Buckshot Parks?" Maria asked the ranger while the townsmen hurried back and forth, gawking at the aftermath of the bank robbery gone wrong.

"He outran his shadow getting out of here," said the ranger. "We'll stay on his trail, but I expect he'll hole up for a while. When he sticks his head up, we'll be on him. Parks is a natural-born thief. He won't sit still for long."

At the Cleland Davis spread three cowhands milled about out in front of the bunkhouse, awaiting the return of their trail boss, Jet Mackenzie. When they spotted Mackenzie walking toward them from the big house with four riflemen flanking him, Jock Brewer, the most experienced of the three drovers, pulled his knife blade from a post he'd been throwing it into and said in speculation, "Boys, it looks like the news ain't good."

The three gathered and stepped forward as Mackenzie and the riflemen stopped ten feet away. Mackenzie raised a hand toward the three and said, "Don't none of you boys go flying off the handle when I tell you this."

"We ain't getting paid," Jock Brewer anticipated before Mackenzie could finish speaking.

Chester Cannidy, the leader of the four riflemen, gestured toward Mackenzie and said to Brewer, "This man was your ramrod. Let him talk."

"I'll handle this, Cannidy," said Mackenzie, seeing Brewer eye the rifleman with a stare of hatred.

"Then get to handling it," said Cannidy with a no-nonsense look. "Mr. Grissin wants you out of here."

"Yeah, you make the yard smell like cattle dung," said another rifleman, Elton Long.

"That's enough out of you, Elton," Cannidy said to the grinning rifleman.

The three young drovers had flared, but Mackenzie spoke up to keep things from getting out of hand. "All right, here's the deal," he said to the three drovers. "Long Pines is no longer Cleland Davis' spread. Davin Grissin bought him out while we were on the drive. Grissin has his own men, so we've been let go."

"I told you something was up when they didn't pay for the herd in cash at the railhead," Brewer said to the other two. Then he said bluntly to Mackenzie, "What about our pay?"

Mackenzie swallowed as if to push down a bad taste and replied, "According to Davin Grissin's bookkeeper, we've got no money coming, leastwise not from Grissin. The bookkeeper says Cleland Davis owed us our wages, but he beat us out of our money. He made no arrangements for us to get paid before he left for California."

"That's bull," Brewer cut in. "Clel never cheated a man in his life. Grissin's bookkeeper is lying."

"Keep your mouth shut, Brewer," Cannidy warned. "This ain't the time to spin your opinion."

"I want to talk to Davin Grissin," said Holly Thorpe, another of the three trail hands.

"No, you don't," said Cannidy. "That wouldn't be a smart thing to do, the mood you're in."

"I can try to talk to the man without raising a ruckus," Thorpe insisted.

"You can catch a handful of your teeth too, if you keep on," said Elton Long.

"I said that's enough, Elton," said Cannidy. But then he turned back to Mackenzie. "Finish up and get moving," he said. "I'm sorry. I'm just trying to keep down any trouble here."

"Well, there it is," Mackenzie said, also trying to avoid any trouble. "If we want our pay, we'll have to go collect it in California. Clel is living there with his daughter, Ida."

"Dang it all!" said Jock Brewer. He yanked off his dusty Stetson and slapped it against his thigh. Dust bellowed.

"You boys don't feel no worse than I do," said Mackenzie. "Being trail boss, I feel responsible for—"

Thorpe cut him off, saying, "We don't blame you for nothing, Mac." He fidgeted with his wire-rimmed spectacles, adjusted them on the bridge of his nose and cut a dark glance toward Cannidy and the other three looming riflemen. "We all know who dealt us this dirty hand."

"Don't talk about it here," said Brewer, before Mackenzie could respond. He gave Cannidy and the riflemen a hard stare. "I say we go to town and pull some cork over this. These snakes are itching to show Grissin how tough they are."

"Say, you're not as stupid as you look, cowboy," said Elton, wearing a cold smile. He fished a coin from his vest pocket and flipped it into the dirt at Mackenzie's feet. "Here, let me buy the first round. I know you're all three a little pressed for drinking money." The other two riflemen chuckled. But Cannidy only stared. It was all he could do to keep from turning and bending his rifle barrel over Elton Long's head and firing him on the spot. But he kept quiet, and calm.

The youngest drover, Tad Harper, started to bend down and pick up the coin. But Brewer caught him by his forearm and pulled him away. "Let it lie, Tadpole. He meant that as an insult."

"I want you to know I ain't happy about doing this, Mac," said Cannidy.

"You could have fooled me," Mackenzie said flatly, running his eyes over Elton Long and the other riflemen.

The four drovers mounted their horses and left the Long Pines spread. When they had ridden four miles along the trail toward the town of Albertson, they stopped and sat in silence for a moment until Brewer said, "Well, I've got two dollars in whiskey money. What about you, Mac?"

"Four and some change," said Mackenzie. The two turned to Holly Thorpe.

Thorpe shrugged and looked at them through his

wire-rimmed spectacles. "A dollar something." The three looked at Tad Harper. "What about you, Tadpole?" Thorpe asked him.

"I don't have any money at all," said Harper.

"Well, lucky for you, you're traveling with a flush crowd," Brewer said with a wry chuckle.

Mackenzie let out a tight breath, seeing the other three had unwound a little. "If we can figure a way to drink on seven dollars for the next week, we can ride all the way up to the Bar Y. Clyde Thompson told me himself he'd be looking to take on trail hands the start of the month."

"Think it'll pay better than out last job?" Thorpe asked with mock sarcasm.

"It can't pay any worse," Mackenzie replied, reining his horse to the trail. "Let's go drinking, wash the taste of Long Pines and Davin Grissin from our gullets. I know the livery hostler in Albertson. He'll stake our horses to keep 'til we get ourselves square."

"I thought you said a while back that Davin Grissin was a crook and a sidewinder," said Harper, sidling up to Mackenzie.

"I did say it, Tadpole," said Mackenzie. "I reckon this is what I get for speaking ill of a man behind his back."

Brewer spit and said, "Just so you won't bear that burden of guilt alone, let me say for the world to hear that Grissin is a no-good, thieving, killing, lying, rotten snake—one that was so crooked, he ended up becoming straight." He turned a look to

Harper and said, "You know a man can do that in business, Tadpole. All he has to do is make so much *dirty* money that after a while people begin to admire him for it."

Harper looked at Mackenzie and said, "You said at the railheads that cheating on a cattle count is the same as stealing a man's money from his poke."

"That is what I said, Tadpole," Mackenzie answered patiently.

"So, do you believe a man can be so crooked he turns straight?" Harper asked.

Brewer cut in, saying, "Tadpole, why do you always want to know what Mac believes? Look at him. Do you see any golden halo above his hat?"

"He was our trail boss," Harper replied.

"*Was*," said Brewer. He reached his arm out and gave Mackenzie a little shove. "Now he's as broke and down in the mouth as the rest of us."

Mackenzie shook his head slightly and said, "Jock is right, Tadpole. It turns out I don't know nothing after all. If it takes a man like Grissin to get ahead in the world, I don't know what's to become of the rest of us."

"We all end up eating dust and driving cattle if you ask me," said Holly Thorpe, adjusting his spectacles up on the bridge of his nose. The four rode on into Albertson.

Chapter 2

For more than a week Stanton "Buckshot" Parks had followed back trails and game paths, until he'd located the hideout of two small-time thieves, Henry Moore and his cousin Benson Carnes. For the next week and a half the three had lain low, made plans and lived on bottles of sarsaparilla, cured hog jowl and airtights of beans and sugar beats that Carnes and Moore had stolen out the back door of a trading post nine miles away.

By the end of the second week, Parks had busted a bottle of sarsaparilla on the plank wall and said, gun in hand, "I don't know about you two, but if I don't steal something soon I'm going to go dung-dipping crazy. Have you boys got any jobs worth doing, or is *talking* about it as far you jakes go?"

Henry Moore and Carnes looked at each other knowingly. Finally Moore turned a sharp gaze to Parks and said, "We thought you'd never ask."

That had been four days ago. Now Parks sat atop his horse, a flour sack with eyeholes cut in it lying on his lap. "What's going on down there, Hank?" he asked Moore. He drummed his restless fingertips on the butt of the Colt he'd stolen in broad daylight from the same trading post where Moore and Carnes had stolen the food staples.

"There's plenty going on," Moore said without turning toward him. A moment later, at first sight of the stagecoach rolling around a bend below, Moore turned, facing the other two as he pulled his bandanna up over the bridge of his nose. "Gentlemen, here she comes, right on time," he said. "Let's skin down there and make ourselves some spending money."

Each of the three wore long riding dusters and wide-brimmed plainsmen hats.

Benson Carnes, as he also pulled up his bandanna to cover his face, said, "I've got the shotgun rider. I've owed greedy Jim Blanton a blasting for a long time now."

Parks took off his hat, laid it on his lap, picked up the flour sack and pulled it down over his head. The other two watched him adjust the flour sack until the eyeholes matched his eyes. Then Parks pulled his hat down over it tightly and adjusted the flour sack again.

"Damn, Buckshot," said Carnes, "why don't you wear a bandanna like everybody else? By the time you get yourself primed and proper, the dance will be over." He chuckled at his little joke and looked to Moore for support. "Right, Hank?" he asked.

But Moore didn't answer. He shook his head and tapped his horse forward onto the steep hillside leading down to the dusty basin below.

"Because I *ain't* like everybody else," Parks replied to Carnes in a stiff tone of voice. "So, mind your own business. I've listened to you flap your mouth nigh three weeks now."

Carnes only smiled to himself behind his bandanna. He waited until Parks put his horse forward behind Moore, then let his animal fall in behind him. "I expect that flour sack is something you learned night-riding in Missouri? I heard *all* the James Gang wears them." His voice had a needling edge to it. "Or did you learn it riding with the Stockton Gang? Now, there was a step down, going from the James Gang to Charley Stockton."

Parks caught the sarcasm and replied over his shoulder, "When we're done down here, Carnes, I'll be pleased to discuss the James Gang or Charley Stockton with you, or any *damn* thing else you'd like to talk about, any *damn* place you care to, in any *damn* manner you like to—"

"Shut it, the both of yas," Moore growled back to them. "Get control of yourselves. We've got a job to do here."

The three rode down the narrow path in silence until they reached a spot where they stood hidden behind a stand of boulders alongside the trail. "When you said '*spending money*,'" Parks inquired of Moore, "just how much do you figure we're talking about here?"

"Yeah, I was kinda wondering that myself," said Carnes.

Moore considered it. "With any luck we'll make ourselves a thousand or so apiece," he said to the other two as they listened intently to the stage rolling along the rocky trail. "Does that suit the two of yas?" he asked with a snap to his voice. "We went over all this before we agreed to do it."

"Suits me," Carnes said quickly. "Of course I never used to ride with the rootin'-tootin' bold-as-hell James-Younger Gang." He shot Parks a look from above his bandanna mask. "So maybe I ain't the one to say."

"Yeah, maybe you ain't." Buckshot Parks stared at him through the jagged eyeholes, the flour sack revealing nothing.

Inside the stage, a big spotted cur sat panting in the sweltering desert heat. The animal stared menacingly at the two businessmen seated across from it. Drops of saliva dripped from the animal's lolling tongue and had formed a wide dark spot on the edge of the seat. The two businessmen had ridden in a stunned silence most of the past fifteen miles since boarding the stage at Albertson.

". . . then the bastards threw me out!" Seated next

to the big short-haired dog, retired army colonel Morgan Tanner sat with his tunic open halfway down his chest, revealing a deep, fierce tomahawk scar. He clenched a bottle of rye whisky in his fist. He had rattled on drunkenly above the creak of wood, the fall of hooves and the rumble of wheel. "Eighteen *got*-damned years! I fit Injuns. I fit John Reb. I fit Injuns again! Now the bastards threw me out!" At his free hand an Army Colt lay cocked on the seat. He picked it up and wagged it drunkenly toward the big dog. "So me and Sergeant Tom Haines here is going as far as we can ride. I'm going to beg the heathen Sioux's forgiveness, then put us both to sleep."

The two businessmen looked at each other uncomfortably. One fidgeted on his seat. He cleared his throat and tried to make more pleasant conversation. "So, that's the dog's name, is it . . . Sergeant Tom Haines?" he asked meekly. "A rather unusual name . . ."

"Unusual . . ." The colonel stared at him drunkenly with a malevolent scowl on his weathered face. After a long tense silence he picked up the slack in the dog's thick leather leash, jiggled it and said, "The dog disturbs you gentlemen, does he not? Eeven with this *got*-damned leash and collar on him?"

"Oh no, sir! Not at all," the two were quick to respond. One wiped sweat from his cheek with a handkerchief and ventured, "Although, if you will allow me to interject, I was taken aback upon finding him here. It is not what one will see these days in, say . . . St. Louis, or even Springfi—"

"Then damn St. Louis and muddy Springfield both to hell," said the colonel. "You see which direction my string runs." He wagged the Army Colt toward the rugged high desert.

"Indeed, sir, we do," said the other man, eager to find some common ground. "May I point out that our string runs in much the same direction as yours?"

"Does it, now?" the colonel asked flatly.

"Most certainly it does." Both men nodded quickly as one.

"God help us all," the colonel murmured under his breath, looking away in drunken disgust, out across the harsh, barren land.

The dog stared. Saliva dripped. The two men looked at each other as the stage bounced along the rocky trail.

Atop the stage, the shotgun rider, Jim Blanton, first caught sight of the three riders as they sprang out into the middle of the trail, blocking it. "Don't brake her down, Baggy, you see what this is," Blanton said, cocking both hammers on the double-barreled shotgun.

"Sure enough!" said the driver, Lionel Baggs. His instincts had sent his hand reaching for the long brake handle. But upon seeing the masked faces of the three riders, his hand went back to the traces in his other hand, raised them high and slapped them down hard onto the stage horses' backs.

"Damn it, they ain't stopping!" shouted Carnes, his horse stepping back and forth restlessly beneath him.

"It's *our job* to stop them!" shouted Moore, his rifle already up to his shoulder. He fired repeatedly at the oncoming stage as it speeded up toward him. The other two outlaws quickly followed suit.

Inside the coach, Colonel Tanner lunged upward with the forward thrust of the stage. The dog lunged forward beside him. The two businessmen were flung back against their seats. A handkerchief flew from one's hand. "My goodness! What now?" one of them cried out.

"We've got ourselves a melee, gentlemen!" shouted the colonel. A strange fierce look came into his bloodshot eyes; a wicked grin lit his face. He stuck the cork into the whiskey bottle and palmed it tightly. Even in his drunken state he quickly hitched the dog's thick leather leash around an iron grab bar overhead. "As you were, Sergeant Tom Haines, until further orders!" he shouted above the sound of gunfire.

"What shall we do? What shall we do?" one of the businessmen cried as the stage rumbled through the mounted gunmen, scattering the robbers even as the three fired relentlessly.

"Fight, *got*-damn it!" Colonel Tanner raged. Another Colt appeared as if from out of nowhere. The colonel pitched it into the man's trembling hands. "Fight or die!" he shouted with a maniacal laugh. Turning, the colonel hurled himself sidelong half-way out the stage window. With a loud war cry he fired shot after shot at the robbers as the coach rolled past them. The big dog bounced on the leather seat and barked and growled. Saliva flew in every direction.

"Fight or die?" the businessman cried, his eyes wide with terror, his knuckles turning white as he grasped the Colt. The two jerked back and forth violently with the rough riding coach. "Give me that, Fenton!" the other man shouted, grabbing the Colt from him. He shoved his arm out the other side window, closed his eyes tightly and fired toward one of the three riders.

Atop the stage, Jim Blanton slumped low in the seat, his empty shotgun still in hand. He could not force his right hand to loosen its tight grip on the gaping bullet hole in his bleeding stomach. Out in front of the fast-moving stage, Stanton Parks had managed to jump from his saddle and land atop the lead stage horses. He crawled down between the two running horses and began pulling back on their traces while the driver tried desperately to yank the traces from his hands.

"Load up, Jim," the driver shouted, "he's dragging us down!"

Blanton struggled with loading the shotgun one-handed, the bleeding too profound to take the pressure off the wound.

"Jim, damn it, man!" shouted Baggs.

"I'm done for, Baggy," Blanton said, holding the shotgun over to the driver.

Baggs only had a second to shoot him a glance. "Buck up, man! I need you shotgunning!"

"Aw, hell, Baggy, I'm dead here," Blanton groaned. He collected himself, stuck two fresh loads into the twelve-gauge and cocked both hammers. But before he could get the shotgun up and aimed, a bullet from alongside the stage hit him high in his shoulder. At the same time, a shot from the other side of the stage grazed across Baggs' lower lip, ripping it away in a spray of blood. His bare lower teeth glared as he kept attending to the horses, yanking at the traces, trying to keep Parks from taking control.

From inside the stage, one of Colonel Tanner's shots hit Moore in his side, causing him to veer away and struggle to keep from falling off his saddle. On the other side of the coach, the businessman with the Colt fired the gun's last shot. The bullet hit Carnes in the side of his throat and sent him flying from his horse and rolling into a thick, wide stand of barrel cactus.

On the floor of the coach the other businessman lay dead in a wide pool of dark blood, his forehead agape from a rifle shot. "Fenton, my God!" the other businessman cried, turning from the coach window with the empty Colt in his hand.

"He's dead, *got*-damn it!" shouted the colonel,

swaying wildly with the bouncing, rocking coach. "You will be too, if you don't *fight*!"

"I'm out of bullets," the terror-stricken man called out above the barking, snarling dog and the insistent gunfire.

"Then *by* God, prepare yourself to use it as a club, sir!" shouted the colonel. His eyes were glazed and wild with battle.

He's insane! the businessman noted to himself. Yet, even as he thought it, he turned the Colt around in his hand and grasped the barrel. The two felt the speeding stage began to lurch downward toward a halt amid shouts and cursing from the wounded driver and the equally wounded robbers. "Surrender, you damn fool!" Henry Moore bellowed at the driver, his own bleeding side causing his voice to sound strained and weakened.

"You shot my mouth off, you sons a' bitches!" Baggs shouted, his voice distorted by his missing lip. The dog remained in a bouncing, barking frenzy.

Feeling the stage begin to slow down, the colonel looked at the frightened businessman and shouted, "Hold your position! I'm going up!"

"Oh God!" the man cried, clutching the empty Colt to his chest. He watched the colonel slide out of the swaying coach window like an angry snake and disappear up the side of the cabin.

In the driver's seat, Baggs looked up in time to see the colonel grab him by his shoulders and yank him aside. "What are you doing?" he shouted. Beside them, Moore raced along, his rifle empty, but his Colt out of his holster now, and firing at the colonel from ten feet away.

"I'm getting us out of this!" the colonel shouted, grabbing the traces from Baggs' hands. Standing crouched in the seat, he lashed the traces wildly up and down, slapping Parks' face with them and sending the stage horses back into a hard run. "We're not licked! Not by a long shot!" he bellowed.

A bullet from Moore's Colt hit the colonel high in his ribs. But he only flinched and kept slapping the traces. Parks fell from between the two lead horses and rolled back beneath the other horses' hooves. Taking hard glancing blow after blow without losing consciousness, Parks grasped wildly at the bottom of the stage in a cloud of choking dust.

He managed to hold on just long enough to see the dirt and rock disappear from beneath him as the rear of the stage swung out off the edge of the trail for only a second. With a scream he turned loose just as the stage swung back onto solid ground and shot forward. He held on to an armful of rock and dirt and scrub juniper root as the stage rolled farther away, the shooting and shouting and barking dog traveling with it.

Beneath Parks lay a straight drop of more than a hundred feet onto sharp rocky hillside. He clung and clawed and wrestled himself back onto the trail and lay staring up at the sky for a moment, catching his breath. Then he rose unsteadily to his feet and limped on along the trail, his hat gone and one boot heel missing, dust streaming from his clothes and hair. His flour sack mask had ripped across the top and gathered down around his chin.

"I bet I kill them both—dragging me into a mess like this," he said to himself.

Chapter 3

The colonel remained crouched in the driver's seat, slapping the traces to the horses' backs. Beside him Baggs and Blanton held on for their lives. Alongside the speeding stage Henry Moore kept firing wildly, blood running down his legs from wounds in his chest, his side and his upper shoulder.

"Stop this damn thing!" Moore bellowed above the sound of the rocking, bouncing stage and the thunder of the horses' hooves.

"My goodness, Baggy, this fool is going to kill us all," said Blanton, his voice and demeanor turning weaker and weaker with each passing second.

"Why won't he stop?" Baggy asked through his bloody disfigured mouth, while being slammed back and forth on the narrow wooden seat. "This ain't the first stagecoach that ever got robbed!" He rose in the seat and grabbed the colonel by his sleeve. "Please, sir, for God sakes, stop the stage!"

"No way in hell!" the colonel roared, jerking his sleeve free and slapping the traces even harder.

Seeing the trail begin to narrow even more as it went into a long curve around the hillside, Moore slowed his horse almost to a halt and shook his head. "Damn it to hell, it's only money!" he shouted after the fleeing coach. He watched the stage sway as it rode deeper into the long curve. Its two right wheels lifted inches off the ground for a moment. He heard a scream from one of the wounded coachmen as the coach wheels touched ground with a jar, then rose again.

"Hold on, cayouse," Moore said to the horse beneath him, "this ain't over yet." He watched the stage careen crazily out of sight around the curve. He flinched and grinned at the sound of a crash, and at a large puff of dust that sprang immediately out across the trail.

"That's more like it," he said, tapping his horse forward, this time at a walk. He jerked the bandanna down from his face.

Keeping a hand to his bloody side, his Colt still in his grasp, Moore rounded the curve and stopped a few yards back to look the situation over. Beyond the stage stood a rise of dust where the horses had managed to break free and get away from the harshness of the leather traces at their backs. The stage had veered off the trail, struck a boulder and bounced along for about thirty yards before it stopped. It was now tipped dangerously to one side, its top resting against a sheer rock wall.

Moore sat for a moment, watching the two raised left wheels spin themselves down. "What a damn mess," he said to himself, still holding his side as he swung stiffly down from his saddle.

The coach's door had spilled open on the side facing the rock wall. The dog had been flung out of the tipped-over stage and hung by its collar and leash, its legs kicking in the air, scratching for the ground that lay four feet beneath it. Walking up closer, Moore aimed his Colt at the animal's head and fired. The dog made a sharp *yip* and hung silent and still.

"Poor . . . sumbitch," a voice behind Moore said, causing him to swing his smoking Colt around. But upon seeing Carnes standing with a face and chest full of cactus needles, one bloody hand pressed to the side of his wounded throat, Moore let out a breath.

"You're lucky I didn't shoot *you* . . . walking up on me that way." He saw the gun in Carnes' hand, pointed at his chest. They lowered their guns in unison.

Carnes limped forward, past Moore, toward the leaning stagecoach. His duster was shredded by the barrel cactus where he'd fallen. "Where's the loco sumbitch soldier that caused all this?" he said, gesturing his gun barrel back and forth. Along the trail both carpetbags and leather travel bags had busted open upon impact. The contents lay strewn about amid spilled mail, newspaper and magazines.

Colonel Tanner's raspy voice called out from a ditch running alongside the sheer rock wall, "Here I am, you saddle tramps." He scrambled up onto the trail and stood facing them, holding the double-barreled shotgun with one hand, but with both hammers cocked and ready to fire. "Let us . . . continue on, then."

The shotgun rose with a heavy kick as its first blast hit Carnes full in his chest, picked him up and hurled him backward to the ground. Carnes' Colt flew from his hand and landed in the thick brush off the edge of the trail.

Moore, even with his gun hand slick with blood, fired the last rounds in his Colt. One bullet hit the colonel squarely in his chest; the second shot nailed him in the forehead. But he didn't fall right away. Instead, he wobbled in place, pulled the shotgun's trigger and sent Henry Moore flying backward, a stunned look of disbelief on his face.

From around the curve in the trail, Buckshot Parks heard the shooting and instinctively flung himself behind the cover of a rock. "What does it take to rob a damn stage here?" he asked himself, staring from around the edge of the rock for a full two minutes before easing out onto the trail and venturing forward.

Having lost his Colt, rifle, hat, horse and boot heel, he limped around the curve, unarmed. He stopped and stood for a moment, staring at the dead, at the debris and at the dog hanging still and silent out the open stage door. "Holy Joe and Mabel," he murmured, limping closer to where the stage leaned at a dangerous angle against the rock wall.

Stepping into the space between the open door and the dog, he took a knife up from his boot well. "I never seen anything like this in my whole worthless life."

Parks cut the leash a few inches from the dog's collar and let the big cur drop to the ground with a thud, giving himself more room to look inside the stage. Stooping down, he peered inside at the two bodies, one of them staring blankly at him through a face covered with blood. "It wasn't our fault, if you want to know the truth," he said to the dead blank face, "it was that crazy soldier. He wouldn't stop fighting for nothing!"

Walking back to where Moore's bloody body lay faceup in the dirt, Parks stooped down, picked up the empty blood-slick Colt, checked it and shook his head. He reached and checked Moore's gun belt for bullets and found it empty as well. He shook his head again and dropped the Colt where he'd found it. Then he pulled off the dead outlaw's left boot and looked it over.

Moments later, he stood up, wearing Moore's black left boot in place of his own heelless brown one. Leaving his broken boot lying in the dirt, he jerked the torn flour sack from around his neck and flung it to the ground. He stamped his feet, getting adjusted to the new boot, then walked among the strewn baggage, looking for the strongbox.

"There you are," he said quietly, finally spotting the metal box lying on its side twenty feet from the stagecoach. "At least I'm going to get something out of all this."

He dragged the box a few feet into the shade of a large trailside boulder and looked all around for something to pry open its brass lock. Seeing nothing, he scratched his head and started to sit down in the dirt and consider his next move. But before he could get seated, he heard the thunder of hooves coming fast from around the curve.

"Damn it!" He scanned the site once more for any usable guns. But seeing none, and knowing the horses were approaching fast, he cursed again and ran into the cover of brush off the edge of the trail. He flattened himself just in time to catch first sight of four cowhands swinging into sight around the long curve.

They reined their horses down hard in a cloud of trail dust and stared all around at the dead, at the leaning stagecoach and at the strongbox lying in the dirt.

"Dang!" said one of the cowhands. "It's the Cottonwood Flagstaff coach! Somebody has robbed the hell out of it!"

"Injuns!" another rider shouted, grabbing his battered range Colt from its holster and spinning his horse in a circle as if not to be caught off-guard.

"Take it easy, Holly," said Jet Mackenzie, the oldest of the four and their former trail boss. "This doesn't look like the work of Indians." He eyed the strongbox lying in the dirt a few feet away. "It doesn't even look like robbery, far as that goes."

"Yeah?" said another cowhand, Jock Brewer. "Then what do you suppose put holes in these ole boys, woodpeckers, thinking they's trees?"

Mackenzie realized his mistake. He stared at Brewer, noting that the coolheaded young Texan appeared to be the only one besides himself who was unshaken by the sight of dead men lying amid the debris from a wrecked stagecoach. "I'm just saying something ain't right, is all, Jock," he said firmly. "Wouldn't you agree?"

Brewer spit and grinned and ticked his head. "Oh, I'd say 'something ain't right' is a fair enough assessment." He tapped his horse forward, stopped close to the leaning stage and looked down at the dog lying in the dirt beneath the open door. Blood lay in a puddle surrounding the animal's big spotted head.

"Careful, Jock," Mackenzie cautioned him.

"Right, *boss*," Brewer said with a touch of sarcasm. "You want to come hold my hand?"

Mackenzie said straight-faced to Tad Harper, the youngest of the four, "Tadpole, go over and hold Jock's hand."

"I'm there," Harper said in earnest, all set to give his horse a boot forward.

But Mackenzie stopped him with a raised hand. "Hold up, Tadpole, that was a joke."

Mackenzie and Brewer had a short laugh. But Holly Thorpe only looked around suspiciously through his wire rims, his Colt still in hand. "Real funny," he said in a stiff, solemn tone. "Let's tom-fool around and get ourselves killed."

"I said, 'take it easy, Holly,'" Mackenzie repeated to the wary cowhand, this time in a firmer tone. But he turned more serious as he swung down from his saddle and led his horse over to where Jock Brewer sat staring all around the leaning stagecoach.

"What do you make of it?" Brewer asked.

"Oh, it was a robbery all right," Mackenzie deduced, looking at the bodies, one of the dead wearing a black boot, a broken brown one lying discarded in the dirt beside him. He stooped and stepped in between the open door and the rock wall, and looked inside. He grimaced at the sight of the two dead men in business suits.

"Anybody alive in there?" Brewer asked from atop his horse.

"No," said Mackenzie. He backed away from the open door and looked at the dead colonel lying in the ditch alongside the trail. He again noted the strongbox lying unopened in the dirt. "I'd say all these stagecoach folks decided to shoot it out with the robbers and this is the outcome. Everybody ended up dead." He shrugged, still a bit bewildered.

At the sound of a heavy thump between the

stagecoach and rock wall where Mackenzie had just been standing, they all turned, their guns coming up cocked and ready. But they all breathed a sigh of relief, seeing that the body of one of the dead passengers had given way, fallen out of the leaning stage and dropped onto the ground.

"Jeez," said Mackenzie, looking at the bloody, blank face staring aimlessly across the land, "we best get word to the law in Albertson about this."

"Yeah, sure," Brewer said absently, his attention drawn to the stagecoach's rear freight compartment. He stepped down from his saddle, walked over to it and began inspecting it curiously.

A few yards away, guns still in hand, Holly and Tadpole had stepped down from their horses for a closer look at the strongbox. "You think there was nobody left alive to open this money box?" Tadpole asked.

"That's what I think, maybe," said Mackenzie.

"Want me to shoot this ole lock off of here?" Harper offered.

"No," Mackenzie said firmly. "Leave the strongbox exactly like it is. You go fooling with it, next thing you know we'll get ourselves accused of something we had no part in."

"Aw, heck, Mac," said Brewer, "anybody that knows us knows that we're not thieves. There ain't no way in the world we'd ever get accused of having a part in something like this."

Mackenzie stared at Brewer as he said to Harper, "All right, Tadpole, go ahead, shoot the lock off.

Shoot a whole bunch of times so anybody near here will hurry in and catch us doing it—maybe figure we're the ones did all this."

Tadpole started to point his range Colt at the lock on the strongbox. But he stopped and gave Mackenzie a confused look. "Was that another joke?"

Still staring at Brewer, Mackenzie said, "Yeah, sorry, Tadpole, that was another joke." But this time neither he nor Brewer laughed.

"We could be in a bad spot here, couldn't we?" Brewer said quietly between the two of them. As he spoke he finished loosening the last strap holding the canvas freight cover in place.

"Yep, I'm thinking that we could," said Mackenzie, "if we don't play this thing right."

Brewer stopped what he was doing and started to refasten the straps he'd just loosened. But without the straps holding things in place, the canvas cover sagged, then spread open enough for several bags, bundles and small wooden crates to spill out onto the ground.

"No harm done," said Mackenzie, seeing Brewer give him a look of apprehension. "Leave it like it is. We'll say we found it that way."

"Right," said Brewer, and he stepped back away from the freight compartment.

"I'm wondering how we should do this," Mackenzie pondered, rubbing the whisker stubble on his chin.

"Two of us rides to Albertson, two of us stays right here," Brewer offered.

"That's what I thought," Mackenzie said. "But whoever stays here has got a lot of explaining to do if somebody shows up before the other two gets back."

They stood in silent contemplation for a moment. Finally Holly Thorpe said, "I say we ought to all go, tell what we saw here and get it over with."

Mackenzie stared down at the loose dusty ground and gave a troubled look. "We've been here," he said. "We've left the tracks to prove it."

"I say we leave and go on about our business like we never saw anything," Tadpole Harper threw in.

The three looked at him, a bit surprised at Harper offering his thoughts on the matter.

"That's right," Harper added. "These folks are all dead. Us riding to Albertson ain't going to bring them back to life. This territory is quick to stretch a man's neck. After that it don't matter much if they find out we were innocent."

"Tadpole's right," Holly agreed. "I'm danged if I want to even answer all the questions we've already brought upon ourselves by finding this."

"Doggone it!" said Mackenzie with a grimace. "This stagecoach never gets robbed. Why now, of all the *danged* times?"

"Oh my goodness!" said Harper, jumping back suddenly as if he'd seen a snake. He pointed at the ground beneath the freight compartment where stack upon stack of green American dollars had began falling one after another into a widening pile on the ground.

The four formed a half circle and stepped closer, staring amazed, guns still in hand. "This just gets worse by the minute," said Mackenzie, giving Brewer a look.

"Yeah," said Brewer, "I never seen so much money in my life."

Chapter 4

When the bound stacks of money stopped falling, Mackenzie, Brewer and Harper stepped in closer. Brewer and Harper stooped down around the pile. Holly Thorpe stepped farther away, his range Colt still up, cocked and ready. He stood with all four horses' reins in his other hand, his wary eyes scanning the area surrounding them from behind his wire-rims.

"How—how much money is this?" Brewer asked no one in particular. He picked up one of the bundles and examined it, thumbing the bills.

"Lot and lots," Harper replied absently, scooping up some of the bundles and letting them fall from his hands.

While the two pondered over the money, Mackenzie opened the canvas freight cover the rest of the way and looked inside. Beneath a false bottom panel that had jarred loose, a large leather-bound carpetbag lay on its side, its top gaped open from the impact of the stage wreck. Inside the bag lay more stacks of cash.

"Uh-oh, guess what I've found here," he said, dragging the bag from amid the rest of the overturned freight and pulling it out.

As soon as he'd plopped the bag onto the ground, the three of them saw the name painted on its side in black letters.

"D. Grissin Enterprises," Brewer read aloud in an awe-stricken voice.

A puzzled half grin came to Mackenzie's face. "Davin Grissin . . . ," he said quietly.

"The same thief who's had us cussing in our whiskey all this time?" Brewer said. "What are the odds on that?"

"Long and troublesome, I'd say," Mackenzie replied. He stared at the bag and the money lying beside it, then said suddenly, as if overcome by some dark premonition, "Let's get away from here. This looks bad, us standing over a pile of Grissin's money after all the bad-mouthing we've been given him in the saloons."

"Good idea. Let's go," said Brewer. He stood and stepped back, wiping his hands on his trousers as if to clean them of the cash.

But without standing, Tadpole Harper looked up with a grin and said, "What's your hurry? Look at all this." He held three stacks of money in his hand, fanned out like playing cards. "Mr. *D. Grissin* chased us off like we was coyotes in his henhouse. The least we can do is play with his money some."

"Get up, Tadpole. Let's go," Mackenzie said firmly to the young drover. "You were right to begin with. We're going to leave here and act like we never seen any of this."

"I know that's what I said. . . ." Harper stood up slowly. He stared down at the money and shook his head. He still held three stacks of cash in his gloved hand. "But that was before. We can't leave this kind of money lying in the dirt."

"Tadpole's right. We better make danged sure we do the right thing leaving this money lying here," Brewer said. "If something happens to it and anybody ever figures out we were here, we'll have Grissin's bodyguards down our shirts before we can spit or whistle."

"We'd be a sight better off without it than we would be having it on us, if we run into a posse searching for it," Mackenzie reasoned.

"Would we?" Harper asked, still holding the three bundles of money. He shook the wads back and forth for emphasis. "If something happens to all this after we leave here, we better hope to God nobody ever figures we seen it. Because they'd never believe we'd be foolish enough to just leave it lying here."

"How come you got so danged smart all of a sudden, Tadpole?" Mackenzie asked, irritated and worried.

Harper gave a dejected look, then lowered his head and started to turn away.

"Wait, I didn't mean nothing by that, Tadpole," Mackenzie called out. "Dang it!" He rubbed his troubled forehead, needing to think things through clearly, but feeling too pressed to do so.

"Tadpole was right, what he said before . . . and he's right what he's saying now," Brewer said quietly to Mackenzie. "If we leave this money lying here and something happens to it, we'll be the ones answering for it, sure enough."

Mackenzie shook his troubled head. He looked all around as if searching for a way to pull his herd out of a box canyon. "Bag it up," he said with resolve, not facing Brewer or Harper. "We'll take it with us to the next town where's there's a sheriff, turn it in there and explain why we did it this way."

"What town is that?" asked Thorpe.

"There's a supply town named Red Hill, thirty, forty miles ahead," said Mackenzie. "They used to have a sheriff. I'm hoping they still do."

"*Hoping?*" Harper said, with more insight than the others were used to hearing from him. "Even if there is a sheriff, he'll more than likely—"

Cutting him off, Mackenzie said with a stare, "He'll take *our word* for it. None of us are thieves, Tadpole. The law don't condemn innocent men for trying to do the right thing."

"Come on, Tad." Brewer gave Harper a slight nudge toward the money. "Don't crowd him right now, give him some room." Without another word, the two stooped down and began stuffing the money stacks into the carpetbag.

Mackenzie walked a few feet away and looked out across the badlands below. He needed to think this thing through, he told himself, drawing a deep breath. But before a clear thought come to mind, Holly Thorpe called out to him, "Mac? What about these stray horses?"

The young trail boss looked around, appearing pressed and put upon by so much hitting him at once.

"Them," said Thorpe, nodding toward Moore's and Carnes' horses, standing off the trail staring at them.

Whew . . . Mackenzie felt the pressure, yet he kept his voice calm. "Drop their saddles and turn them loose."

But no sooner had he'd spoken than Harper called out from over beside the bag of money, "It'll be a sure sign somebody else was here after the shooting if we turn them loose now."

"Quiet, Tad," Brewer said, still stuffing money into the bag.

"No, Tadpole's right again," said Mackenzie. He let out a tense breath. "All right, we'll take the horses with us. Like as not, we'll find the stage horses somewhere ahead. We'll have to take them too." He shook his head, looked back out across the rugged terrain and murmured to himself, "I just hope we can lay all this on the law before the law lays it all on us."

In the thick brush alongside the trail, Buckshot Parks stayed hidden, watching and listening as closely as he could until the four drovers mounted and rode out of sight, leading Moore's and Carnes' horses along behind them. Then he ran out onto the littered trail, looked all around and kicked the unopened strongbox.

Damn it! Damn it all to hell! He had no idea how much money he'd just watched the four cowhands ride off with, but there was not a doubt in his mind that it was *his* money. After all, it had been him, Moore and Carnes who'd robbed the stage. He'd heard them mention Davin Grissin's name. If that money had belonged to Davin Grissin, the four cowpokes had more trouble coming than they knew what to do with, he told himself. But all that aside, it was *his* money now, regardless who it had belonged to before.

Red Hill, huh? Hurriedly he walked to where the double-barreled shotgun lay in the dirt near Jim Blanton's dead hand. He stooped over Blanton, picked up the weapon and searched Blanton's body until he found four fresh loads shoved down in his vest pocket.

Standing, shotgun loaded and in hand, Parks searched all around until he found a canteen he'd seen lying in the dirt earlier. He picked it up, shook it, determined it was half-full and slipped the strap over his shoulder. He looked back and forth for his horse. Not seeing the animal, he pressed his fingers to his mouth and let out a loud whistle.

Hearing no sound of the horse's hooves or the breaking of brush and twig, he'd turned to leave when he heard a deep moan coming from the direction of the leaning stagecoach. He turned and walked warily over to one of the businessmen who had fallen from inside the tipped stage.

"Are you still alive, you bloody sumbitch, you?" Parks asked, staring down at the blank dead eyes. He kicked the bloody face and watched it wobble limply back and forth. The blank eyes remained unchanged. They continued staring straight ahead.

"All this craziness has got me hearing things," Parks said. He looked at the expensive new derby hat lying in the dust near the body, with only a streak of dust on its rolled-edge brim to prove it had been in a stagecoach crash.

"Well, now, I don't mind if I do," said Parks. He stooped down, picked up the derby and slapped it against his thigh. He shoved it down atop his bare head, turned and looked back and forth along the trail again. He gave another loud whistle, then walked away, following the hoofprints on the ground, tracking his money.

Three hours later, in the fading afternoon light, Millard Kinnard rode around a turn in the trail and came upon the ghastly sight so suddenly that it caused him to jerk back sharply on his reins and startle his horse. The frightened animal reared, nickered loudly and turned in a full circle on its rear hooves. While perched high and hanging on to the horse's mane, Kinnard got a close-up, wide-eyed look at the dead, the crashed stage and the money box lying in the trail.

The frightened schoolmaster let out a loud shriek as his horse came down, its direction reversed, and raced back along the winding trail toward Albertson, out of control.

At the bottom of a hill where a fork led in one direction toward town and in another out toward the badlands, Maria and Sam both stopped at the sound of hooves and the shouting, pleading, cursing voice of the schoolmaster approaching them.

"I've got him," Sam said quickly, the two sidling off the trail to keep the racing horse from veering off the trail into rocks and brush.

Maria reined back and watched as the ranger's white barb with its black-circled eye shot out like a dart and swung alongside the spooked animal. In a second, Sam had reached out and slowed the animal to a walk and turned it alongside him and headed back along the trail. The man in the saddle straightened with a worried and embarrassed look on his sweaty face. He appeared relieved to see the badge on the ranger's chest.

"My goodness! I thought this horse was never going to stop!" Maria heard him say as the two drew to a halt in front of her. Seeing Maria, the man reached to tip his hat, only to realize that his hat had flown off somewhere back along the winding uphill trail.

"What spooked it?" Sam asked, seeing Maria offer the man a curt nod.

The schoolmaster turned to Sam as he fished a handkerchief from his lapel with a nervous hand. "Ranger, a terrible thing has happened up there," he said, nodding toward the uphill trail. "The stage to Albertson has been crashed and robbed, there are dead everywhere!"

"Calm down, mister," the ranger said, looking off in the same direction. "Who are you? What were you doing up there?"

"Oh, excuse me, I'm Millard Kinnard, I'm the schoolmaster in Alberston," said Kinnard in a shaky voice. "I was on my way to Wakely to advise them in starting a school there. And who are you, sir, ma'am?" he asked.

"I'm Arizona Ranger Sam Burrack. This is Maria," Sam said. As he spoke, he sidled in, lifted the flap on one of Kinnard's saddlebags and looked inside. Seeing only three leather-bound books and some food wrapped in canvas, he dropped the flap and stepped his horse back. "How far up the trail is the stage?"

"A mile, I estimate," the schoolmaster replied. "This horse has been running so long, everything is a blur to me." He looked back and forth between Sam and Maria, then looked at the white barb with the black spot circling one of its eyes. Recognition came to him and he said, "Oh my. You're *the ranger*, aren't you?"

"Yes, I am," Sam said. "I'm going to ask you to ride back up there with us, show us what you saw."

"What I saw?" Kinnard looked frightened at the prospect. "Ranger Burrack, I hardly see how riding back up there with you is helpful in any way. Shouldn't I ride back to Albertson and tell everyone what has happened?"

"It's only a mile," said Sam. "You'll have plenty of time to ride back to Albertson afterward."

A look of realization came to the schoolmaster's eyes. "Do you think I might have had something to do with this, Ranger Burrack?"

"No," Sam said cordially, "I'm not thinking that at all, and I won't think it unless you start trying to stall us." He nodded toward the trail. "Now, what do you say? You want to ride up with us?"

"Oh yes, of course," said Kinnard, "anything to help."

As they turned their horses, Maria reached out with her gloved hand and offered Kinnard an uncapped canteen of water. "Oh yes. Thank you, ma'am," he said, grasping the canteen and drinking from it eagerly.

They rode upward until they reached the turn in the trail. Along the way the ranger and Maria had both kept an eye toward the trail beneath them, seeing zigzagging wheel marks, hoofprints, boot prints and drag marks, getting a picture of what had gone on. Before rounding the turn and stepping down from their saddles, Sam said quietly to Kinnard, "Stay back a little," which the schoolmaster did gratefully.

Kinnard stood back with his eyes averted while Sam and Maria walked among the dead and the debris, recognizing Moore's, Carnes', Baggs' and Blanton's bloody bodies. When Sam reached the spot where the colonel's body lay in the ditch alongside the bottom edge of the rock wall, he called out to Maria, who had walked over closer to the stagecoach.

"This is Colonel Tanner over here," he said. "That explains things a little. Between him riding as a passenger and Jim Blanton riding shotgun, I'd say these two took on more than they'd bargained on."

"Sam," said Maria, "the colonel had Sergeant Tom Haines with him."

"I know," Sam said, looking down at dark bloody paw prints in the dirt.

Kinnard had ventured closer. "Who—who is Sergeant Tom Haines? The colonel's orderly?" he asked.

"No, Tom Haines is his dog," Sam said. He followed the dog's paw prints in reverse, over to where Maria stood crouched between the leaning stage and the rock wall. Looking in, Sam saw her hold up the cut leash in her hand. On the ground lay a wide dark puddle of blood. From the dark puddle the dog's paw prints had led to the colonel's body, then off into the brush.

Kinnard asked, "Do you suppose the dog is . . . ?"

"Dead?" said Sam, looking off into the brush. "I don't know. He might be wounded, wandering around out there somewhere. He won't last long if he is."

Walking to where Moore lay dead, his black left boot missing, Parks' heelless brown boot lying in the dirt, Sam said quietly, his Colt still in his hand from when they'd ridden in, "There's another one somewhere."

Maria eased over closer and looked down with the ranger. "This is the heelless boot print we saw back there along the trail?"

"Yep," said Sam. He looked around, glimpsing only Kinnard's high-topped shoes. As he walked to the edge of the trail he asked the finicky schoolmaster over his shoulder, "Is there a sheriff in Albertson now?"

"No," said Kinnard, "Peyton Quinn is acting as a temporary sheriff. If you want to consider him a sheriff, I'm certain he won't mind." His voice carried a heavy note of unveiled sarcasm.

"Quinn the gunman?" Sam asked skeptically. "I never knew of him upholding the law."

"Nor has anyone else," Kinnard said in the same dry tone. "But he was appointed to office by Davin Grissin. If you know Mr. Grissin, you must realize that he is the final authority over anything that goes on in Albertson these days."

Sam shook his head and made no comment on either Peyton Quinn, Davin Grissin or the town of Albertson itself. Instead he said, "Ride back, tell everybody what happened here. Bring back some help and a team of horses to pull the stage. I'll lay the dead inside once I pull it up onto its wheels. Tell them Maria and I might already be gone, searching for the other robber." He noted the fading light. "But if they see a campfire, tell them to approach it wisely."

"Yes—yes, right away, Ranger Burrack," said Kinnard, already stepping back into his saddle, anxious to get under way.

Only when the schoolmaster was out of sight did Sam and Maria give each other a knowing look. "Please tell me I heard him wrong," said Maria. "Davin Grissin has appointed Peyton Quinn, the *hired killer*, as temporary sheriff for the town of Albertson?"

"I'm as surprised as you are," said Sam. "But if he shows up wearing a badge, I'm obliged to treat him the same as I would any other lawman."

"You mean with '*respect and cooperation*'?" Maria asked, having a feeling she already knew what his answer would be.

"With *cooperation* for now," the ranger replied, already turning away from the matter of Peyton Quinn. His eyes darted from the dead and to the debris strewn on the ground. "There's been a lot gone on here," he added quietly. "You saw all the tracks, the overlapping, the different group of riders."

"*Sí*, I saw them," Maria said. "But I decided that

you didn't want to say too much while the schoolmaster was here."

"You were right." Sam walked closer to the leaning stage and looked down at the boot prints and scrape marks in the dirt beneath the rear freight compartment.

Chapter 5

As the ranger pulled back the canvas cover and looked down at the opened secret compartment, Maria said, "I always wondered: What good is a secret hiding spot when everyone knows where it is?"

"I've often wondered that myself," the ranger replied. He gave a thin smile and gazed off along the trail. After a pause he said, "We both know there were other folks who came along and found this stage before the schoolmaster did. Why do you suppose those folks didn't want anybody to know?"

Maria considered it. "They got spooked. They thought they would be blamed for what happened here?" She stirred the toe of her boot on the ground amid the disheveled dirt where the stack of money had fallen, as if discerning something from the earth itself. "They were not thieves, or else they would not have left the strongbox lying here unopened."

Sam looked at the strongbox, the boot prints around it. "Sometimes folks don't start out to be thieves, but temptation falls upon them so sudden and powerfully it makes them do things they ordinarily wouldn't do."

"*Sí*, I understand," said Maria. She gestured a gloved hand toward the strongbox. "But here lies the sudden temptation you speak of. What would make them turn away from the money in there?"

"Maybe there was more money lying here." Sam nodded at the dirt beneath the toe on her boot.

"Perhaps . . . ," Maria mused, pondering the notion. She looked between the open hiding compartment lying empty and its plank panel cover lying beside it. "But why would they not take all of the money—this money too?"

"Because these folks aren't thieves, remember? At least they haven't talked themselves into it yet. They're still thinking about it—flirting with the notion, so to speak."

Maria only nodded.

As the ranger spoke he walked over to the broken-heeled boot and the ripped flour sack lying beside it in the dirt. He looked down at Moore's stockinged foot. He left the broken boot where it lay, but he picked up the flour sack and shook dust from it. "Now, the fellow who wore this," he said, running his gloved hand inside the ripped sack and poking his fingers out the eyeholes, "is a thief to the bone."

"Aw," Maria said, seeing that the dusty sack was a bandit's mask and making a connection, "Stanton 'Buckshot' Parks?"

"Yep, I'm betting on it," said Sam. "He's known to be partial to these old-fashioned train robber flour sacks. Most robbers have stopped using them. Having one in his saddlebags could get a man hanged under the right circumstances. It's easier using a bandanna since everybody wears one anyway."

"You said Buckshot Parks wouldn't be able to sit still long." Maria gave a slight smile and shook her head. "He would stoop to riding with the likes of these two after all the big gangs he rode with?" She pointed back and forth from Moore to Carnes.

"Like I told you, he's a born thief. He's got to be up to something all the time. He can't help himself."

"And now," said Maria, "is he riding with whoever came along and found this stage wreck?"

"That's a good question," said the ranger. "Is he riding with them, or he is riding after them, shadowing them?"

"How do we know these others have whatever money was in the hiding compartment instead of him?" Maria asked.

"We don't," Sam said, considering it. "But my hunch is, if Parks had his say over things, this box would be lying here open and empty—"

The ranger cut his words short when he heard a sound from the brush. Together he and Maria swung their guns around at the same time. "Who's there?" Sam demanded. "Come out with your hands up and empty."

The sound moved closer toward them through

the brush, but instead of a reply, they heard only the soft whine of a wounded animal in pain. After a second the colonel's big cur staggered out of the brush and fell to the ground without giving them a glance. Dark blood from the gaping bullet graze on his head covered most of his face.

"He doesn't know we're here," said Maria. She took a step forward, but Sam cautioned her back with his raised hand.

"Careful, Maria," Sam said as the big cur struggled up onto his paws and staggered forward to where the colonel's body lay on the ground. "He's dazed. But it could wear off any minute. When it does, we won't know how he's going to act. The colonel always said he's a one-man dog."

"I know," Maria replied, stopping, letting her rifle down. The two watched the dog whine pitifully and poke the colonel with its nose as if to awaken him. "But we've got to do something to help him."

"We will," the ranger said quietly, "just as soon as he gives us an opportunity."

The two watched for a moment as the dog staggered in place beside its dead master. Finally, overcome by the loss of blood and still dazed from the impact the bullet graze had had on its brain, the big animal curled down against the dead colonel, let out a deep breath and slumped in the dirt.

"I'll get my canteen, and my needle and thread," Maria said almost in a whisper. "He will need many stitches to close his wound."

"I'll get some rope and make a muzzle for him,"

said Sam, already on his way to his horse where a coiled rope hung from his saddle horn. "We might need it if his head clears and he feels what we're doing to him."

Within minutes Maria had chosen a length of heavy surgical thread and a curved surgical needle from her saddlebags. When Sam finished slipping a double loop of rope around the dog's muzzle and looped it again around the dog's neck, Maria washed the open wound with a clean cloth and tepid canteen water.

Sam watched her thread the curved needle and upon seeing her signal that she was ready, he held the dog down firmly by the rope and the short length of its cut collar while she made the first stitch.

The dog's eyes opened, but only for a second when the needle made its way through both edges of the gaping wound and drew them together. When the dog's eyes closed again, both Sam and Maria breathed a sigh of relief. With a nod from the ranger, Maria systematically hooked and drew stitch after stitch until the gaping wound closed and only a thin line of blood drained from one end of it.

"You do good work," Sam said with a slight smile, his gloved hands only resting now on the dog's neck.

"This is the first time I have sewn stitches in an animal," Maria said. "I hope he will be all right." She reached down a bloodstained hand and stroked the dog gently.

"He's breathing good," Sam said reassuringly. "If

this was all that's wrong with him, he should be just fine."

"We will see," Maria said. Beneath her hand the dog stirred only a little, then let out a breath and once again lay silent and still.

Sam looked around in the growing darkness. "By the time I get the stage righted and get the dead inside it, it's going to be dark traveling." He stroked the dog's neck as he spoke. "I'd hoped we could get out of this hill line before dark, but attending to Sergeant Tom Haines here changed everything."

"I would like to be here when he awakens, so I can see for myself that he is all right," said Maria.

"Okay, we'll camp here overnight," said Sam. "It'll be easier tracking come daylight."

"Good," said Maria, "I'll build a fire and prepare us some food and coffee."

Standing and dusting his trousers, Sam said, "While you do that I'll pull the stage back onto all fours and attend to the dead. Someone from Albertson should be heading here in another couple of hours, if the schoolmaster hurries to town."

Rummaging through a tool compartment beneath the driver's seat of the stagecoach, the ranger found two more coiled ropes and an iron pry bar. While Maria boiled a pot of coffee and prepared a meal of beans, salt pork and flatbread, the ranger strung his rope around the trunk of a stout pine. He tied one end of the rope to the leaning stage and the other end to one of the coach's ropes he'd tied between the saddle horns on both his and Maria's horses. The third rope he tied atop the stagecoach and over to the rock wall, to keep the coach from tipping too far and falling in the other direction.

With no more than moderate effort the two horses righted the leaning stagecoach with one long pull. As soon as the two raised wheels touched back onto the ground and the big coach rocked back and forth stiffly, the ranger halted the horses and gave them both a pat on their muzzles for their effort.

Moments later he had checked the stage wheels over good and found no cracked or broken spokes that might prevent the big coach from carrying its grizzly cargo back to Albertson once a team of horses arrived. Then he went about the task of carrying the bodies over and stacking them inside. When Maria called out to him that the meal was ready, the ranger closed the stage door, dusted his hands together and walked over to the campfire. "All finished," he said. He sat down and poured water over his hands from a canteen, washing them.

"Yes, I see," Maria said quietly, "and look who is finally waking up."

Sam looked over at the dog in time to see the dazed animal roll onto his belly. The animal had a strange, wild look in his eyes as if he awakened in some world he'd never seen before. He steadied himself with his forelegs spread wide on the ground, his body swaying limply for a moment.

"Here," Sam said quietly, "you've got to be hungry after all this time. Maybe this will help clear your head some." He picked up a piece of pork from his tin plate and flung it easily over in front of the dog.

The dog only gave the meat a glance. Then he rose and staggered over to the closed door of the stagecoach and stood staring up as if expecting the colonel to appear and let him inside.

"The poor thing," Maria whispered, the two of them standing and walking toward the dog. "This is heartbreaking to watch."

"Yes," said Sam, "what becomes of this *one-man* dog now that the one man is gone?"

Easing forward, the two had to stop in their tracks when the big cur turned, facing them, his hackles up in spite of his weak and shaky condition. A deep menacing growl resounded in his broad chest. "Easy, boy," Sam said softly. "Nobody's going to hurt you."

"I don't think he believes you," Maria whispered as the dog's growl only grew more intense, his paws spreading as if going into a fighting stance.

"I think you're right," Sam said, taking a slow step backward. Maria did the same.

The dog turned away from them and stepped back to the stagecoach, its growl turning into a whimper, a plea for its master to appear and assure him that all was well.

"What do we do for him now?" Maria asked with a quiet sigh.

"There's nothing we can do for him right now," Sam replied. "He's still a little dazed. We'll give him some room overnight and hope he'll settle down enough to either ride on with us a ways or go on back to Albertson with the townsmen when they get here."

"*Sí,*" Maria said, watching the poor dog whine and try to scratch its weak paw at the stagecoach door, "and if he goes back to Albertson, what will become of him?"

Sam made no reply, which in itself was answer enough for Maria.

"Someone will shoot him, won't they?" she answered for herself.

"Yes," Sam said quietly, "I'm afraid so. That's what usually happens to an animal like this if no one can take the place of his master. They can't just turn him loose and let him run wild. It's no good for him or the folks around him. A wild dog becomes dangerous real quick, especially one this big and powerful."

"Perhaps he will settle down and listen to you?" Maria offered.

"I doubt it, Maria," Sam replied, "so let's not get our hopes up."

"But if he will settle down, do you think he could stay with us? I hate to think that he must be shot simply because the man he belonged to was killed. That only compounds the injustice of what has happened here."

Sam listened and considered, but before he could reply he saw the big cur loop unsteadily around the coach. The dog scratched once again at the door, then turned and moved away into the brush. "Uh-oh, there he goes." As he hurried to catch up to the big dog, he called back to Maria, "Do you know what the colonel called him? Was it 'Sergeant,' or 'Tom' or what?"

"I don't know," Maria replied. "I only know his name is Sergeant Tom Haines."

"Nobody calls a dog by a name that long," Sam said as he hurried to the edge of the brush. "Sergeant," he called out, "come back here, Sergeant." He paused for a moment, then called out, "Tom, here, Tom."

The two listened closely, but they heard only the sound of the dog breaking farther and farther away, deeper into the thickening brush. Finally Sam walked back to where Maria stood. "Are we going after him?" she asked.

"No," Sam said, "that's too big of a dog to be tracking into brush, him in the shape he's in. We best leave him alone. He might wear himself down and come back here, to where he left the colonel. As weak as he is he can't go far."

"If he doesn't come back, then what?" Maria asked with a concerned look on her face.

"I don't know," Sam said. He did not want to talk about all of the things that could happen to a wounded dog, on his own in rugged unforgiving terrain. "I expect we'll just have to wait and see. Things like this aren't always in our hands."

"I understand," said Maria. For a moment the two stared out into the dark hillsides in silence, and then she added, "We say things are not in our hands, yet isn't it up to us to decide which things *are*, and which things *are not*?"

The ranger didn't answer. Instead he walked back to the fire and sat down. Maria watched him sit there for a long time, his hands wrapped around the tin cup, his eyes staring into it as if matters of great importance lay beneath its metal rim.

Chapter 6

As Maria lay wrapped in her blanket beside the fire, Sam sat for a long time, his rifle across his lap, his blanket thrown across his shoulders against the chilled night air. Finally, in the middle of the night, he stood and walked to the stagecoach at the edge of the firelight and took a folded handkerchief from the dead colonel's tunic pocket. He unfolded the cloth enough to find four pieces of jerked elk meat inside, then refolded it and stuffed it into his trousers pocket.

Moments later, Maria awoke to the feel of Sam's hand on her shoulder. "Maria, wake up."

Her eyes blinked as she looked all around the outer edges of the shadowy campfire light. "What is it, Sam?"

"I'm taking a torch and going after the colonel's dog." On the ground lay an unlit torch he'd made while he'd contemplated the task before him.

She sat up, awake now. "But you said 'some things are not in our hands.'"

"I know what I said," Sam replied, "and you said it's up to us to decide which things are. I decided this one must be in my hands"—he grinned—"because here I go." He handed her a cup of warm coffee. "I saved this for you, to help keep you awake until I get back."

"*Sí, gracias,*" she said, taking the cup. "So I will know I'm not dreaming this?"

He reached out a hand and brushed a strand of dark hair from her face. "No, it's not a dream, you're hearing me right." He stood, his duster and sombrero already on. Taking his rifle, he picked up the unlit torch in his right hand. "I figure he hasn't gone very far. He should be worn down enough for me to get close to him."

"But if he is still dazed from the bullet . . ." Maria let her words trail.

"His thinking ought to be a little clearer by now. He took a hard knock on his skull, but that's been a good while ago." On the ranger's shoulder hung one of the coiled ropes.

She nodded in agreement. "Be careful, Sam. I will call out to you if anyone arrives from Albertson."

Sam nodded, then said as he walked away toward the brush in the direction the dog had taken, "I won't go too far. I just figured he might have wanted to come back but couldn't make it. I wouldn't feel right leaving him here thinking that was the case."

"I understand," Maria said with a slight smile. She watched him walk out of sight.

Inside the brush, with only the pale light of a half-moon overhead, the ranger followed a meandering path of brittle, parted brush as far he could. A thousand yards deep into the rocky hillside, when he reached a small clearing where the brush was replaced by scrub juniper and young pine saplings, Sam stooped down, took out a match, lit the torch and moved it back and forth near the ground, finding the dog's paw prints.

Seeing no blood on the dog's path was a good sign, he thought. It meant that the big confused animal had not opened any of the stitches in the tangles of brush.

"Sergeant . . . Sergeant," he called out quietly as he moved along in the flickering firelight, not liking the idea of searching for a dazed and wounded animal in the dark.

He stood in silence listening for any sort of response, a growl, a whine, a rustling on the ground, anything. But he heard nothing. Moving forward out of the clearing, he followed the paw prints for another fifty yards and stopped beside a dead standing aspen. "Tom," he called out, trying another variation of the dog's name. "Tom." He stopped and listened, still hearing no response.

He walked deeper into a taller, older stand of pine and juniper and said to the darkness before him, "Sergeant Tom Haines."

He waited for a moment, then started forward.

But before he'd taken a step he heard a weak whimper and the thrashing of bracken and pine needles only a few feet away.

"Sergeant Tom Haines," he said again. This time he expected a response and got it. In the darkness beneath a large pine less than twenty feet away, he heard the dog whining and thrashing harder as it rose onto its tired paws.

Hurrying forward, his torch high, Sam found the big dog standing shakily in a bed of dry pine needles, it paws spread for support. Sam could see that the stitches in its head were holding up well, save for a thin dry line of blood from the end Maria had left open for drainage. "Easy, Sergeant Tom Haines," Sam said, feeling almost foolish calling a dog by such a formal-sounding name.

The dog looked exhausted, yet much clearer in his eyes as he stared at the ranger and offered a slight but uncertain wag of his tail. "Good boy, Sergeant Tom Haines," the ranger said softly. "If that's what you're used to being called, I expect that's what I'll call you."

Stepping forward slowly, giving the big dog all the time it needed to catch his scent and understand his intentions, the ranger lowered the coiled rope from his shoulder and held it low for the dog to see. "Come on, Sergeant Tom Haines, it's about time you and I got acquainted."

The dog's nose probed the air before him, his eyes glittering with curiosity in the flickering torchlight. His hackles rose only slightly as the ranger stepped closer. The big cur even took a short step forward himself, his nose going toward the ranger's trouser pocket. "That's it, you check me out all you need to," Sam said in a soothing tone. "I'm known as an honest man hereabouts."

He eased his gloved hand close to the dog's probing nose, holding the rope for the dog to see, smell and understand. "I've got no surprises here, no tricks or sudden moves," Sam said. The dog stood still as the end of the rope slipped under his collar.

Feeling the dog's skin ripple a bit as he tied the rope in place, Sam rubbed his neck gently, up near the thick jaw muscles that had supported the animal while he'd hung in the air. "You've got a sore spot there?" Sam said, taking his hand away when the beginning of a low growl rumbled in the dog's chest. "All right, duly noted," Sam added quietly.

Standing with the rope tied to the dog's collar, the ranger took a step forward, giving only the faintest tug on the rope. "Come on, Sergeant Tom Haines," he said, "let's take you home."

The dog sniffed the ranger's trouser pocket, looked up at him in the torchlight and walked along beside him as if they'd known each other for years. Sam breathed a sigh of relief. He hadn't been afraid of the big cur, but he had dreaded what he knew he would have had to do if the dog refused his help.

But this was good, Sam told himself as the two walked along quietly through the rocky, brushy terrain, Sam holding the torch high. Getting the dog used to him made it more likely that the animal would get used to others. He was certain someone in Albertson would want to make a home for a big strong dog like this one. *Wouldn't they?*

The two proceeded without incident until they reached a spot less than thirty yards from the campsite, where suddenly the dog stopped and gave a low growl toward the darkness lying ahead of them. So intense were the dog's actions that the ranger took heed and crouched down beside him. "Easy, boy," he whispered, "I got your message."

The dog's growl ceased; he stood stiff and silent, his full attention riveted on something in the darkness to the right of the campsite ahead. *The men from Albertson?* Sam asked himself. He hoped so. But to be on the safe side, he rolled the torch back and forth in the rocky dirt until the light disappeared, replaced by a gray plume of smoke that dissipated sidelong through the brush and trees.

Standing in a crouch, he stepped forward, the dog right beside him. "Come on, Sergeant Tom Haines," he whispered, "let's see how good you are at your job."

Peyton Quinn and Grady Black sat in the grainy darkness, awaiting the return of Antan Fellows. Fellows, a half-breed, had slipped down from his horse and scouted ahead on foot to investigate both the campsite and the torchlight that they'd seen moving across the hillside. "I figure it was just one of them had to go to the jake," said Black. He spit a long stream of tobacco juice.

Peyton Quinn looked at him. "That light was a long way from camp just to be going to the jake." Behind them stood a team of large powerfully built workhorses they'd brought to pull the big coach back to town.

Black grinned and shrugged in the darkness. "Maybe he took that dark-haired woman on a moonlight stroll. What else is there for a man to do, a night like this, a woman like her? If you know what I mean." His voice carried lewd suggestion.

"Yeah, I know what you mean all right. I can think of a thing or two, a night like this, a woman *like her*," said Quinn, crossing his wrists on his saddle horn. "Nothing that would require a torchlight or a walk in the woods either."

"So you've seen her too, I take it?" asked Black. He spit again.

"Oh, you bet I've seen her," said Quinn. "I've seen much more of her than you or anybody else ever saw her. She didn't know I saw her, but I saw her."

"Huh, what do you mean?" asked Black.

"I never told anybody this, but I saw her bathing herself in a stream down near Cottonwood, over a year ago." He grinned in the darkness.

"Holy cats and rabbits, you didn't!" said Black, sidling his horse over closer.

"What did I say, Deputy?" Quinn replied in an abrasive manner. "Don't you believe me?"

"Yeah, I believe you, but, my Gawd, Quinn!" said Black. "Did you see her you-know-whats?" As he spoke he held his hands up in front of his chest, his fingers wide and cupped.

Quinn grinned again, slyly. "Oh, I saw her *you-know-whats* all right. I saw them standing proud as ripe peaches, wet and shiny in the morning sunlight—saw her wash them for me nice and slow-like. I watched her wash all over. I mean her belly, her thighs. I'm talking *all over*."

"Gawd, I can't stand it!" said Black. He fidgeted restlessly in his saddle.

"Are you going to need to be alone for a while, Deputy Grady?" Quinn said sarcastically.

Black ignored the question, but settled down and sat more still. "Tell me more about it, Quinn—you know, what you saw, how she done and all," he coaxed.

"No, we've got important business to take care of out here," said Quinn. He nudged his horse forward a step. Black nudged his right along beside him. A lead rope in Black's hand jerked the team of work-horses along behind him.

"Did you see her out of the water—I mean see her real good when she walked out and got dressed?" Black asked, not having enough.

"I saw everything," said Quinn, giving him more to visualize. "I mean *ev-ery* thing. Front to back, top to bottom." He paused for a moment as if in wistful and tortured reflection. "And I'll tell you the truth, I saw almost nothing but her bathing naked in that stream for the next solid month."

"Jesus . . . ," Black whispered. He pushed up his

hat and wiped a hand across his moist brow. "Just hearing about it makes me feel like I was right there."

"Yeah, it was something all right. Some of yas go squirrel-tail crazy at how well she fills out a shirt," Quinn said smugly. "But me, I've seen the goods that gets it done." He nudged his horse another step forward.

"Jesus . . . ," Black repeated.

"Where is that half-breed?" said Quinn. "We need to get cracking, see if the ranger happened upon Mr. Grissin's special cargo shipment."

"I still don't understand Grissin shipping money that way," said Black, trying to recover from what he'd heard and pictured in his mind. "It seems awfully risky to me."

"He's got his reasons," said Quinn, "and don't make me sorry I told you about it. I figured it would make things easier, you knowing it, in case that ranger has seen it and we have to kill him."

After a pause of consideration, Black said, "That kind of makes me wish the ranger has found it."

"Oh?" said Quinn.

"Yeah," said Black. "I mean, what if the ranger wasn't around?"

"What do you mean, if he *wasn't around*?" Quinn replied, acting dumb about the matter.

Black said bluntly, "I mean, *the woman*. If I was to kill the ranger, do you suppose I could have the woman?"

Quinn smiled to himself in the darkness. "I expect you'd best ask her, not me."

"I wouldn't *ask* her," said Black. "Once Burrack's dead, I'll take what I want. She'll have no say in the matter. I'm just asking you if it's all right, me *taking* her. After all, you are the sheriff."

"That's right, I am the sheriff," said Quinn, "and don't you ever forget it."

After another quiet pause, Black said, "So? Is it all right—with you, that is?"

"Is what all right?" Quinn asked, still playing Black along.

"*Damn it*," said Black under his breath. "Is it all right that I take the woman," he said to Quinn, "after I kill the ranger?"

"Look at you, Deputy," said Quinn. "We don't even know if Burrack has come upon the money. You've already got him lying dead on the ground and the woman spread beneath you like a spring mare." He shook his head with a dark chuckle and said, "I'm not telling you any more *naked-woman stories* if this is what it does to you."

"*Naked-woman stories?*" Black gave him a skeptical look.

"Don't worry," said Quinn, "it's all true. Maybe someday you'll see her that way yourself. Then you'll know what I'm talking about." He nudged his horse forward to a tall aspen standing at the edge of a narrow path, and stepped down from his saddle.

Stepping down beside him, Black began hitching his reins and the team horses' lead rope to the tree beside Quinn's big dun. "That day might come quicker than you think, Sheriff," Black said.

"Where the hell is Fellows?" Quinn asked in a lowered voice as he drew a Spencer rifle from his saddle boot and checked it.

"I don't know," said Black, stoked with nervous energy at the thought of the same woman Quinn had seen bathing naked in a stream being only a short distance in front of him on the rocky hillside. "He said you're going to make him a deputy too," he added, also drawing a Spencer rifle from his own saddle boot. "Is that true?"

"Not based on what he's showing me tonight," Quinn whispered. "I'm starting to wonder if he's gotten himself lost."

"They say a Ute never gets lost," Black whispered, rifle in hand.

"Fellows is only *half* Ute," Quinn reminded him. He stepped forward quietly, walking along the path through knee-high brush. He held his Spencer rifle up and ready at port arms.

Chapter 7

Maria had heard a thrashing, then the quick, strange sound of a muffled yell followed by total silence in the endless darkness surrounding the campsite. What was the sound? How close had it been to the camp? She couldn't answer either question with any certainty. The sound had come and gone too quickly to be identified or pinpointed.

"Sam?" she ventured warily, her hand setting her second cup of coffee aside and wrapping around the stock of her rifle. "Sam . . . ?" she repeated as she rose from her blanket and stepped out of the flickering firelight.

After a moment when she received no reply from the rocky hillside, she went back to her blanket, laid her rifle down against her saddle long enough to pick up her coat and slip it on. She had started to reach down for her weapon and hat, but the jacking of a rifle lever caused her to freeze.

"Huh-uh, little lady, just leave that big ole Win-chester where it lies," said Peyton Quinn. As he spoke, he and Grady Black stepped into the firelight and stood at its edge. Both men held their rifles pointed at her.

"Raise your hands so we can see them," Black added, his voice sounding strained and harried.

Maria did as she was told, her empty hands raising slowly chest high as she stayed calm and looked the two up and down appraisingly. "You are the sheriff from Albertson?" she asked Quinn, eyeing a shiny new badge on his chest that peeked from behind the loose lapel of his riding duster.

"We'll ask the questions here," said Black before Quinn got the chance to answer. "You just answer and do as you're told."

Do as you're told? Quinn gave him a sidelong look, getting a good idea of just how far Black would go, left to his own judgment. "Yes, I'm Sheriff Peyton Quinn," he said, taking a step forward away from the edge of firelight and the perimeter of woods. "This is Deputy Grady Black. He's what you could call a *recent admirer* of yours."

All right, Maria thought, she understood. A woman alone in a campsite in the middle of a dark night. She saw where this would soon be headed if she couldn't manage to put a stop to it. Ignoring the remark, she asked, "Did you bring a team of horses to pull the stagecoach?"

Quinn stopped. He looked back at Black, then back to Maria with a thin, flat smile. "Didn't you hear my deputy? We'll ask the questions. You do as you're told." He stepped closer. "Who are you, and where is Ranger Burrack?" He looked at the ranger's blanket lying crumpled on the ground near the fire.

He knew perfectly well who she was before he'd ever walked into the firelight, she told herself. "I'm Maria," she said, staring at him in a way as to make him understand that she knew this was all a game of his.

"Oh, Maria," he said with a grin.

"Ranger Burrack went into the woods for a moment. He is on his way back right now," Maria said, hoping her voice sounded convincing, enough to defuse any explosive situation these two might try to create. "May I lower my hands now and pick up my rifle?" She tacked on "Now that we know we are all on the same side."

"Not so fast, little lady," said Quinn, enjoying himself, still wanting more. "How do we know you are who you say you are?"

"That's right," said Black. "As far as we know, you could be part of the ones who robbed this stagecoach. The ranger could be lying dead somewhere for all we know." He remained standing at the edge of the firelight and the woods line in a strained, awkward position, as if embarrassed to step closer right then. She understood. . . .

All right, trouble had arrived. These two had talked themselves into it on their way here, perhaps even as they had watched her from a spot in the darkness, like two hungry wolves. She thought about her gun belt still lying at her saddle, the butt of her Colt beneath the edge of her blanket.

"What is it you want from me?" she asked almost as if in submission. But she knew the answer. She had to make a move. She couldn't wait for Sam, and she didn't want him walking into danger unknowingly.

Quinn gave a suggestive smile. "I don't know what you have in mind, ma'am," he said, even his voice sounding lewd and filled with double meaning. "We're just hardworking lawmen doing our job. But now I'm starting to wonder myself if maybe you've done something to the ranger."

"He will be back any second," Maria repeated in a cool, level tone. She knew that when the moment came she would make a leap for the Colt instead of the rifle, simply because that was the move they wouldn't expect her to make.

"Then I think we best be prepared to meet him," said Quinn. "First of all, my deputy is going to search you all over, *real thorough-like.*"

"I am warning both of you to keep away from me," Maria said. "You've had your fun, now let it drop." She was ready. In one fast leap, she would land on the blanket, grab the Colt and keep rolling. She rehearsed it in her mind, standing tense, ready to do it.

To Grady Black, Quinn said, "Deputy, would you mind searching this woman, real thorough-like? I mean, take your time, make sure you don't overlook any part of her." His cold smile widened. "See to it she's not carrying any hidden weapons that she might use to inflict bodily harm on us." He stared intently at Maria. "I'll kind of watch how you do it, and keep an eye out for the ranger."

"Jesus," said Black. He swallowed hard. "Yeah, I'll do it." He yanked off his hat and held it low in front of himself as he started to step forward. But as Maria looked past Quinn at Black, she saw the ranger's rifle butt jab out of the darkness and slam into the back of Black's head. The man fell forward to the ground in a puff of dust and pine needles. Quinn never noticed.

"Do you know what Sam is going to do to you?" Maria asked, keeping Quinn distracted, appearing to make one more attempt at trying to stop this without bloodshed.

Quinn just stared at her with a dark, cold smile. "He can't fault us for just doing our job." To Black he said over his shoulder as he turned in his direction, "Deputy, you best get a move on, else the ranger might show up before we both get a chance to properly administer the law to this young wom—"

Maria watched him turn unexpectedly into the upswing of Sam's rifle butt, catching the full force of it under his chin. But even as Quinn staggered back and forth like a drunkard, knocked out on his feet, Maria forgot about leaping for her Colt. Instead, she reached down, grabbed her rifle and stood up quickly.

In front of her Quinn had turned, facing her in his

blind staggering state. Instinctively, she drew back her rifle and jabbed it hard, the butt striking him in the center of his forehead, the bridge of his nose. He hit the ground at her feet. "This pig," she murmured, stepping back, letting her rifle relax in her hands.

"Are you all right?" Sam asked quietly, stepping over close to her and taking her free hand.

"*Sí*, I am now," Maria replied. "You arrived at just the right moment."

Sam squeezed her hand, then turned it loose and stepped away. He rolled Quinn over roughly with the toe of his boot. Looking at the badge on the knocked-out man's chest, he shook his head. "My sympathy to the good folks of Albertson if these two are their lawmen."

Maria looked past the ranger to where the dog paced back and forth beside Grady Black, staring down at him as if daring the knocked-out man to make a move of any sort.

"I see you found the colonel's dog," she said. Near the pacing dog lay Antan Fellows where Sam had dropped him off his shoulder. Antan lay staring at the dog in wide-eyed fear, handcuffs on his wrists, a bandanna gag tied tightly around his mouth. The big cur had left a line of deep bite marks down both of his bloody cheeks.

"Sergeant Tom Haines found him about thirty yards out," said the ranger. "Lucky for him I was there, or else the dog would have eaten him alive."

"I did not hear anything louder than a yelp of

some sort," Maria said, looking surprised to hear that such a battle had gone on so close to the campsite.

"I know," said the ranger. "This dog shot out, grabbed him by his face and took him down as slick and quiet as anything I've ever seen. I wouldn't have believed it had I not witnessed it for myself." He turned a gaze toward the dog. "Now look at him. He looks like he's on guard duty."

"His army training?" Maria asked.

"I suppose." Sam stared at the big cur with a curious expression. "I've never seen a dog attack without making a growl, or a sound of some kind. He clamped his big jaws over the man's face and pinned him to the ground until I took over and cuffed him." He shook his head in amazement. "The colonel or his Apache scouts must have spent a lot of time teaching Sergeant Tom Haines how to stay alive in hostile country."

Maria offered a faint tired smile. "Perhaps that is why he is a *sergeant*," she said.

"I wouldn't attempt to call him anything less," the ranger returned, "not if I was standing anywhere close to him."

"What will we do with these three?" Maria asked, gesturing toward the men on the ground.

"They're going to deny any ill intent," Sam said. He looked at her closely. "Are you sure you're all right? They didn't lay hands on you in any way?"

"Would they still be alive if they had?" Maria asked matter-of-factly.

"I expect not," Sam said. The two turned toward Quinn as he let out a painful moan and raised his battered face from the dirt. "I found their horses and a team of stage horses in the woods. You tell me what you want to do about these two."

"We are on Parks' trail," said Maria. "We cannot waste time with these pigs—they will have Davin Grissin's protection anyway." She looked back and forth from the stagecoach full of corpses to the men slowly awakening on the ground. "Send them back to Albertson with the dead. Let's go on."

"I think I knew you were going to say that," the ranger said. He started to step away, over to where Antan Fellows sat rigid, his eyes still fearful of the big cur.

She stopped him with a questioning look. "What about the dog? We can't trust these men to take him to Albertson and see to it he finds a good home."

"Right," said Sam, sounding as if he'd already given the matter some more thought, "maybe Sergeant Tom Haines would be better off riding with us . . . for a while anyway." He looked at her closely. "What do you think?"

Upon hearing his name spoken, the dog turned to face them and stopped pacing for a moment, as if awaiting orders. Noting the dog's action, Maria asked, "Why do you call him by his full name? It is such a long name for a dog."

"His full name was the only name he responded to," Sam replied. "I expect that must be what the colonel called him." Also noting that the dog had stopped and stood looking at them, Sam called over to him, "As you were, Sergeant Tom Haines."

The dog stood staring blankly for a second, then turned and resumed pacing back and forth. The ranger and Maria looked at each other as if in disbelief. "*Sí,*" said Maria, turning an astonished gaze back toward the pacing animal, "perhaps he *should* stay with us . . . for a while anyway."

Peyton Quinn awakened leaning back against the stagecoach wheel. Beside him sprawled Black. Both men's left hands were cuffed together between two wooden spokes. Antan Fellows stood beside them, leaning on the wheel, his right hand cuffed to it. He held a wet cloth to the line of dog bite down his cheeks. The dog stood ten feet away, watching the three men.

"Who—who did this to me?" Quinn asked in a thick voice, cupping his bruised and swollen chin. Even as he spoke and tried to shake his stalled mind back to consciousness, his free hand eased down to his empty holster.

"I did," the ranger said, watching Quinn's hand search the empty holster. "Don't give me cause to do it again." He stared at Quinn from a few feet away where he sat on the unopened strongbox, sipping coffee. Behind him, the three men's horses and the team of stage animals stood watching with disinterest.

Quinn said defiantly, "You had no cause to do it the first time." But his hand left the holster, gave up its search and fell to his lap. "I'm an officer of the law, the same as you." He jerked his throbbing head toward Grady Black, who sat coming to slowly. "So is this man. I'll see to it you pay for this, Burrack. As soon as I get back to Albertson, I'll wire the circuit judge—"

Sam cut him off. "You'll take the stagecoach and the dead back to Albertson and forget all about your cracked chin and the goose egg on your forehead, if you're wise, Quinn."

"Sheriff Quinn to you," Quinn snapped.

"Stop testing me, Quinn," said the ranger. "You and this man dishonored your badges. You don't know how hard it is for me to keep from wearing this rifle butt out on the two of you."

Quinn fell silent, seeing the fire in the ranger's eyes grow more intense.

"I'm going to turn all three of you loose," said Sam, holding up the handcuff key in his gloved hand. "But first, tell me what was in the hidden freight compartment."

"Nothing," said Quinn, a little too fast, a bit too harshly. He caught himself and shrugged. "I mean, nothing that I know of. Why, is it empty?" But the look on his face had already told the ranger he was lying.

"Yes, it is empty," said the ranger, watching Quinn's eyes.

"Oh well, that's too bad," said Quinn. "It could have been private mail, personal business documents."

"Come on, Quinn," said Sam, "you know about everything coming and going on the Albertson stage. You're bought and paid for by Davin Grissin." He gestured toward Antan Fellows. "This one has already told me that Grissin owns a big piece of the stage lines. What was on the stage that was more important than the money in this strongbox?"

Quinn gave Fellows a hard look. "What?" said the dog-bitten half-breed. "It's not a secret that Grissin owns everything that's worth anything around here."

"You talk too much, *breed*," Quinn growled. To the ranger he said, "As soon as I get this coach back to town, me and my deputy here will be headed out after whoever did this. So this is one time when your services will be neither welcomed nor required. I've got everything under control."

"Are you sure you want to play it this way?" Sam asked. "I'll be on the trail after whoever done this whether you like it or not. If there's anything going on that I need to know about, this is the time to tell me."

"You've got some nerve, Burrack," said Quinn, "after what you've done to me." He shook his cuffed hand. "If this wasn't on my wrist and I had my gun in my hand, I'd kill you."

The ranger levered a round into his rifle chamber and left the hammer cocked. "My hand isn't cuffed. I am holding a gun. Every time you think about how wrongly you've been treated, remind yourself I could've killed you. Don't make me sorry that I didn't."

Quinn looked away, too proud to admit to himself that the ranger was right.

The ranger continued. "It won't help either one of us or your boss, Grissin, either, if you and I keep bumping heads out here."

"We take care of our own business in Albertson, Burrack," said Quinn, turning a cold stare back to the ranger. "You'll do well to keep your nose out of things here."

Sam stepped in with the handcuff key and unlocked Fellows' cuffs first. The half-breed rubbed his wrists and stepped back, not wanting any trouble.

Sam turned from Fellows and stepped over to Quinn. In an even tone he said as he reached down and stuck the key into the handcuffs, "You've made your threats, Quinn. Now here's something you'd better know as the gospel. Don't ever come into my camp the way you did tonight, or badge or no badge I'll treat you like the vermin you are."

Quinn struggled up onto his feet, his head still pounding. "What about our guns?"

"You don't have any guns," Sam said flatly. He reached down, unlocked Black's cuffs and poked him with the toe of his boot to help awaken him.

"You can't send us back to town unarmed," Quinn raged. "You can't disgrace us that way!"

"You'll be more disgraced if I ride in with the three of you handcuffed and tell the town what you were up to out here," said the ranger. "Now get your horses and get out of my sight."

The other two started for their horses, but Quinn would have none of it. He stood with his feet spread shoulder width apart, still rubbing his wrists. Nodding toward his Colt sticking up from behind the ranger's gun belt, he said, "Give me that gun, Burrack. We'll see who gets *out of sight*. You might be a big wind out on the badlands, but for my money you're just one more—"

Before he'd gotten his words finished, his Colt landed with a plop in the dirt at his feet. The ranger leaned his rifle against the wagon wheel and dropped his right hand down beside his holstered Colt. "There it is, Quinn. Make use of it, or crawfish back away from it like a coward."

Chapter 8

The big dog stood back, watching from the side, his head lowered slightly, his ears back. His paws spread wide beneath him, he looked prepared to spring forward with no further warning. Antan Fellows noted the animal's fierce demeanor and eased a step farther away toward his horse, the wet cloth to his cheek. Black was still too groggy to understand what was about to happen. He stood staggering in place, his palms out flat toward the ground as if stabilizing him.

Stunned by the ranger's pitching the gun at his feet, Quinn eyed the weapon lying in the dirt. He considered his odds while a drum pounded hard, sharp beats inside his forehead, inside his swollen chin. He looked back up and caught the cold, killing look in the ranger's eyes and heard Maria say quietly, "Sam, don't do this. Don't kill him."

"See what he's doing?" Quinn said over his shoulder to the other two. "He *wants* me to make a move for my shooting iron. He wants me to grab it and come up fighting. But I see through his plan." Staring at the ranger, he gave a tense, knowing grin. "He took all the bullets out of my gun. Didn't you, Ranger? My gun's not loaded, is it?"

Sam stood staring calmly, at ease, yet with his gun hand poised at his side. "There's only one way you'll ever know for sure, Quinn."

"Yeah, that's it, I get it. I see what you've done, Burrack." Quinn straightened and put any thought of going for his gun from his mind. "I'm not making a move. See this, boys? I'm not making a move. I want you both to see that I'm not going for my Colt . . . not getting myself shot down while I reach for an unloaded gun."

Antan Fellows eyed the big Colt lying in the dirt closely and said, "Sheriff, I didn't see him unload it. If you ask me it's still—"

"That's just it, Antan!" Quinn said angrily. "Nobody asked you a damn thing." He pointed at the ranger. "This man is no fool. He knows my reputation with a gun. He's not about to lay a loaded gun at my feet and invite me to pick it up and use it." His cold, sly grin came back as he stared at the ranger. "Some other time, Burrack. I'm not falling for any tricks tonight. I've got business that needs attending." He backed away.

"Suit yourself, Quinn," Sam said coolly. He stepped forward, picked up the Colt and held it up. He let bullet after bullet fall to the ground until all six lay in the dirt at his feet. "But don't leave here with your shirt in a knot, feeling like I took unfair advantage."

Fellows shook his head; Black blinked his unsteady eyes. Quinn clenched his fists and gritted his teeth in humiliation. "I hope to hell we meet again, Burrack."

"Careful what you hope for, Peyton Quinn," the ranger said before the gunman had hardly finished his words. He made it a point not to put the word "Sheriff" before Quinn's name, not acknowledging the man having any moral claim to the title.

"He wasn't lying, Quinn," Black said in a thick, still addled voice, "the gun was as loaded now as it was ever going to be—"

"Let's get a damn move on!" Quinn snapped fiercely. "We've wasted most of the night dealing with this blasted stagecoach! We need to get it back to Albertson and get on after the men who robbed it!"

Sam stood beside Maria, the two of them watching closely as the three shamed and beaten men hitched the team of stage horses to the coach and hefted the strongbox up behind the driver's seat. He returned Quinn's cold stare while the gunman made one final look in his direction as the stage rolled away.

"I've got a feeling there'll be some lively conversation going on when these three explain everything to Davin Grissin," he said when the stagecoach lurched forward. Antan Fellows sat in the driver's seat. The other two rode alongside, Quinn slapping his reins hard to his horse's rump as if blaming the poor animal for all of his woes and degradation.

"He is right about one thing," Maria said. "The night is nearly gone. Should we break camp and get an early start? Parks is wasting no time finding himself a hole to crawl into."

"Yes, we can do that," Sam replied, knowing Maria, realizing that she wanted to ride away from this place and the events that had nearly occurred here. "First, let's give credit where it's due." He looked over at the dog and saw the big animal standing as if at attention, watching the two of them closely. "Sergeant Tom Haines, come right over here, front and center," he called out in a feigned military tone of voice. "You've earned yourself a nice strip of jerked elk."

The big cur loped over and sat down near their feet, facing them. "This one is certainly recovering fast," Maria said, stopping and rubbing the dog on his shoulder, his head still too tender and swollen to be patted. "Do you suppose he will ever take up with anyone the way he did with the colonel?"

Sam gave a slight smile, taking a piece of elk jerky from the colonel's handkerchief in his trouser pocket. "We'll find out soon enough, I expect," he said, reaching out, letting the big cur take its reward from his gloved fingertips.

The big dog swallowed the elk morsel without so much as a chew, then stood up and licked his flews. Maria nodded toward the hoofprints leading away toward the north and asked the ranger, "Where you suppose these tracks are going to lead us?"

"To Red Hill," the ranger said with confidence.

"The supply town?" Maria queried. "Won't they try to lie low for a while first, hide themselves until their trail turns cold?"

"That's what most robbers would do," Sam said. "But I've got a feeling this isn't thieves we're dealing with here . . . not yet anyway." He gazed in contemplation along the dark trail ahead of them as the first glimmer of dawn wreathed the eastern horizon. "These folks are still wondering whether or not they're going to keep the money or turn it in."

"Oh?" said Maria, raising a brow at his keen perception. "And which of the two choices do you predict they will make?"

"I don't know," Sam admitted. A troubled look came to his face as he considered it. "I expect they realize by now that either choice can be dangerous."

Maria nodded. "And if they are headed for Red Hill, we can bet that Parks is hot on their heels."

"That is my thought, exactly," the ranger said, his gloved hand at his side. He felt the big dog sniff at his fingertips, then sit back down at his side, gazing ahead in the same direction.

Jet Mackenzie rode his claybank dun onto the dirt street of Red Hill. Jock Brewer rode his brown-speckled barb beside him, followed closely by Tadpole Harper on a white-faced roan and Holly Thorpe atop a salt-and-pepper barb. Thorpe led the two spare horses behind him. Harper led three of the four stage horses they'd gathered on their way, having stripped the animals bare and discarded their harnesses along the trail.

"Here goes nothing," Brewer said under his breath to Mackenzie, feeling eyes on them as they rode toward the large weathered wooden star hanging out in front of the sheriff's office. "I sure hope you know what you're doing," he added almost in a whisper.

"*Me?*" said Mackenzie. "I thought we all agreed this was the right way to handle things?"

"Yeah, we did agree," Brewer said with a worried half smile. "But the more eyes I feel on me, the more I'm wanting this to be your doing."

"Much obliged," Mackenzie replied under his breath, veering his horse over to the hitch rail. The others followed his lead and stepped down from their saddles as one. Mackenzie said to Holly Thorpe as Thorpe and Harper hitched the spare animals beside their horses, "Holly, you and Tadpole stick here while me and Jock go see the sheriff."

"Right," said Thorpe. The four had already discussed it while they'd stopped miles back and divided the money. Each had rolled a portion of it in his slicker, bedroll and saddlebags rather than be seen carrying the cash into town in a bag bearing Davin Grissin's name. There would be time to haul the money into the sheriff's office after they explained everything that had happened. He hoped so anyway, Thorpe said to himself, standing near his horse, a hand on its rump near his bedroll.

A few townsfolk gathered along the boardwalk as Mackenzie and Brewer walked to the door of the sheriff's office and Mackenzie tried the door handle.

"If you boys are looking for the sheriff, there ain't any," an old man said from the boardwalk. He wore the ragged clothes of a prospector, scuffed and worn-down boots and a tattered broad-brimmed flop hat.

"There used to be one," said Mackenzie, looking back and forth with a concerned expression. "What happened to him?"

"If you mean Jake Sutterwhite, a rattlesnake bite is what happened to him," the old man said. "That was nigh three years back."

"No," said Mackenzie, "I heard of a sheriff here only last winter—a man by the name of Delbert something or other."

"That would be Delbert Jamison," the old man said with a crooked grin. "But he's dead too—consumption ate his lungs out. He coughed his way plumb to hell and stopped right there. The nearest thing we've got to lawman here is 'Fearless' Fred Mandrin. He was Jamison's deputy. He's dead too, only unlike the others he's *dead drunk*." He let out a rasping laugh and looked all around to see if any townsfolk shared his good humor. When no one joined him in his laughter, he grumbled under his breath, "Mirthless sons a' bitches."

"All right, then," said Mackenzie to the old man,

giving Brewer a look of uncertainty, "where will we find this Fred Mandrin?"

The old man gestured with his rough hand. "Just pull the cork on a whiskey bottle and fan your hand back and forth across the top of it. He'll land on you quicker than a blue fly. Just don't let him hold that bottle if you want to get any sense out of him—"

"Excuse me, gentlemen," said a bearded man in a swallow-tailed business suit. He stepped forward from along the boardwalk, an ivory-handled cane in hand. "Pay Art Mullens no mind." He looked the old man up and down with distaste. "Art, go have Sweeney set you up a drink on the house. I'll talk to these gentlemen, if you please."

"There you have it," the old man said, tossing a rough hand. "When it comes to a free drink, I expect I am your huckleberry, no less so than the man I just maligned." He turned on his worn-down heels and walked away toward the saloon.

"Art Mullens is a good old man, but he's spent too many hard days in the sun and cold nights with his head on a rock," said the bearded man. "I am Bart Frazier, owner of the Blue Belle Saloon, at your service, of course, gentlemen." He touched his fingers to the brim of his black bowler hat. "Now, do I understand you are looking for a lawman, someone with legal authority? May I be so forward as to ask *why?*"

"We, uh—" Mackenzie stalled, not sure he wanted to explain what had happened to anyone other than a man wearing a badge.

"Saw some Indians not far from here," Tad Harper cut in. He suspected that Mackenzie thought the same thing he and the others thought. They all knew how quickly things could get out of hand in a town like Red Hill with no lawman keeping the peace. Once a crowd tossed a noose over a limb, it was too late to stop them, right or wrong.

The gathered townsfolk gave one another a curious look.

"Oh, Indians? Do tell," said Frazier, looking back and forth among the four, noting the three big team horses standing at the rail beside the two spare horses. The crafty saloon owner could tell there was something afoot. He noted the gathered townsfolk and decided the four young drovers weren't about to say much more on the matter unless they did so in private. "Good of you to come tell us," he added, eyeing Mackenzie knowingly. "But we haven't had any trouble with Indians around here for a long time. Perhaps it was just some peaceful Utes moving north with the game."

"Yeah, maybe so," said Mackenzie. He was still having a hard time getting his thoughts centered on what to do next.

"Hear that, folks?" said Frazier to the gathered onlookers. "Nothing to worry about, just some Utes moving through, I'm betting." He turned from the townsfolk back to the four drovers. "But I sure want to thank you young men for coming to tell us. I hope you will accept the hospitality of my drinking establishment as repayment for your thoughtfulness."

Mackenzie looked warily at Brewer.

"Free drinks, gentlemen?" said Frazier as if he hadn't made himself clearly understood. In a lowered voice he said just between himself, Mackenzie and Brewer, "Along with some, shall we say, *private conversation,* if you feel so inclined?"

Mackenzie let out a tense breath. "A private conversation sounds good right about now."

"Follow me, then." Frazier turned and gestured his walking stick toward the batwing doors of the saloon a block away. "I have a private office behind the Blue Belle. We can pull a cork and sit and discuss whatever is on our minds."

Mackenzie glanced at Harper and Thorpe standing among the animals. Catching the exchange among the men, Frazier said, "Feel free to lead the horses along and hitch them out front of the Blue Belle. I'm sure we can make room for them. I can have one of the boys from the livery barn come get them if you prefer."

"Huh-uh," Mackenzie said firmly, "we're keeping the horses with us."

Brewer offered in a quiet tone, "Mac, we could send all these spare horses to the livery. It would give us less to have to fool with." The expression on his face told Mackenzie that it might be a good idea to get the stage horses off the street. "Out of sight, out of mind . . . ?" Brewer added.

Mackenzie nodded. "Good thinking," he whispered.

Outside town, Stanton "Buckshot" Parks slid his tired horse to a halt and reined it back and forth as he squinted and watched the four drovers and the man in the swallow-tailed coat walk along the boardwalk toward the Blue Belle Saloon. "Frazier, you greasy-thumbed son of a rattler," he growled to himself. "Touch one dollar of my money and I will open the top of your head and stir my fingers around in your brains!"

But he settled down as he watched the young drovers follow Frazier into the saloon. "Who do I know in this one-horse miserable gnat's ass of a town?" he asked himself.

Keeping the worn-out horse running back and forth in a frenzy, the shotgun he'd taken from the site of the stage coach robbery in hand, he finally stopped abruptly as a name and face came to mind. "Hell yes, that's my man!" he said aloud. Then he smacked the shotgun barrel on the horse's rump and rode away, wide of the town's streets and off along a littered alleyway behind a long row of buildings.

PART 2

Chapter 9

Former deputy Fred Mandrin awakened to the sound of a rocking chair creaking slowly back and forth on the bare wooden floor. Before he opened his eyes, he slipped his hand beneath his pillow and felt around for the butt of his big Remington pistol. When he noted that the gun wasn't there, he froze for a moment trying to remember where he might have put it, knowing that any second he might be called upon to use it. He'd been drinking hard the night before; he recalled that much. . . .

"Looking for this, *Fearless* Fred?" said Stanton Parks, cocking the Remington, holding the tip of the barrel only a few inches from Mandrin's face.

Mandrin opened his bloodshot eyes and blinked a couple of times to get rid of the cobwebs and get a focus on Parks. "Nobody calls me *Fearless*," he said in a gravelly, testy voice, "leastwise, not to my face. Not if they don't want to die bloody." He raised himself onto an elbow and raked his hair back from his eyes.

"You're awfully prickly for a man staring down the barrel of his own gun," said Parks.

"A man staring down his own gun barrel might as well be prickly," Mandrin said. He looked around at the nightstand for the bottle of rye he'd placed there the night before, saving it as an eye-opener. "Did you drink my whiskey?" he asked, his face becoming grim at the prospect of having nothing to drink.

"No," said Parks, "you must have lost it wallowing in the dirt last night, like a pig."

Mandrin gave him a curious look. "Were you here last night?"

Parks gave a slight dark chuckle. He reached behind his back, produced Mandrin's corked bottle of whiskey and pitched it over onto the bed beside him. "I'm only funning you, Fred."

"You're a real funny man," Mandrin said in a stiff, dry tone. He picked up the bottle, pulled the cork and drained the two inches of rye with one deep swallow. Then he let out a whiskey hiss and tossed the bottle aside. "Unless you're going to shoot me, point that smoker another direction," he said, reaching out and shoving the barrel of the Remington away from his face. "I'm shaking so bad I might cause it to go off."

Parks chuckled again, but he eased the hammer down on the big Remington and laid it on the nightstand.

Mandrin felt the whiskey go right to work, soothing him, filling in all of the raw jittery holes it had left in him overnight. "What brings you up this way, Buckshot?" he asked with a more steady voice.

Parks shrugged. "I'm on the run, sort of," he said as if uncertain of himself.

"Yeah?" Mandrin stared at him through his puffy bloodshot eyes. "I don't know as I've ever heard of a man *sort of* on the run. Most will tell you flat out, they either are, or they ain't."

"Are you still toting that badge Delbert Jamison hung on you?"

"No," said Mandrin, "the town made me take it off. Said I drank too much. Said I'd get it back if I ever sobered up enough to pin it on without stabbing myself to death. The smug sons a' bitches." He coughed. "I told them to kiss my ass." He coughed again, deeper. "Why'd you ask?"

Parks looked disappointed. "That's too bad. I've got some business in the works that would've made you rich had you still been wearing a deputy badge."

"Well, I ain't wearing one," said Mandrin, "so close that door behind you." He reached back, took a wadded-up pillow and adjusted it, ready to lie back down. As an afterthought he took the Remington from the nightstand and slipped it roughly under the pillow.

"We might be able to do some business anyway," Parks said, giving the matter some thought. "Get up and let's talk about it."

Mandrin rose a little, an aggravated look on his face. "Listen, Buckshot, and don't take this the wrong way. I have never liked you much. I always thought you'd stab your best friend in the back if it would make you a dollar or two."

"What's that got to do with anything?" Parks asked, not the least bit offended. "Do you want to hear what I've got afoot here?" He looked all around the weathered, sun-bleached shack. "Or is this about as far as you ever planned on going in life?"

"Don't make yourself my judge, Buckshot Parks," said Mandrin. "I ain't the one *sort of* on the run here. I turned to upholding the law just to keep from getting hung by it. But badge on or off, I've stolen as much as the next man, over my natural time." He pushed himself up in the bed, swung his feet over onto the dusty plank floor and let out a breath. "I'm just what you could call 'off my game' right now."

"And I'm just the ace who can put you back onto your game. Do you want to hear what I've got going on here or not?" Parks asked.

"I might as well, I'm already up," Mandrin replied.

Parks gave a crafty smile. "I've got two words for you, Fred: Davin Grissin." He stopped as if he need say no more.

Mandrin just stared at him. After a dull pause, he said, "So?"

Parks shook his head slightly. "There's four cowhands in Red Hill who stole a bunch of Grissin's money from a stagecoach that I robbed. I was going to offer you a fourth of that money if you still wore your deputy badge, and for helping me kill them and get me that money back. It's rightfully mine anyway."

"Hold on," said Mandrin. "They stole money from a stagecoach that *you* robbed?" He wrinkled his brow trying to understand it.

"I'll fill you in on everything," said Parks. "The question is, are you in, or not?"

"A fourth?" Mandrin eyed him again.

"That was when I thought you still had your deputy badge," said Parks. "I figured you could pin it on and buffalo them a little. These boys are not outlaws. They'll do what the law tells them to do."

"I said I don't have my *deputy* badge," said Mandrin. "But I've got a sheriff badge I stole out of a desk once whilst I was delivering a prisoner to Yuma to be hanged."

"Well, hell, that's even better," said Parks. "Let me take a look at it."

"In good time," said Mandrin, not trusting Parks with such a rare treasure. "All we've got to do is kill these four cowhands, take the money and ride away?"

"Yep, that's it, more or less," said Parks, "if you can pose as a lawman when we catch up to them."

"I can do that easily—I've got enough practice at it." Mandrin stood up. "Let's go kill them and get done with it."

Parks stood up and said, "We're going to have to lure them out of town first."

"Why?" Mandrin asked. "There's nobody here to stop us. We can do as we damn well please."

Parks grinned "I like your way of thinking, but we want to do this in a way that neither the law nor Grissin and his men ever suspect us of anything. After acquiring this much money, I don't want to be looking over my shoulder for the rest of my life, do you?"

Considering it for a moment, Mandrin said, "No, I don't." He rubbed a hand across his dry lips. "Let's go get a bottle and you tell me everything I need to know about this deal."

"Now you're talking, Mandrin," said Parks, "or should I say, *Sheriff* Mandrin?"

As soon as a boy had been summoned from the livery barn and the spare horses taken away, the drovers moved their own mounts to the hitch rail out in front of the Blue Belle Saloon. Tad Harper had volunteered to stay with the animals while the other three accompanied Bart Frazier to his office in the rear of the barroom.

Frazier sat listening closely to everything Jet Mackenzie told him, about the stagecoach, the dead robbers and coachmen, the unopened strongbox and the bag of money belonging to Davin Grissin. The only thing Mackenzie didn't tell him was that the money was out front, divided and hidden among each of the drovers' personal affects.

"Just where is all of this money?" Frazier made a point in asking, showing great concern. "Somewhere safe, I hope?"

"Very safe," is all Mackenzie replied in a tight-lipped voice. Then he went on with the story, mentioning how they had gotten a raw deal from Grissin and were afraid that this fact alone might cast suspicion on them.

"Yes, I see how one might think that," Frazier said, rubbing his chin thoughtfully.

When the young drover finished, Frazier picked up the half-full bottle of whiskey standing on his desk, poured himself a shot, tossed it back and sighed. He looked studiously at Brewer, then at Thorpe, then back to Mackenzie.

"It's most fortunate for you young men that you came to me," he said. He pointed at Mackenzie and told the other two, "Your ramrod here has a head on his shoulders. I always admire a man who can think on his feet."

Mackenzie stared at him. He didn't need to be told what a good job he was doing. He only wanted to get things straightened out. "Obliged, Mr. Frazier," he said humbly. "Do you think you can help us out? All we want to do is get this money to the stage line and get shed of it. We don't want to get blamed for something we didn't do."

"Certainly I can help you out," Frazier said with confidence. "Put your minds at ease." He gave an even pearly white smile. "Can you do that for me, while I go send a wire to some of 'the right people' I know in Flagstaff?"

"We can sure try," said Mackenzie, making an effort to return Frazier's smile.

"Very good," Frazier said. "I'll bring you back

their reply, so you can read it for yourself." He reached out with the bottle and filled the empty shot glass sitting in front of Mackenzie. Then he filled Brewer's and Thorpe's shot glasses as they held them out toward him. "Of course I have to say, it would be much easier to declare your innocence if I could tell 'the right people' that I have the money sitting safely in front of me."

"Don't worry," said Mackenzie, "as soon as we know that your folks believe us and will get us off the hook, we'll put the money at your feet."

Frazier considered the matter. "Well, I certainly can't ask for better than that, now, can I?"

"No, you can't," Jock Brewer replied.

"Well, then," Frazier said, appearing undisturbed by the reply, "please make yourselves at home, gentlemen, while I get a wire off to Flagstaff." He turned, walked out and shut the door behind himself.

After a moment of tense silence, the three listening to the sound of Frazier's footsteps walking away across the plank floor, Brewer and Thorpe stepped closer to Mackenzie. "Do you trust this man?" Brewer asked.

"Yeah," Mackenzie said quietly, "but only because I don't see that we've got much choice."

The three remained quiet for a long moment, the only sound in the room that of a tall pendulum clock. Mackenzie finished his glass of whiskey. Brewer did the same. Then he glanced at the clock, poured himself another glassful and sipped it.

"I think he's a slick, grinning rattlesnake," Holly Thorpe finally said in a whisper, eyeing the closed door as if Frazier might be standing on the other side, listening all this time. "I think we'd best get out of here while the getting's good." He looked to Brewer for support.

"As soon as your *grinning rattlesnake* shows us a reply from Flagstaff, we *are* getting out of here," said Mackenzie. "We're not going to trust him any longer than we have to." He looked all around. "But, pards, we've got to get this money off our backs. Once Grissin hears about this, I've got a feeling he's not going to listen to anything we've got to say on the matter."

Brewer said to Thorpe, "I'm sticking with Mac on this. He's still our ramrod. He's never steered us wrong yet, has he?"

Thorpe settled. "Sorry, Mac. I just get a bad belly listening to the man talk." He fidgeted with his wire-rims and pushed them up on the bridge of his nose.

"Take it easy, Holly," Mackenzie said firmly, the ramrod giving his trail hand an order as if the two were seated atop their horses alongside a moving herd of longhorns. "A few minutes, it'll all be over."

Thorpe only nodded. "You're the boss, Mac."

Something had been gnawing at Mackenzie ever since Frazier had told them he knew *the right people* in Flagstaff. There was something he had noticed riding into Red Hill, but he couldn't quite put his finger on it. *What is it?* he asked himself, sipping his whiskey, looking across the room and out the window. Finally, he stood up, set the shot glass down, walked over and leaned both hands on the windowsill. Behind him, Brewer and Thorpe only gave each other a puzzled look and remained silent.

Through the dusty wavy windowpanes, Mackenzie gazed back and forth along the dirt street. He caught a glimpse of Frazier's swallow-tailed coat hurring into an alleyway; he saw two men with rifles hurry in behind him. Then he searched back and forth again, this time up along the rooflines, until suddenly he stopped and stood as if frozen for a second.

"Mac, what is it? What's going on?" Brewer asked, seeing a change come over the young trail boss.

Mackenzie didn't answer. Instead he turned from the window, walked past the desk and swiped his hat up and shoved it atop his head. "Let's go, pards. He's jackpotting us."

"Who's jackpotting us, Mac?" said Thorpe. He noted the pale, drawn look on Mackenzie's face as he and Brewer fell in behind him and started toward the door. "What do you mean, he's jackpotted us?"

"Yeah, boss," said Brewer, squeezing through the office door right beside Mackenzie, "jackpotting us how? What did you see out there?"

"Nothing," Mackenzie said in a clipped tone as he walked on toward the batwing doors leading out to the street.

"Nothing?" said Brewer. "It sure don't appear that you seen nothing, the way you're—"

"I saw *nothing*," said Mackenzie. He lifted his Colt from his holster as he walked, checking it and keeping it in his hand. "I looked from one end of this town to the other. There's not a telegraph pole in sight."

"That grinning rattlesnake," said Thorpe.

"Stay close 'til we hit the street and get Tadpole covered, then spread out and get ready for a fight. But don't shoot until I tell you to. Both of you got that?"

"Got it, boss," said Brewer, his Colt already up, checked and cocked.

"Thorpe?" said Mackenzie, pushing his way through the batwing doors.

"Right behind you, boss," said Thorpe, his right hand levering a round up into his rifle chamber.

Chapter 10

Out in front of the Blue Belle Saloon, Tad Harper had already caught sight of Bart Frazier and three riflemen step out of the alleyway and start walking in his direction. Along the dirt street, buggies and wagons hurried away as if in premonition of a coming gun battle. On the boardwalks people ducked into doorways. Atop the roofline to his right, Harper saw the glint of gunmetal in the harsh sunlight.

Easing away from the hitch rail, he started toward the batwing doors to warn the others. But before he'd made it halfway there, the three barged out. "Mac!" Harper said. "There's gunmen everywhere!"

"We saw them, Tadpole. Good work," said Mackenzie, staring past Harper toward Bart Frazier. Two of the three riflemen flanked the saloon owner. The third had drifted off to the side, covering the entrance to a narrow street leading out of town.

In the middle of the dirt street, Bart Frazier said to the gunman nearest him, "Damn it, they caught on to me too soon! If we'd surprised them in my office, there wouldn't have been a shot fired."

"But that ain't how it worked out, Frazier," said one of the riflemen.

Frazier stopped suddenly, raised his voice and called out loud enough for the whole town to hear, "Those four drovers robbed the Albertson stage. They killed the driver, the guard and three passengers! One of them was Colonel Tanner, a man this territory held in the highest esteem—"

Mackenzie cut him off with a raised voice. "You're a liar, Frazier, you grinning rattlesnake! Don't listen to him, folks," he called out to faces peeping from behind closed doors and windows. "We come here to tell the law about the robbery—"

Now Frazier cut him off. "I am the law when it comes to dealing with bandits and far-handed rogues like you," he shouted for the townsfolk to hear. "If you're truly innocent, throw down your guns. The whole town is backing me up on this. Am I right, folks?" He looked back and forth along the street.

"We'd like to hear what the young man has to say about it," a voice called out from the cracked-open door of the barbershop.

But Frazier ignored the voice. "Tell your men to throw down their guns, Mackenzie," he demanded as the young drovers spread out along the boardwalk in front of his saloon. He brought his own gunmen forward with a gesture of his hand. "You're not leaving Red Hill," he called out to Mackenzie.

"They're getting too close, boss," Brewer said in a harsh whisper, getting anxious. "Say the word, let us commence!"

"Hold your fire," Mackenzie said sidelong to the two drovers. In front of him Tad Harper stood watching quietly, his rifle in hand, cocked and ready. Then Mackenzie called out to the listening townsfolk, "Frazier told us there's no sheriff here, but that we could trust him. We told him that we found the robbed stage, but we wouldn't tell him where the money is hidden until we knew we were safe. Now he figures if we're his prisoners, he can force us to tell him—"

The young trail boss's voice was cut short by a rifle shot resounding from the street. The bullet whistled past his left knee and thumped into the front of the Blue Belle Saloon. Splinters flew from a large hole in the clapboard siding.

"Damn it, Sadler!" said Frazier to the gunmen flanking him. "Don't shoot up my place. Wait until they make a run for it. Take that trail boss alive, but kill the others."

"Yes, sir," said the rifleman who had just fired at Mackenzie's leg. He levered a fresh round into his rifle chamber and gave a hand signal to two more gunmen atop the roofline. "Wait until they try to make a break. Leave the trail boss to me, boys, we want him alive," he said, repeating Frazier's words up to them. "Kill the others."

Hearing part of the rifleman's words, Thorpe and Brewer glanced at each other, then stared at Mackenzie, their hands tight around their guns. "You heard him, Mac!" Brewer said through clenched teeth. "Say the word before they kill us."

"Hold your fire," said Mackenzie, noting how low the bullet had been zipping past his knee. "Wait until I tell you."

"Dang it, Mac, let's do something!" said Brewer, his nerves pressing him hard.

"Do as you're told, Brewer," Mackenzie said in a harsh rigid tone. To Harper he said, "Tadpole, unhitch the horses. Get ready to make a run with them."

"Right, boss." Harper stepped forward, reached out and quickly unhitched and gathered the reins to all four horses along the rail.

"Jock, you and Holly get ready to cover him," Mackenzie said to the other two.

"What are we fixing to do here, Mac, try to make a run for it?" Brewer asked, his confidence in the trail boss wavering a bit. His eyes darted back and forth between Mackenzie and the men advancing slowly along the dirt street.

"No," said Mackenzie, "we just left the best cover in town." He gave Brewer a determined look. "We're going back inside Frasier's saloon . . . only we're taking our horses with us. If he wants us out of there, he'll have to burn us out."

"You're danged right, boss," Brewer said, the look on his face changing quickly. "Give Tadpole the word, we've got him covered."

"We've got to let him know," said Mackenzie, raising his cocked Colt and taking careful aim at the rifleman who had fired the first shot, "that we'll stand together or let his place burn down around us." He pulled the trigger. The Colt bucked in his hand. The rifleman nearest Frazier flew backward to the ground, his life's blood splattering on the saloon owner's face.

"Fire," Mackenzie said to Brewer and Thorpe. To Harper he said, "Go, Tadpole!"

As bullets began to fly, Frazier watched Tad Harper rush through the batwing doors, the horses filing in behind him. "What the hell are they doing, Bryson?" he asked the gunman left standing beside him, above the roar of gunfire from both directions.

"What are they *doing*? They're taking their damned horses inside your saloon," Nate Bryson replied, firing as he spoke. "That's what the hell they're doing."

On the boardwalk, Mackenzie gave the last of the four horses a slap on its rump. As the animal slipped inside the saloon, a batwing door fell from its top hinge and hung at a crazy angle. Hurrying inside behind the horses, Thorpe gave the door a hard kick and sent it bouncing and sliding along the plank boardwalk. Mackenzie braved the heavy gunfire until Brewer was safely inside behind Thorpe.

Then he fired three shots as he backed inside the saloon.

"Jesus!" said Frazier with a wince, seeing the butt of a rifle crash through a large front window. "This is not what I intended! They're going to bust my place to pieces!"

"We've got a fight on our hands, Frazier," said Bryson. "You might not have intended it this way, but you best get used to it. When they killed Sadler, they called it on to the end."

Bryson ducked away, Frazier right beside him as rifle fire from the broken front windows grew too intense to stand up to. Inside the saloon, Brewer called out to Mackenzie, "The ones in the street are backing away to cover, boss." He fired another shot as Frazier and Bryson disappeared behind a stake of wooden shipping crates out in front of the freight office.

"Good. Hold your fire," shouted Mackenzie, noting that the gunshots from the rooflines had ceased. "Tadpole, get a count, see how much ammunition we've got between us."

Harper hurried to the milling horses, who stood huddled at a battered upright piano as if studying its yellowed ivory keys. He flipped open saddlebag after saddlebag, rummaging through them and laying boxes of ammunition and loose handfuls of rifle cartridges onto a green-felted poker table.

"*Whooiee!* I never realized we all were so flush with bullets!" he said.

"What does it look like, Tadpole?" Mackenzie asked in a stern tone of voice.

Counting quickly, Harper said, "It looks like we've got near a hundred and fifty rounds amongst us, Mac."

"A hundred and fifty?" said Mackenzie. "Are you sure, Tadpole, that sounds like a lot."

"Want me to count it again?" Harper asked.

Before Mackenzie could answer, all four men swung their guns toward the bar, where a crash of glass resounded, followed by a curse, then a sharp cry. "Don't shoot! I just work here," a voice called out as the bartender stood up behind the bar with his hands in the air. "I'm not on Frazier's side—I'm not on anybody's side. All I do is sling whiskey for Frazier! I swear it! You can ask ole Art here."

Beside the bartender, the old man, Art Mullens, stood up with his hands raised too. "He's not lying," said Mullens. "His name is Thesis Sweeney, and I've never seen him take sides agin a man on Frazier's account."

"I heard shooting and ducked down," said the tall, thin bartender.

"Is there a shotgun back there?" Mackenzie asked, his hand relaxed but still holding his Colt in the bartender's direction.

"Yes, sir, there is," said Sweeney. "But I never intended to—"

"Pick it up by the barrel and lay it on the bar," said Mackenzie, cutting him off.

"Here I go, easy-like." The bartender sidestepped

along the bar, slowly raised a shotgun and laid it down along the bar top.

"Ask him what that *grinning rattlesnake* Frazier drinks," Harper called out to Mackenzie.

Mackenzie and Brewer gave each other a curious look until they both caught on to Harper's reasoning. "Good thinking, Tadpole," said Brewer.

"Yeah, good thinking *again,* Tadpole," Mackenzie repeated. He gave a slight smile and said to the bartender, "You heard our pard. What does your boss drink?"

"Mr. Frazier drinks only the finest Kentucky bourbon," said Sweeney, not seeming to realize what the drovers had in mind. "He has it sent here all the way from Bardstown, where it's made at."

"Get it up, bartender," said Mackenzie. "We could all use a good long drink about now."

"What?" Sweeney looked dumbfounded. "I can't serve you his sipping bourbon—he'll have a straight-up conniption fit! His bourbon and cigars are the pride of his life!"

"Are you going to make me ask you again?" Mackenzie said in a stronger tone. "Get the bourbon." He cocked the Colt even though he had no intention of shooting the wide-eyed bartender.

"The cigars too," Harper called out from his position at one of the broken front windows.

"You heard him, Thesis Sweeney," said Mackenzie, "get out the cigars too."

"Yieeehi!" From the broken window, Brewer called out to the street, "Much obliged, Bart Frazier.

We're fixing to help ourselves to your bourbon and cigars."

Behind the shipping crates, Frazier watched Nate Bryson reload his rifle and wave the gunmen along the roofline to come down to the street. "Did you hear what he said? They're going to start looting my place."

"Tough luck, Frazier," said Bryson. "Me and the boys were in a serious game of poker at the River Palace when you come asking us for help. We agreed, for one thousand dollars. Now it's sounding like you're ready to crawfish out of the deal."

"Don't worry about your money, you'll get it," said Frazier. "But my plan was to take them as prisoners without incident. I didn't consider getting my saloon shot to pieces in the bargain!"

"Like I said, *tough luck, Frazier.*" Bryson levered a round into his rifle chamber. "But we're not stopping, not after them shooting Sadler down like a dog."

"I understand you feeling that way about losing one of your own," said Frazier. He wiped sweat from his forehead. "But there must be a way to get them out of there without destroying the Blue Belle! For God's sake, it's the only decent saloon in Red Hill."

"Then you best hope we can get these cowhands to come out," said Bryson, "else we're going to level it to the ground if we have to." He rose quickly, threw his arm atop a wooden shipping crate, leveled his rifle and began firing.

"Level it to the ground? Good Lord, man! You must be out of your mind!" Frazier shouted. But his words went unheard beneath the renewed volley of gunfire from the rooflines, from the corner of an alley and from Bryson right beside him.

Inside the Blue Belle, Mackenzie hurried around the bar in a crouch while the other three drovers returned fire from the broken windows. Huddled back down behind the bar, Sweeney and Art Mullens looked at Mackenzie wide-eyed. "Are you going to shoot us?" Sweeney asked. "I warned you he'd have a fit over his bourbon and cigars."

"I'm not going to shoot you," said Mackenzie. "I'm going to get you out of here before they shoot you and we get blamed for it."

"Why don't you just hold us hostage?" Art Mullens grinned, holding a bottle of Frazier's Kentucky bourbon, a black cigar gripped between his teeth.

"Because I don't think holding you two hostage would do a thing for our predicament," Mackenzie said.

"You never know until you try," the old man offered with the wink of an eye.

Mackenzie looked at him. Then he nodded toward the rear door, saying, "Come on, both of you follow me."

"You know danged well Frazier has a gunman or two covering the back door," said Mullens, not wanting to give up his unique situation. "He knows every lowlife in the territory."

"They'll see it's us and they won't shoot us, Art," said the bartender, eager to get out of there. "Now stop jawing and get moving." He gave the old man a shove to get him started.

"All right, then," Mullens said grudgingly. He hurried along in a crouch behind Mackenzie, gunshots spitting through the air all around them.

At the back door, Mackenzie crouched to one side, lifted the latch and swung the door open wide. The tall, lean bartender and the old man stepped out, hands held high and hurried forward. "Don't shoot! It's me, Thesis, and old Art!" the bartender called out. Mackenzie glimpsed a man stepping out from behind a tall saguaro cactus with his rifle to his shoulder.

"Get the hell away from that open door," the gunman called out.

Seeing that the gunman wasn't going to shoot at the bartender and the old man, Mackenzie waited a moment until the two were safely out of the way. Then he fired three rapid shots and swung the door shut. "It looks like Frazier has thought of everything. He's got us surrounded," Mackenzie called out through the gunfire.

At the broken front window, Harper peeked out. "You mean they've got us circled?" he asked. On one side of the street the gunmen from the roofline had hurried down and taken new positions. On the other side of the street, Frazier and Nate Bryson remained behind the cover of the shipping crates.

"I'm afraid so, Tadpole," Mackenzie called out in reply.

"That's good," said Harper. "It they're all around us, they'll have to shoot at each other when we ride through them."

Brewer and Mackenzie looked at each other through the heavy gunfire. "Don't he beat all?" Brewer said.

Chapter 11

When the gunfire reached a lull as both sides reloaded, Frazier ventured a long look at the front of his bullet-riddled saloon. "Oh no . . . ," he lamented. A bullet had broken one of the chains holding a large wooden sign above the doors. The sign hung from one end, bullet holes having splintered it so badly it was no longer readable.

"What's the matter?" Nate Bryson asked, turning with his smoking rifle in one hand, a palmful of bullets in the other.

Broken window glass sparkled like piles of diamonds on the boardwalk. Bullets had chopped off the hitch rail, leaving two post stubs standing in the dirt. "Nate, we've got to stop this!" said Frazier. "It's gotten entirely out of hand."

"You ask for it, you got it," Bryson said, hardly giving the saloon owner a glance as he shoved bullet after bullet into his rifle. He nodded at the empty Colt in Frazier's hand. "You best get yourself reloaded. My pa always said, 'an empty gun never solved anything,'" he said with a dark chuckle.

"Damn it, your pa was right." Frazier stared at him, seething with shock and anger, and jammed bullets into the big Colt.

As soon as Bryson had finished loading his rifle, he stepped back to where the riflemen could see him and waved an arm back and forth in the air.

On the other side of the street, at the corner of an alley, one rifleman eased up into his saddle and took three burning torches from another gunman's hand. Catching a glimpse of what was going on, Frazier asked Bryson in a voice near panic, "Wait a minute, what the hell is he doing?"

"Just what I'm wanting him to do," Bryson said without a glance at the saloon owner. "He's fixing to burn them *the hell* out of there. These sons a' bitches ain't getting the upper hand here."

"Jesus! God, no! You can't burn the Blue Belle to the ground!" Frazier shrieked, jumping up and waving his arms back and forth wildly, trying desperately to get the gunman's attention and stop him. But he was too late. The mounted gunman raced his horse forward and made three short, fast circles in front of the Blue Belle, hurling one of the flaming torches with each pass.

"I've got him, Mac," said Holly from inside the saloon. He adjusted his wire rims and tucked the butt of his rifle up against his shoulder. He took close aim while the other drovers began shooting toward the gunman who stood at the corner of the alleyway providing cover fire for the circling horseman.

The last torch streaked through the air, through the open window past Thorpe's head and bounced off a felt-topped table just as his rifle shot exploded. "Got him," Thorpe said under his breath as the gunman flew from his saddle and landed sprawled in the dusty street.

"Look out, Tadpole!" shouted Mackenzie.

Harper had snatched up each torch as it landed on the saloon floor, and tossed it back out through the broken window. The first two torches lay in the street, burning harmlessly in the dirt. But the third torch had bounced off the table, off a wall and landed where an earlier bullet had knocked an oil lantern to the floor.

A large circle of the spilled oil flamed up suddenly, burning high and fierce. Harper turned away quickly, slinging his arm madly in the air as flames danced along his wool shirtsleeve. At the sight of the licking flames, the horses spooked, one of them spinning and kicking the upright piano over on the floor.

Mackenzie made a long dive, tackled Harper to the floor and beat at the fire with his hat. Thorpe and Brewer left their positions at the front windows and grabbed the horses' reins, trying to settle the terrified animals. Bullets streaked through the air, one of them slicing across Mackenzie's shoulder as he and Harper hurried out of gun sight.

"Here it comes, they're burning us out, Mac!" Thorpe shouted. "It's going up fast!"

"Mount up! Let's go! The danged fool is burning his own business!" Mackenzie shouted in reply.

Jumping atop their horses, Brewer struggled to keep his horse bounding in one spot long enough to ask Mackenzie, "How do you want to play this, boss?"

"I'm coming last, giving you boys some cover. Ride hard, shoot straight!" said Mackenzie above the licking, bellowing flames as the fire leaped upward against the ceiling and rolled back down inside itself. "Don't stop for nothing!"

"Don't worry, we won't!" Thorpe shouted, nailing his boot heels to his horse's side even as the animal reeled on its own and shot out through the large broken window.

"Who's going to cover you?" asked Brewer.

"Don't argue with me, Jock!" Mackenzie shouted at him harshly. "Do like you're told! Get out of here!"

On the street, Bryson and Frazier watched the flames that had traveled across the ceiling and now rolled out and up along the broken window frames. "Burn or fight, you no-good saddle tramps . . . ," Bryson said in a low growl almost to himself.

As the four drovers streaked out the window in a broiling cloud of black smoke and raced past him, Bryson fired repeatedly. His shots caused his men across the street to have to duck down and take cover from him as well as from the shots coming from the guns of the fleeing drovers. Beside Bryson, Frazier stood staring pale-faced, red-eyed and stunned at his burning saloon.

He heard Bryson's rifle explode. He heard Mackenzie's horse let out a fearful whinny as Bryson's bullet struck its bulging saddlebags.

"I got one!" Bryson shouted. He jumped up and down, his rifle smoking as the bullet's impact caused Mackenzie's horse to lose balance and go tumbling headlong in a cloud of dust. "See it? I got one!"

The bullet had struck the saddlebags solidly enough to stagger the animal. As it tumbled, a bundle of money jumped from the saddlebags, high in the air, and broke open in a shower of green U.S. dollar bills. "I got one! I got one!" Bryson repeated over and over.

"You got *one . . . ?*" Frazier stared at him fiercely from behind while the gunman continued to jump up and down.

Having heard Mackenzie's horse whinnying behind him, Brewer circled sharply and saw Mackenzie staggering to his feet, scrambling to his horse as it stood and spun wildly in place. "Mac's down!" Brewer shouted, nailing his boots to his horse's sides and racing back into the fray.

"You got one?" Frazier repeated to Bryson, his voice swelling with rage, the smell of his burning saloon heavy in the air.

"Yeah!" Bryson spun, facing him wide-eyed, wearing a broad openmouthed grin. "Did you see—"

Holding the big Colt at arm's length, Frazier shot him in his forehead.

On the other side of the street, the riflemen had renewed firing now that Bryson's shots were no longer pinning them down. By the time Brewer had slid his horse down beside Mackenzie, the young trail boss was back up in his saddle, his horse rearing, dust flying from its mane and tail. "I told you all not to stop!" Mackenzie scolded him.

"Let's go, boss," said Brewer, "you can fire me later!" As he spoke he fired at the men positioned at the corner of the alleyway.

Mackenzie caught sight of Frazier standing over Bryson's body. But before he could even think about what might have happened, he heard Thorpe and Harper firing as the two raced back along the dusty street. "You can fire them too," Brewer shouted.

Mackenzie shook his head and wiped dirt from his eyes. The firing from the corner of the alley continued but only halfheartedly, as the drovers turned their horses as one and raced away toward a hill line. No sooner had the four ridden out of range than the riflemen ran from the alleyway and began snatching up the money lying in the dirt and drifting along on a breeze.

When Red Hill become barely visible behind them, the four drovers stopped at a triple fork in the trail for a moment and looked back at the black rising smoke. "I never want to leave a town that way again," said Tad Harper.

"It was all your fault, Tadpole, drinking the man's whiskey, smoking his cigars," Brewer joked, his nerves settling some. He reached over and pulled Harper's hat down over his eyes. "In case you didn't hear back there, Mac is firing us."

"What for? We don't even have a job," Thorpe said, his hand pressed to his side.

"He said we did wrong coming back to get him," Brewer replied.

"We wouldn't have had to come get him if he had known how to sit his horse," Harper tossed in.

"All right," said Mackenzie, taking his ribbing good-naturedly, knowing it was their way of winding down. "I expect I'll give the three of you another chance."

"Fellows, I'm not feeling so good here," Thorpe said all of a sudden, drawing their attention to his hand pressed to his side. A circle of blood showed behind his palm.

"Dang, Mac, Holly's shot," said Brewer. He sidled up to Thorpe and pulled his hand away from his bleeding side long enough to take a look.

"I'm all right," Thorpe said, even though his face had turned pale and he sat a bit slumped in his saddle.

"You sure don't look it," said Brewer. "Get down from that saddle, let's take a look at your side."

"My side ain't none of your business, Jock," Thorpe said, his voice sounding weak. He jerked his horse away from Brewer.

Nudging his horse over closer to Thorpe, Mackenzie said to him, "Do like he said, Holly, we've got to take a look at it."

Thorpe's jaw tightened, but he did as he was told. He slid stiffly down from his saddle, walked over to a rock and sat down on it, pulling his bloody shirttails from his trousers. "I never seen such a nosy bunch in my life," he grumbled, unbuttoning his shirt. As he took off his shirt, a fresh rush of blood spilled from the round hole in his flesh and poured down onto the rock beneath him. "See, it ain't nothing," he said, spreading his shirt open.

"While it's *nothing* is a good time to get it taken care of," said Mackenzie, "before it does turn into *something.*"

Harper stepped down from his horse and walked over carrying a clean bandanna he'd taken from his saddlebags. Brewer took it, laid it against Thorpe's wound and placed Thorpe's hand over it. "You two are turning into old parlormaids," Thorpe said to Brewer.

Mackenzie stepped back and looked off in three directions. "There used to be a doctor in Creasy," he said. "I expect that's our best bet."

"We ought to split up," said Harper, "just in case Frazier and his bunch comes looking for us."

"No, Tadpole," said Mackenzie, "we're sticking together. Four guns are better than one if Frazier, or anybody else, comes hunting us."

"That ain't what I mean," Harper said. "I mean right now we ought to split up. One of us takes Holly into Creasy, the other two each take a different trail. Frazier has seen the money—he knows we've got it with us. If we split up he won't know which one of us has it. He'll have to split his men to follow each one of us."

"That means fewer men riding into Creasy on us while Holly gets patched up," Brewer speculated. "It makes sense."

"Once we get a few miles up the trails, we can cut away, cover our tracks and meet up in Creasy."

Mackenzie considered it for a moment, then looked at Brewer. "Tadpole has turned out to be smarter than he looks, boss."

Brewer shrugged.

"Okay. I'll take Holly into Creasy," said Mackenzie. "Don't neither one of you go any farther than ten miles along the other two trails. When you cut off, make danged sure they won't see your tracks right away. That ought to keep them all busy until we've gotten Holly patched up and get going." He looked back and forth between them. "Has everybody got that?"

"I've got it, boss," said Harper, taking a step back toward his horse. "Ten miles, cover our tracks, meet in Creasy," he reiterated.

"Got it, boss," said Brewer, stepping forward to help Mackenzie get Thorpe back up into his saddle.

"You don't have to do all this for me," Thorpe protested as the two drovers shoved him upward onto his horse. "I'm telling you I'll be all right, just as soon as this thing stops bleeding."

"Shut up and take it easy, Holly," said Mackenzie. "I ain't planning on losing a man here." He laid Thorpe's reins into his bloody, gloved hands.

"But I can ride my own danged self into town," Thorpe insisted, gripping the reins. Sunlight glinted off his spectacle lenses. Even as he spoke, the three noted that his voice had begun to slur a little. His eyes swam aimlessly.

"Sure you can," said Mackenzie, waving the other two away, getting them off onto the two different trails. "I'm just tagging along with you to make sure I don't get myself lost."

When the drovers had slipped up onto their respective trails and ridden out of sight, no sooner had the dust settled than Stanton Parks and Fred Mandrin rode up off the rocky hillside at a hard run and had to slide their horses to a dust-raising halt. "Damn it all to hell!" said Parks, looking back and forth along the three separate trails, each trail full of crisscrossing hoofprints, some older, some newer.

"I told you so," said Mandrin, shaking his head as he took out a bottle of whiskey from inside his ragged riding duster. "Once they got here, it would be hard to tell which trail they took." He turned up a drink and let out a whiskey hiss. "*Whew!* That was a hard ride, drunk or sober."

Parks gave him a hard-eyed stare, seeing how the former deputy seemed to slump into his saddle as if the day's work was done. "It ain't over, Mandrin," he said. He stepped his horse back and forth where he'd been examining the start of each trail.

"Hell, I know that," said Mandrin, straightening in his saddle and taking on a more committed countenance. "I just took myself a breather, is all."

"You better know it," Parks warned. "You better draw your nuts up in that saddle and act like you think all this money is worth going after. You do not want me thinking you've lost interest." He didn't wait for a reply. He looked back at the ground and searched back and forth, trying to determine what he could from the fresh tracks on all three trails.

Mandrin nudged his horse over, looked back and forth and said confidently, "They split up here."

Parks glared at him with a snarl. "How the hell can you just ride over after me looking my ass off, and tell that they split up?" He gestured toward the ground. "Tell me just how the living hell you can read all that in these prints!"

"I didn't read it in any hoofprints," said Mandrin in the same confident tone. "I'm a former lawman and a former outlaw. Both my *lawing* and my *outlawing* tell me this is where I'd split up if I didn't want to be followed. Don't it you?"

Parks stared at him coldly, his fingers tapping on the butt of his Colt. "Yeah, it does," he said. "What else does your lawing and outlawing tell you here?" He gestured toward the ground.

With a finger pointing to the two sets of fresh prints, Mandrin said quietly, "The one with all the money is headed for Creasy. He kept one man with him as a guard, and the other two split off to fool anybody following them. That's what I would have done, and so would you." He grinned, raised the bottle to his lips and took another swig. He took out a handkerchief to pat his sweaty forehead. When a shiny sheriff's badge fell out of it, he caught it quickly and shoved it into his vest pocket, hoping Parks had not seen it.

But Parks had caught a glimpse. Without mentioning the badge, he gave Mandrin a glance, considered it and replied, "I believe you're right, Fred. But you know what?" As he spoke he raised his Colt from his holster, cocked it and laid it on his lap. "I don't think you and I are going to make it as pards after all."

"What the hell?" said Mandrin. "I thought you said you needed some help with this deal?"

"I thought I did," said Parks, "but now that I know where they're going, I can handle it myself." He shrugged.

Mandrin wiped the handkerchief across his lips quickly, letting the bottle fall from his hands. "It's because I drink a little? If it is I'll just stop it right here and now."

"It's not that, *Fearless* Fred," Parks said with sarcasm, picking up the Colt and looking at it as he hefted it in his hand. "I just don't think your heart's been in this." He turned the Colt and fired one shot through Mandrin's chest. The former deputy, former thief, hit the ground in a puff of dust and lay staring stone-eyed dead at the wide blue sky.

"Call it *poor hiring judgment* on my part," Parks

said. He stepped down from his saddle long enough to take the sheriff's badge from Mandrin's vest pocket, look at it and put it away. Remounting, he turned his horse onto the trail toward Creasy and nudged the animal forward.

Chapter 12

The ranger, Maria and the big cur rode into Red Hill the following morning, having seen the slim spiral of smoke on the evening sky the night before. Arriving on the dirt street, they saw the ashy gray-black pile of rubble that had been the Blue Belle Saloon. In front of his vanished saloon, Bart Frazier sat rocking back and forth slowly in a high-backed rocker.

The ranger and Maria stopped their horses as they watched three armed townsmen walk toward them from the boardwalk out in front of the sheriff's office. On the ground the big cur gave a low warning growl, but then sat down in the dirt when he saw the ranger's gloved hand point to the ground and heard the ranger say, "At ease, Sergeant Tom Haines," feeling a little foolish doing so.

Upon seeing the ranger's badge and recognizing him by his horse, his pearl gray sombrero and the dark-haired woman riding at his side, the lead townsman said as he approached, "I can't tell you how glad we are to see you ride in, Ranger. I take it you *are* Ranger Sam Burrack?" Without pausing to take a breath or hear a reply, he continued, saying, "I'm Al Sheer? I own Sheer's Mercantile?" His every sentence ended as a question, as if he wasn't quite sure of anything. "As you can see, we've had a terrible tragedy here?"

"Yes, so it appears," said Sam. He gazed toward a body lying wrapped in a tarpaulin in the rear of a freight wagon sitting at a hitch rail, in front of the River Palace Saloon. "We're tracking four riders from over near Albertson," he said. "I wonder if they had anything to do with this." He didn't mention the stage robbery or the killings, or Stanton Parks just yet. He didn't say any more than he had to, wanting to hear what the townsfolk had to tell him.

"These are the ones who robbed the stage near there, if that's the ones you're tracking," said Sheer.

"How do you know?" Sam asked. He gazed up the street, spotting four more canvas-wrapped bodies lying on the boardwalk in front of the barbershop.

"He told us. That's Bart Frazier," said Sheer, nodding toward the saloon owner who sat dejected, rocking in his chair and staring at the burnt stubs and ashes of the Blue Belle Saloon. "He owns the Blue Belle—that is, he *did* own it. Frazier and some of his gambling associates tried trapping the four drovers inside the Blue Belle. . . . You can see how well that turned out. The drovers killed three of them. The other body is our former deputy, Fred Mandrin. I tracked the robbers up to Three Forks and found Fred lying there dead. Once a lawman always a lawman, I suppose."

Not in "Fearless" Fred Mandrin's case, Sam felt like saying. But he kept himself from commenting on the matter, knowing that if Mandrin was there it was to get the money for himself, not as an act of upholding the law.

Sheer nodded toward the rubble. "The drovers confessed the killings and stage robbery to Frazier. So now there are four more murders and an arson charge you can arrest them for. I'll formalize the complaint myself if you wish me to."

Now, why would they confess to Burt Frazier . . . ? Sam only stared at Sheer, still offering no reply. "Hold up on the complaint," Sam said, "until I get to the bottom of all this."

"To the bottom of this?" said Sheer. "My goodness, Ranger Burrack, isn't it obvious, giving what we saw, and what Frazier said—"

"Frazier was lying," Art Mullens said abruptly before Sheer could finish his words. "He's also a *grinning rattlesnake,*" Mullens added with a chuckle, he and Thesis Sweeney having eased in behind the armed townsmen. "That's what the four cowhands called him—*a grinning rattlesnake.*"

"Art, stay out of this," said Sheer. To the ranger he said, "Pay him no mind, Ranger Burrack, that's old Art Mullens. He's always got to put his two cents' worth into anything that happens here."

But the ranger ignored Sheer's advice and stared at Mullens. "Lying about what, Mr. Mullens?"

The old man's chest swelled a little at hearing himself called *Mr.* "Hell, about everything. Them drovers didn't rob no stage—"

"Of course the drovers robbed it," Sheer cut in impatiently. "Where else would cowhands get something like this?" He handed a broken money band up to the ranger. "A stack of bills flew out of one of their saddlebags. This was all that was left of it, of course, after Frazier's *gambling associates* began plucking it out of the dirt and the air."

"Having the stolen money doesn't make the cowhands thieves, Sheer, any more than having a red rabbit jump out your ass makes you think you're going—"

"Hey, that's enough of that," said the ranger, cutting Mullens off.

"Begging the lady's pardon," said Mullens, snatching his flop hat from his head with a repentant expression.

Beside him, Sweeney said, "But what he's saying is true, Ranger Burrack. I'm Thesis Sweeney. I tended bar at the Blue Belle. Them drovers was as polite and respectful as any bunch I've ever met. They didn't rob no stage, and they didn't burn down the Blue Belle." He pointed at Frazier in his rocking chair. "That idiot had his pals from the River Palace throw torches through the window to smoke out the drovers."

"See?" said Sheer. "That makes no sense at all to

me, or to anybody with their wits about them. Why would Frazier do something like that?"

"Because it all got out of hand on him, Sheer," said Sweeney, getting irritated. "Are you an idiot too, that you can't see that?"

Sam handed Maria the broken money band. "Take a look at this," he said to her while the men argued back and forth. Maria read the printing on the band and gave it back to the ranger. She looked at him with a raised brow. Then she cut into the conversation between Sweeney, Mullens and Sheer, saying, "Excuse me, Mr. Mullens. My horse is thirsty. Will you please accompany me somewhere so I can water it?" She stepped down from her saddle and stretched, a hand to the small of her back. Mullens and Sweeney watched, their mouths agape. "Perhaps we can talk some more?"

"Uhhh . . ." Mullen looked dumbfounded for a moment, as did Sweeney. Then, snapping out of it, Mullens said, "My God, *yes, ma'am*! I most certainly will." He grabbed the reins from her with a trembling hand, almost spooking her horse. The dog sat watching her walk away, the two men flanking her. But sensing no danger, he made no sign of wanting to follow.

"Thank goodness," said Sheer, seeing what he thought was Maria leading the two away so he and the ranger could talk. Looking back at the ranger, he gestured at the dog. "I recognize this dog, he belonged to Colonel Tanner."

"Belonged?" Sam said, eying him closely.

"Yes," said Sheer, "Frazier told us the colonel is dead, that these four drovers killed him." He shrugged. "I suppose it was part of what they must have confessed to him."

He could see he needed to talk to Bart Frazier, Sam told himself, studying the broken paper money band in his gloved hand. "I'm also searching for another man . . . a fellow named Stanton Parks," he said.

"Buckshot Parks?" said Sheer.

"You've heard of him?" Sam asked.

"Oh yes, indeed," said Sheer, "I know the name. I've seen his face on many wanted posters. I haven't seen him in person, though, I'm happy to say." He paused in reflection, then said, "But wait. I did see a lone rider approaching Fred's shack. . . ." He considered it further. "I wondered why he was riding off the trail, through the brush and weeds, as if he did not want to be seen. I thought that was odd. You don't suppose . . . ?" He let his words hang for a moment, then tacked on "No, I hardly think Fred Mandrin would have any dealings with a man like Buckshot Parks."

Yep, it made sense to him, Sam thought, not replying to the naïve townsman. Parks was after the money and threw in with Mandrin, he surmised to himself. He closed his hand over the band and looked over at Frazier.

"You'll find Bart Frazier *very* upset, Ranger Burrack," said Sheer, anticipating what the ranger had in mind.

"I bet I will," Sam replied, nudging his horse forward. He glanced at the pile of debris, then at the back of Bart Frazier's head as the former saloon owner sat rocking back and forth slowly. The big cur loped along beside him.

"I know it's you, Ranger Burrack," Frazier said without turning to face him when Sam stopped his horse a few feet behind him and stepped down from his saddle. "I'm not receiving any company just now, so you can feel free to ride on."

"I'm here on business, Frazier," Sam said calmly, walking up behind him, the big cur at his side. "I need to know the truth about everything that happened here. I don't want to go away searching for four innocent men."

"Innocent? Ha! Innocent of what?" said Frazier with a bitter tone.

"You know what I'm saying, Frazier," Sam pressed. "If these four have really broken any laws, I need to know about it. If they haven't I need to know that too."

"I've never cared much for you, Burrack," Frazier said, still staring at the black and gray pile of ashes and debris, "and I know you have never cared much for me."

"I'd say that's a fair assessment both ways," Sam replied. "But I am sorry to see the Blue Belle burnt to the ground."

After a sigh and a pause Frazier said, "Let me ask you something, Burrack. How would you feel if you saw everything you've worked for go up in a black puff of smoke? Wouldn't you want to see the ones responsible for it punished?"

"Only if they really were *responsible* for it, Frazier," said Sam. "That's why I want to know everything about this shoot-out."

After another pause, Frazier said, "Ask away, Burrack."

"I'm curious as to why these four drovers came to you and confessed that they had robbed the stage," said Sam.

Frazier shook his head slowly and said without looking around at him, "You must not know much about the drinking and gambling business, Burrack. People get a little whiskey in them, they tell you everything when you own a saloon."

"I know a *bartender* hears a lot, Frazier," Sam replied. "But thieves don't tell saloon owners their business. Thesis Sweeney was tending bar, not you."

"So?" said Frazier.

"So tell me why these four drovers would come and confess robbing the stage to you?" Sam said firmly.

"Well, you've got me there," said Frazier with the toss of a hand. "Perhaps I just have a fatherly way about me." He finally turned and faced the ranger, his hair disheveled, his eyes red-rimmed and hollow. "They burned my precious Blue Belle to the ground, Burrack," he said grimly. "Can you not understand why I want to see them dead?" He eyed the big dog who sat staring at him intently.

Sam didn't answer.

"That's Colonel Tanner's dog," he said. "Does he bite?"

"Only when he thinks it's necessary," the ranger relplied. "How well do you know Davin Grissin?"

"Grissin, hmmph," said Frazier, turning away from him and staring once again into the ashes. "Well enough, I suppose. He's a businessman, like myself. Why do you ask?" He turned his bloodshot eyes back to the ranger in curiosity.

Sam played a hunch just to see what Frazier might know. "Because it was Davin Grissin's money those four drovers had on them," he said. He studied Frazier's eyes closely. "If you know Grissin, I figure you might have been trying to get your hands on the money for him, gain yourself some favor with him."

"I knew it was Grissin's money," Frazier said. "This Mackenzie fellow told me Grissin's name was on the money bag. He said they stole the money because Grissin bought the spread they worked and fired them," he lied.

"So these four drovers knew Grissin's money would be on the stage?" Sam asked, knowing there was no way the four could have known the bag of money would be in the hidden compartment.

"That's right, Burrack," said Frazier, "that's what he told me."

"I see." Sam realized now that Frazier was lying through his teeth. There was no way for four cowhands off the grass range to know anything about Grissin's money or his method of shipping it.

"I hope you catch them, Burrack, and I hope you bring them here, for Red Hill to deal with. They also killed a lawman, in case you don't know it."

As they spoke, Sam took note of a man approaching them with a rifle in his hand. Yet he continued with Frazier as if paying the man no regard.

"I heard they killed Fred Mandrin," Sam said.

"*Deputy* Fred Mandin," said Frazier, correcting him.

"*Former* Deputy," said Sam, countering him. "If these men are guilty of anything, you can bet I'll bring them in," he added. "You can also bet that I'll get to the truth about what happened here, and why."

The man with the rifle stopped a few feet away and looked at the back of Frazier's head with a cold, bitter stare. "Ask him who killed Nate Bryson," he said.

"Mind your own damned business, Hughly!" said Frazier.

Sam only observed in silence as Frazier rose with a snap from his rocker and turned toward the man with a look of rage. "Those four murdering bandits killed him, that's who! They killed Bryson, they killed Sadler, they killed Duffey and Yates—"

"He a lying son of a bitch, Ranger," the man said, raising his rifle as he spoke.

"Hold it," said Sam, his big Colt up, cocked and pointed at the man at arm's length. "Lower that rifle."

The man caught himself, lowered the weapon and let it hang from his hand. "We were all of us playing poker at the River Palace until this turd came in wanting to pay us to go shoot those cowhands," he said.

"Not to *shoot* the cowhands, you idiot," Frazier growled at him. "I asked all of you to *capture* the cowhands, did I not?"

"Shoot, capture, what's the difference?" said the rifleman, Hughly Rhodes. "My pards are *dead* either way." His anger began to rise again. "And you killed Bryson, there's no ifs or buts about it! I all but saw you do it!"

"Let me hold that rifle for you," said Sam. He stepped in closer, reached out and took the rifle from him as he asked, "What do you mean you 'all but' seen him shoot your friend Bryson?" The big cur sat watching, his head going back and forth as the men spoke, as if following their conversation.

"I didn't exactly see him pull the trigger," the man said, "but I heard his gunshot, and when I looked over he was lowering his pistol and Bryson was on the ground, deader than hell . . . shot in the head."

"Don't be ridiculous," said Frazier, dismissing the man. "If you didn't *see* me shoot Bryson, you'd do well to keep your mouth shut."

Rhodes started to say more, but Sam cut him off, saying, "He's right. Unless you can truthfully swear that you *saw* him shoot your friend, you're wasting your breath."

"And if I said I did see him do it, would you haul him off to jail?" Rhodes asked.

"Yes, but make sure you're not lying to me, mister," said Sam. "Murder is a very serious charge." He stared at Rhodes expectantly, until finally the man slumped in submission and said, "Hell, I didn't *see* it, even though I *know* he did it."

"There you have it, Ranger, are you satisfied?" said Frazier. "Can you stop wondering about me, and get on after the real criminals?"

Sam turned and walked away toward the livery barn to join Maria. "What about my rifle, Ranger?" Rhodes asked, hurrying to catch up with him.

"I'll give it to you as soon as you're a safe distance from Bart Frazier," Sam replied. "I've got enough to do without keeping you two from each other's throats." Beside Sam the big cur walked along, observing the dirt street in both directions.

Chapter 13

Maria met the ranger at the livery barn where she had just finished watering and graining her horse. Sam turned his horse's reins over to a stable boy. He noted that neither Art Mullens nor Thesis Sweeney was present. He gave Maria a curious look.

"I sent them to the River Palace," she said, without him having to ask.

"They were easier for you to get rid of than I thought they would be," Sam remarked.

"I gave them enough money to buy themselves a drink," she said, "after I convinced them of how much help they've been."

Sam gave a thin smile. "Did they have anything else to say worth hearing?"

"No, they didn't," Maria said. "But I thought it would be worth a drink to keep them out of the way while you finished talking to Sheer. Did he have anything else to say?"

"Not much," said Sam. "He did say that he saw a

stranger riding through Red Hill. Said the man avoided the trail and rode in the weeds and brush, like he didn't want anybody seeing him."

"Stanton Parks?" Maria asked.

"I've got a feeling it was."

"Why didn't he simply keep an eye on the saloon if he wanted to keep track of the drovers?" she asked.

"I figure he didn't want to start any trouble in Red Hill," said the ranger. "I also figure he didn't want to tangle with these four young men alone. He was looking up Fred Mandrin, knowing Mandrin carried a badge—or that he used to anyway. I can think of lots of schemes those two could've cooked up with a badge on their side."

"You don't think the drovers killed Mandrin up at Three Forks," Maria said, "you think Parks killed him."

"Yep." Sam nodded. "Parks killed him, once he saw the drovers had made out of Red Hill with the money, and he figured he'd no longer need Mandrin and his badge."

"Interesting," said Maria. "It sounds like all the four drovers are doing is trying to stay alive."

"That's the way I'm calling it," said Sam. "Unless something shows me otherwise, I think the drovers are the only honest players in a dangerous game."

"*Sí*, and they are the ones holding the money," Maria mused.

"Yep," said Sam, "and I bet they have no idea Buckshot Parks is trailing them."

"Which puts them in a bad position, honest players or not," Maria added.

"Oh yes," said the ranger. He took out the broken paper money band and examined it again. "Parks is not the only person out for their hides. I imagine that by now Davin Grissin is spitting fire over this, if Peyton Quinn and his two pals had the nerve to go back and face him after we took away their guns."

"We need to catch up to these young men before somebody else does," Maria offered, looking toward the livery boy as he grained the ranger's horse. "Do you think Frazier will send any more men after the drovers?"

"No, I think Frazier has learned his lesson, and so have the men he hired to capture the drovers," said Sam. "Whoever these young men are, they seem to know how to look out for one another." He gestured toward the door. "Let's go get some food ourselves, while these horses rest awhile."

Three blocks from the livery barn, the two found a small restaurant and ate a hot meal of eggs, biscuits and gravy and thick-sliced bacon. When they had finished and paid for their meal, they walked back to the livery barn, saddled their horses and rode away. As they passed the spot where Bart Frazier sat rocking, he didn't so much as glance in their direction.

The pair rode upward along the high-reaching trail, following the newer hoofprints Sheer and his party had left when they'd ridden up and discovered Fred Mandrin's body. Reaching the Three Forks in the trail, Sam and Maria sat their horses for a moment, looking from one trail to another. "This is the perfect place for a group of riders to part company and lie low for a spell," said the ranger.

"The question is, which riders went in which direction?" Maria stepped down and walked her horse from left to right, looking in turn out along each trail.

Examining the trail to the right, Sam noted the dark patch of dried blood on a rock and on the ground. He nudged his horse over, stepped down and gazed out along the meandering trail leading away from it. "It looks like one of the cowhands might've taken a bullet."

"*Sí*," said Maria, studying the dark bloody spot alongside him. "From the looks of it, this one was bleeding bad."

As the ranger spoke, the dog trotted purposefully back and forth, its muzzle to the dirt, picking up the familiar scent of Stanton Parks. "If they split up here, you can bet it won't be for long. These young men are going to stick together. They've learned the hard way that four guns are better than one."

"They have themselves to be the bundle of sticks that cannot be broken . . . ," Maria said with contemplation. "When the time comes, let's hope they will allow us to get close enough to show them that we are not their enemy."

"Yes, let's hope," Sam said. He watched the dog sniff out the various scents in the dirt beneath his busy nostrils. After a moment, the dog stopped and concentrated intently on one spot. "It looks like Sergeant Tom Haines has found something of interest."

When the dog raised his nose from the ground he turned, facing the ranger and Maria, and barked as he bounced slightly on his front paws. He spun in the dirt, faced them and barked again, this time with more urgency.

"All right, boy, we're coming," said Sam. To Maria he said, "I don't know if he's following the drovers or Buckshot Parks, but it doesn't matter. As long as these young men have Grissin's money, their trail and Parks' will be one and the same." They turned and mounted and rode forward, seeing the big cur disappear around a turn in the trail.

In Creasy, a small half-abandoned mining town that appeared to be clinging to a steep mountainside, Mackenzie helped Holly Thorpe down from his saddle and to the door of a doctor's office along a dusty boardwalk. Thorpe had weakened with the loss of blood. He stood with an arm looped over Mackenzie's shoulder as Mackenzie beat urgently on a wooden door where a sign read DR. HIRAM ROSS, PHYSICIAN.

"Am I going to die on you, Mac?" Thorpe asked dreamily.

"No, you better not die on me," said Mackenzie. "We're going to get you looked after by the doctor. You're going to be feeling better before you know it."

"All right, boss. . . ." Thorpe's head lolled back and

forth. He gave a weak half-conscious smile, a smear of blood on one spectacle lens. "Whatever you say."

Before Mackenzie could knock again, a young woman opened the door. She only glanced at Mackenzie. But she looked Thorpe up and down closely.

Mackenzie spoke quickly. "Ma'am, my pard here has been shot. We've rode all the way here to see the—"

"Bring him in," the young woman said just as quickly, before Mackenzie could finish his words. She reached out to Thorpe as she spoke, helping Mackenzie get him through the doorway. "My father isn't here, but he'll be back shortly."

"Much obliged, ma'am," said Mackenzie as she looped Thorpe's left arm over her shoulder.

"Right in here." The young woman guided them across a parlor and straight into the doctor's treatment room.

"Who—who are you?" Thorpe asked, giving her a weak sidelong glance.

"I'm Beth Ann . . . Beth Ann Ross," the young woman replied as she and Mackenzie eased the wounded man onto a canvas surgical table.

"Like the woman who made the flag?" Thorpe asked, dreamily.

"Yes, only *her* name was Betsy, mine is Beth Ann," she replied cordially. Yet as she spoke she deftly went to work. She plucked his spectacles from his face and laid them in a metal tray beside the surgical table. Crossing the room, she returned with a pan of water and a clean washcloth. She set the pan and washcloth down beside the metal instrument tray and began unbuttoning Thorpe's shirt. "Please remove his boots," she said sidelong to Mackenzie.

"Yes, ma'am," said Mackenzie, immediately doing as she instructed. "You said your father will be home real soon?" He took Thorpe's right boot toe and heel between his hands and pulled the boat from his foot.

"Please to meet you, Miss Beth Ann," Thorpe said in a thick incoherent tone.

"And I you, sir," Beth Ann said quietly, patting Thorpe's shoulder. To Mackenzie she replied, "Yes, he should be home soon. But not soon enough, I'm afraid." She picked up a packet of gauze from the metal instrument tray. "Your friend has lost a lot of blood. I have to stop this bleeding right away."

"You?" Mackenzie looked at her.

"Yes, me," said Beth Ann.

"No offense, ma'am," said Mackenzie, "but I brought Holly here to see a doctor."

"And so he shall," said the young woman, "just as soon as my father returns." She dipped the cloth into the water, then wrung it and washed all around the wound as a thin braided stream of blood trickled steadily down over her fingers.

"Ma'am . . ." Mackenzie started to say something but his words trailed.

"Don't worry, I've done this before," the young woman said without facing him. "What's your friend's name?"

"Holly Thorpe, ma'am." Suddenly remembering

his manners, he took off his hat. "Begging your pardon, ma'am, I'm Jet Mackenzie," he said, watching her attend to the weeping dark hole in Thorpe's side. "It's not that I doubt you being capable of—"

"Hold this in place and help me roll him onto his side." She held a square thick packet of gauze out to him.

"What's she doing to me, Mac?" Thorpe murmured. He appeared on the verge of trying to rise up on the table.

"She's taking care of your bullet wound, Holly, now lie still," Mackenzie said firmly. "I'm helping her."

"Here it is," said Beth Ann, as the two settled Thorpe onto his side. "I hardly had to look for it." She touched a finger gently to a raised and reddened welt on Thorpe's back.

"That's the bullet, in there?" Mackenzie asked in disbelief.

"Yes, that's where the bullet stopped," said Beth Ann. She touched the welt appraisingly, pressing her finger on it carefully. "I'd say it's lying no more than an inch deep beneath, perhaps less."

"But the hole is down here," said Mackenzie, gesturing toward the spot of the bleeding wound in Thorpe's side.

"Yes, but bullets don't always travel in a straight line," said Beth Ann, not stopping, not slowing down. She stepped away from the table, over to a cabinet and took out a small blue bottle of laudanum. "Nor are they always this easy to locate. Lucky for your friend this bullet has stopped near the surface. If it hadn't I would have had to widen the wound entrance and go in and probe for it in order to take pressure off and slow the bleeding. That would have been dangerous to a patient who has already lost a lot of blood."

"Oh . . . then what will you do now?" Mackenzie asked.

"I'll sedate him very carefully," she said. "After a moment when he's unconscious, I'll cut in, remove the bullet, let the wound drain from behind for a short time. Then I'll close it."

Mackenzie watched her step back over with the laudanum bottle in hand. She poured a measured amount into a small metal cup and had Thorpe swallow it. "I'd like for you to be here with me while I make the incision in case the laudanum doesn't sedate him enough."

"Yes, ma'am," said Mackenzie. He swallowed a dry, tight knot in his throat. "I'll help any way I can."

Beth Ann smiled. "Thank you, Mr. Mackenzie."

"Ma'am, you can call me Mac if you like, or Jet, either one."

Beth Ann nodded. "When we're finished, we'll let him rest. My father will look in on him as soon as he returns home." She put the cork back into the blue bottle, walked over to the cabinet and put the bottle away. As she walked back to the surgery table, she unbuttoned her long dress sleeves and rolled them up halfway to her elbows, ready to go to work.

"Let's get started," she said calmly.

"Yes, ma'am," said Mackenzie.

Standing behind Thorpe, he laid a hand on his unconscious friend's shoulder, ready to pin him to the table if need be. But to his surprise, Beth Ann Ross worked quickly and expertly with the sharp surgical scalpel. With one swift deep stroke she made an inch-long incision into the red welt on Thorpe's back. Blood spurted, then reduced to a trickle as she laid aside the scalpel, picked up another instrument, shoved it into the incision and withdrew the bloody bullet and dropped it onto the metal tray.

"There," she said with a sigh, "that went nicely."

"That's it, we're finished?" Mackenzie looked at her, taken aback.

"Yes, with that part," said Beth Ann. "Your friend was lucky, he never felt a thing."

"Ma'am, I can't call it luck," said Mackenzie. "I saw how quickly you did that. Ole Holly's *luck* was finding you here."

"Thank you, Mr. Mackenzie," said Beth Ann, without stopping for a moment. "That was the quick part. But now I need to finish up and clean and dress the wound. You can take a seat in the parlor. I'll call you if I need you. There is a pot of tea in the kitchen. I boiled it only moments before you two arrived."

"Much obliged," said Mackenzie. "As soon as you say it's all right, I'll take our horses to the town livery barn and have them looked after."

"Of course," said Beth Ann. "This shouldn't take too long. I'll come tell you as soon as I'm finished."

Mackenzie nodded and walked out to the parlor. He took a seat on a long soft divan and closed his eyes, only for a moment, just long enough to relax and shed the weariness of the trail. . . .

Chapter 14

When Mackenzie opened his eyes, he did so with a start, realizing that he'd been asleep, and that sleep was not a luxury he could afford.

The long shadows of evening reached through the open front window and across the parlor floor. *Oh no. . . .* He sprang up and hurried out the front door and looked out at the hitch rail. His and Thorpe's horses were gone. A one-horse buggy stood in their place. He turned looking in each direction, dumbfounded, until he heard a man's voice say from the door behind him, "Don't worry, young man, your horses are fine."

Mackenzie spun toward the door, keeping his hand from instinctively going to his Colt.

"I'm Dr. Ross. My daughter had a stable man come get the horses so you could get some sleep. . . . Apparently you needed it." He gave a friendly smile.

"I—yes, I did," said Mackenzie, not wanting to appear too anxious about the horses. Remembering his manners, he said, "I'm Jet Mackenzie. My friend in there is Holly Thorpe—"

"Yes, I know," said the doctor. "Why don't you come inside, Mr. Mackenzie? Your friend is doing fine. Miss Beth Ann is preparing supper for the three of us, some hot beef broth for your friend."

"Yes, I will, Dr. Ross," said Mackenzie. "I need to check on our horses first."

"You cowhands," said the doctor, shaking his head slowly. "Go along with you, then, I'll tell my daughter you'll be here shortly."

"Obliged, Dr. Ross," said Mackenzie, eager to get on to the livery barn and make sure no one had discovered the money in his and Thorpe's bedrolls.

Across the street, Stanton Parks had stepped down from his horse a moment earlier and looked back and forth along the dirt street, searching for sign of the drovers or their horses. Cursing his luck at having seen no sign of either, he'd turned to walk into a saloon when he spotted Mackenzie in his brush-scarred chaps and battered Stetson.

"Well, now," Parks remarked to himself, "maybe Lady Luck ain't so fickle after all." Fingering the two badges inside his shirt pocket, he stepped off the boardwalk and followed Mackenzie from a safe distance.

Inside the livery barn, Mackenzie looked back and forth, stall to stall, seeing no sign of either a livery man, or of his and Thorpe's horses. "Hello the barn," he called out. But he heard no reply. A bad feeling began to creep inside him. Had the livery man found the money? Had he alerted the townsmen? Were there guns aimed at him from hiding right now, ready to cut him down before he had a chance to explain anything?

When he sighted both horses standing in the last two stalls, he felt a little relieved. Seeing their saddles on racks outside the stalls, both of their bedrolls and saddlebags still bulging with the money, he stopped and let out a breath before reaching out and flipping up the leather saddlebag flaps. "Thank goodness," he murmured. The stacks of money were still in place.

He patted his horse on its muzzle. Both animals had been rubbed down and looked fed and contented. He stepped away and found a wooden bin full of empty feed sacks. Carrying one sack draped over his forearm and another open in his hand, he hurried back to the saddle rack and flipped open the flap on his saddlebags.

He had begun stuffing the stacks of money into the feed sack when he froze at the sound of the creaking barn door and the fall of soft footsteps walking closer and closer. "Don't think of it, cowpoke, or I'll save Arizona the cost of a trial and hanging," said Stanton Parks as Mackenzie's right hand tensed over his holstered Colt. Parks cocked his big revolver, making sure the young trail boss understood.

Mackenzie moved his gun hand away from the butt of his Colt.

"Now raise your hands and turn around slow-like," said Parks.

Mackenzie obeyed. He turned slowly, raising his hands, the feed sack of money hanging from his left. "Are you a lawman?"

"Am I a lawman?" Parks gave a cruel grin. "You tell me."

Mackenzie noted the stolen sheriff's badge on his chest. "Yeah, I reckon you are."

"You *reckoned* right," said Parks, liking the immediate respect the stolen badge brought him. "I'm Sheriff Fred Mandrin. I've been following you and your pals. I know you robbed that stage and killed those innocent folks," he said convincingly. "You're thieves and murderers, the four of yas."

"You're wrong, Sheriff," said Mackenzie. "My pards and I come upon the stage after it had been robbed. We found this money and have been looking at every way in the world of turning it in. Had we been able to come to you, we already would have—"

"Save your breath, cowpoke," said Parks, enjoying himself. "You'll wish you had it when that rope snaps taut and chokes the last ounce of it from your squirming body."

Mackenzie swallowed a tight knot in his throat. "I swear, Sheriff, we're not outlaws, we're just working drovers. We wouldn't know what to do with this kind of money if we had it."

"Is that all of it?" Parks asked. "Don't try to lie to me about it," he warned. "It'll only go worse on you for lying." This was the most fun he'd had in years, he told himself, seeing the look on the drover's face, hearing the way this fool answered his every question as if it were being asked by the voice of God. He'd have to do some more of this kind of play-acting someday, he decided.

"I won't lie, Sheriff," said Mackenzie. "This is about half of the stage money."

"Where's the rest of it?" Parks asked, already having a good idea the four had split it for safekeeping.

"I don't know," Mackenzie said in a knee-jerk reaction to try to protect the other three. "But you've got me, Sheriff. If anybody is going to hang for robbing that stage, I expect I'm the one."

"You're not a good liar, cowpoke," said Parks.

"I've never had any practice," Mackenzie said, meaning it.

"Most every cowboy I ever met is too damned dumb to lie," said Parks.

"Or too *honest*," said Mackenzie.

"Honest? Ha!" said Parks, taunting the worried young man. "You ought to be ashamed of yourself."

"I'm not ashamed of being honest. I was raised to be," said Mackenzie in a firm tone, in spite of the gun pointed at him.

"Don't try playing the ole innocent and honest game with me, cowpoke. I'm not buying it," said Parks. "Now, where are you and your pals meeting?"

Mackenzie stalled. "Sheriff, you've got me, I'm giving up. That's all I can do for you."

"Oh?" said Parks. "I bet a good pistol-whipping will soften your attitude and wear a little bark off."

"You can bend your barrel around my head if it suits you, Sheriff, but I'm not jackpotting my pards."

"They would you, if it was the other way around," Parks said.

"I suppose I'll die never knowing that," said Mackenzie. "But they're no more guilty than I am. I'm not jackpotting them. I might hang for something I didn't do, but I won't do nothing to cause them to."

"I am so touched by all this cow manure," Parks said sarcastically. He shrugged. "I already figured your pards have the rest of the money. The other two of yas split up at Three Forks to throw off any followers. Now you will all meet up again just as soon as your wounded pal is able to ride. You'll tell me where before I'm through with you."

Mackenzie just stared at him, a determined look on his face.

Parks stepped in closer. "Last chance, cowpoke, before I wear this gun barrel out on—"

Mackenzie suddenly swung the bag of money up hard, catching Parks full on his chin. The blow sent the man staggering backward, dazed. Before the outlaw could collect himself and swing his revolver back toward the young trail boss, Mackenzie was upon him.

Snatching the gun from Parks' hand, he swung a

hard right with the barrel and slammed it against the side of Parks' head. Parks fell back again and down, spinning as he did so and striking the other side of his head on a stall gate.

"You should have settled for me, Sheriff Mandrin," Mackenzie said to the knocked-out gunman, who was lying limply at his feet. "My pards and I kept one another alive all up and down this hard country. I won't have them hang for something they didn't do."

Holly Thorpe was awake and sitting propped up on his good side in a convalescent's bed when Mackenzie returned from the livery barn and knocked quietly on the door. Stepping into the room with his battered Stetson in hand, Mackenzie said to Beth Ann, who sat spooning warm beef broth into Thorpe's mouth, "My apologizes, ma'am, for being late for supper."

"No apology necessary, Mr. Mackenzie," said Beth Ann. "I appreciate your concern for your horses. I set aside a plate for you."

"My daughter sees to it that no one leaves the Ross house on an empty stomach," said the doctor. He stood up from a desk in a corner and stepped forward, his necktie loosened and hanging at his chest, his white shirtsleeves rolled up from inspecting the work his daughter had preformed on Thorpe. "Come, I'll join you while you eat, if you'd like some company."

"Yes, some company would suit me just fine, Doctor," said Mackenzie, putting up a calm pleasant front that only Holly Thorpe could see through.

"How are our horses?" Thorpe asked, his voice still weak. He stared at Mackenzie through his spectacles that Beth Ann had slipped back on him at his request.

"They're both good and well attended to. But they're eager to get going," said Mackenzie, hoping to give Thorpe some indication that they had trouble licking at their heels.

Dr. Ross and his daughter exchanged glances, both understanding right away that there were urgent matters pressing these two. "Well, Mr. Thorpe," said the doctor, "if you've had enough broth to refuel your blood system, perhaps my daughter and I will retire to the kitchen and see that Mr. Mackenzie's supper is still good and warm."

"Obliged, I'm full," said Thorpe, even though he could have eaten three times as much and still been hungry.

"I'll save you some more for later," said Beth Ann, knowing he needed to bring his strength up after losing so much blood. She stood, soup bowl in hand, and followed her father out of the room.

No sooner were the two alone than Mackenzie shot a glance at the closed door and whispered to Thorpe, "How soon before you're able to ride?"

"I'll ride right now if need be," said Thorpe, making a gesture as if to rise to his feet.

"No, not tonight, Holly, you'll ruin all these two have tried to do for you," said Mackenzie. "But you can't stay any longer than two days."

"What's happened, Mac?" asked Thorpe, seeing his former trail boss try to mask a troubled look.

"A lawman has caught up to us," said Mackenzie. "A sheriff by the name of Fred Mandrin. He's convinced we robbed the stage and killed those folks. I just knocked him cold and tied him up. He's in the loft of the livery barn. He'll be coming to anytime. I'm leaving tonight and I'm taking him with me."

"Holy Moses," said Thorpe. He shook his head as if to clear his mind. "Take him with you?"

"Yes, while he's still knocked out I'll take him somewhere where he can't get back to you, or go on after the rest of us."

"I'm getting dressed and helping you, boss," said Thorpe, "that's all there is to it." He started to try to stand, but Mackenzie placed a firm hand on his shoulder, holding him down.

"Listen to me, Holly, this is an order," Mackenzie said in a tone of authority. "You're staying here and getting your strength back. You'll be no good to us if you can't ride and take care of yourself." He gripped his shoulder firmly. "Have you got that?"

"But, boss—" Thorpe didn't get his protest out of his mouth.

"Do I look like I want to argue with you about this, Thorpe?" Mackenzie cut him short with a harsh snap to his voice. "I'm telling you what to do, and you're going to do it. This ain't just for you, this is what's best for all four of us. Now, can I count on you, or not?"

"You can, *boss*," Thorpe said, relenting. "Tell me where you want me to meet up with yas, and when. I'll be there."

"Good man," said Mackenzie, easing down on his harsh manner. He patted Thorpe's shoulder before he took his hand away. "When you leave here, head northwest toward the Colorado. Follow the river toward Marble Canyon. Wait for us in País Duro. Have you—"

"Yeah, I've got that," said Thorpe, finishing his words for him.

"All right, that's our plan," said Mackenzie. "I tied a bandanna around the sheriff's mouth, but as soon as he wakes up, he'll start stomping or raising a ruckus some way until somebody hears him."

"So you've got to get going," said Thorpe.

"Yep, I got to, and fast." Mackenzie pitched some gold coins on the bed for Thorpe to pay the doctor and his daughter for their services. "I'm heading out the back door there." He gestured toward another door on the back wall. "Tell these kind folks how sorry I am to have to leave this way. If ever I come this way again, I'll come apologize in person for my rude behavior."

"I'll tell them you're this way all the time, rude and belligerent," said Thorpe with a poker-faced expression.

"I figured you would," said Mackenzie with the

same deadpan look. "Watch your back trail," he added, stepping over to the rear door.

"Watch yours too," said Thorpe, looking at him through his spectacles until he disappeared from sight and closed the door behind himself.

Chapter 15

Stanton "Buckshot" Parks awakened slowly, his chin, jaw and both sides of his forehead pounding in pain. He tried to say something aloud to himself, but the bandanna drawn tight around his mouth prevented him from doing so. As he started to reach to loosen the bandanna he realized his hands were tied securely behind his back. In his addled state, he at first thought the dark grainy substance moving past his eyes was the night sky overhead. Yet as he became more coherent he realized that there were no rocks and wagon ruts in the sky—were there?

Of course there aren't! he told him himself angrily, struggling in vain to get himself upright. When it came to him in a flash that he was riding tied face-down across a mule's bare lumpy back, he slumped and cursed silently. Then he lay limp for a moment, allowing the events that had happened inside the livery barn to catch up to him.

He looked ahead of him and saw Mackenzie riding along in the moonlight, holding a lead rope to the mule. Not knowing where to find Parks' horse, the young trail boss had found the mule in the rent and purchase corral behind the barn and left payment for the animal in a tin box set up for just such a purpose. He wasn't sure how far he should take the knocked-out lawman, but he was certain that with every passing mile he made it that much safer for Thorpe and the others.

"Muuumph! Muuumph!" Parks raged into the bandanna, causing such a stir that the mule swayed back and forth a step, on the verge of spooking.

"Whoa now, Sheriff!" said Mackenzie, stopping quickly and jumping down from his saddle. He stepped back to the mule, gathering his lead rope, and rubbed its mallet-shaped head to calm it. As the animal settled he stooped down and looked into Parks' face. "Sheriff, I don't know how much you know about mules, but if I were you I'd do my best not to send him into a frenzy."

"Hummm, moompfh foo!" said Parks in his bandanna-muffled voice. He rolled his eyes up and down and jerked his pounding head, gesturing for the young trail boss to take off the gag.

Mackenzie took a hold of the bandanna with his thumb and finger and said, "I'm going to lower this, Sheriff, but you'll have to promise not to start getting loud."

"Ummm-huum," said Parks, vigorously nodding his aching head.

Mackenzie pulled the bandanna down off Parks' sore chin. Parks spit lint from his mouth and started right in, saying quickly, "Listen to me, you dirty cowpoke! You're just making things worse on yourself! You better cut me loose—"

"Making things worse?" Mackenzie knew he had the upper hand. He remained calm. "Sheriff, you said me and my pards would hang. How much worse does it get? Was you gonna give us a sound scolding first?" He started pulling the bandanna back up over Parks' mouth. "If that was all you wanted, I'd rather listen to the coyotes talking."

"No, wait," said Parks, causing the young trail boss to stop. "I've got to tell you something! You and your pals don't have to hang! I wish I hadn't said all that. I was just sort of funning with you."

"It didn't seem very funny to me," said Mackenzie.

He started to raise the bandanna again. But again Parks said, "No, please, listen to me. I'm not really a law—"

"Enough out of you." Mackenzie jerked the bandanna back up over Parks' mouth and led the mule up beside his horse. He had stepped up into his saddle when he saw two riders round a turn only twenty feet in front of him and stop and look toward him in the light of a wide full moon.

"Hello the trail?" a voice called warily. "We heard voices," he added. As he spoke his hand went to the rifle lying across his lap. The rifle hammer cocked slowly. The other rider sidled his horse a step away;

his hand also rested on a rifle across his lap. They stared at Parks as he raised his head toward them and began grunting and trying to shout through the bandanna.

Mackenzie froze for a moment. He knew how bad this looked now. He could only imagine how it would look once these two men saw the sheriff's badge. He wasn't about to shoot it out with two innocent travelers.

"What's going on here?" the other rider asked, both men nudging their horses forward slowly.

"Yes, speak up," the first rider insisted. "Why is that man tied over the mule? Is he ill?"

"Is he your prisoner? Are you a lawman?" the other asked.

There was no way he could explain this, Mackenzie told himself. Unable to think of anything to do that would not cost somebody their life, he dropped the mule's lead rope and spun his horse quickly. He nailed his boots to the animal's sides.

"Hold it! Stop!" he heard the men shout behind him. The two spurred their horses forward and stopped where the mule stood with its tied-down rider. "This man's wearing a badge!" he heard one man say above the sound of Parks' muffled grunting voice.

"Halt there, or we'll shoot!" the other rider shouted.

But Mackenzie never looked back. His horse raced away into the moonlit night. The first rifle shot he heard was a warning shot one of the men fired straight up. The next shot whistled past his head. The third shot hit him hard through his right shoulder and knocked him forward onto this horse's neck. But he held on, managed to right himself in his saddle and keep moving, the horse taking in the rocky trail at a fast dangerous run.

At the mule, one man had slipped his rifle in its boot and leaped down from his saddle. He ran to Parks and jerked the bandanna down from his mouth while the other gave chase for only a few yards before slowing and turning back. Parks had twisted himself up onto his side enough to make sure they had seen his badge when they rode up.

"Gentlemen, it's a damned good thing you come along when you did," he said, spitting lint again as he spoke. He motioned for the nearest rider to untie his hands. "That man is a dangerous killer! I was on my way, taking him to jail, when he managed to overpower me!"

"Who is he?" asked the rider still in his saddle.

"That's none other than Buckshot Parks," Parks said as the man on the ground worked quickly, untying his hands and feet and loosening him from the mule's back. "He's truly the baddest of the bad. He makes the James Gang look like a bunch of schoolgirls. I have no doubt he would have killed me if you two hadn't come along. He's the toughest, smartest, most cold-blooded, daring—"

"I've head of Buckshot Parks, sure enough," said the one in his saddle. "But I never heard of him being all that smart or tough. I heard he was a chicken thief and a whore's towel boy who got lucky and fell in with a bold crowd."

"Hmmmph." Parks fell silent and stared coldly up at him as the man on the ground finished setting him free.

"Why'd he have you tied down over a mule?" the man in his saddle continued as Parks slid down from the mule, rubbing his freed wrists. "What was he intending to do to you, Sheriff?"

"Who knows?" Parks said. He looked back and forth between the two of them. "I'm most obliged to you two for your help." He stared back along the trail in the direction Mackenzie had taken. "I'm going to need a horse."

"You can swap the mule for one as soon as you get to Creasy," said the one in his saddle.

"Yep, good idea," said Parks. He held his hand up to him and said, "Let me take a look at that sharpshooter's rifle."

"My long-shooting rifle, what for?" the man replied. He gripped a big fifty-caliber rifle with a brass scope mounted along its barrel.

"Go on and give the *sheriff* your rifle, Red!" the other man demanded. "Don't ask so many questions."

"Begging your pardon, Sheriff," said the man in his saddle. He handed the big sharpshooter rifle down to Parks. "It's late and I ain't thinking."

"I understand," said Parks. "Give me your reins."

"My reins? Why?" the man asked, even as he handed the reins down to him.

Parks took the reins, tilted the rifle barrel up, cocked the hammer and shot him through the heart. He held the reins taut as the spooked horse settled and realized it couldn't bolt away.

"Oh my God, Sheriff! What have you done? What have you done? You've shot him! You've—"

"Shut up, idiot." The rifle bucked again in Parks' hand. The bullet hit the man high in his chest and flung him backward. He landed flat on his back. He groaned and dug at the ground with his boot heels while Parks stepped into the other man's saddle. Turning the horse, Parks looked down and spit at the body lying on the ground. "There's your *whore's towel boy*," he said. Then he gigged the horse soundly and rode away.

For a day and a half Holly Thorpe had rested and regained his strength in the narrow bed inside the home of Dr. Ross and his daughter, Beth Ann. With his renewed strength came an intense restlessness to get back on the trail and rejoin his friends. He couldn't stand the thought of something bad happening to any one of them while he was laid up. It was almost with a strange sense of relief that he spotted the ranger and Maria from the front window as they rode into Creasy from the south.

In the thin light of early morning, Thorpe caught a glimpse of the ranger's badge on Sam's chest. Without wasting another second, he turned from the window and had started to his room in the rear when he almost ran headlong into Beth Ann Ross.

"Oh, there you are," she said, more than a little surprised at Thorpe being in the front parlor. "I'm preparing breakfast for you. I'm afraid my father won't be joining us. He was summoned in the night to deliver a baby for the Carlsons."

"Miss Beth Ann, listen to me, please," Thorpe said, taking her by her shoulders, his voice deliberately calm, unhurried. "There's a lawman coming into town. I've got a feeling he'll be asking around about me."

"You're—you're running from the law?" she asked, with an almost hurt look on her face.

"Yes, ma'am, but it's not like you think. My pards and I haven't broken any law, but there's some who think we have."

"What laws do they think you've broken?" she asked hesitantly.

"The law thinks we robbed a stage and killed some folks, ma'am," Thorpe replied bluntly, bringing a slight gasp from the young woman. "But it's not true. I give you my word it's not." As he spoke he directed her away from the parlor, farther back into the house. "Come with me, please," he said. "After all you and your pa has done for me, I want to tell you everything. . . ."

On the dirt street, Sam and Maria rode first to the sheriff's office, where they stepped through a creaking unlocked door. They found a desk stacked high with wanted posters and unopened mail, all covered with a sheen of dust. In a kindling box in a far corner a skinny mother cat raised its head and stared at them above the meowing of a litter of small kittens. "Another town without a sheriff," Maria commented.

"Yes, I'm afraid so," said the ranger. "Earl Buckley was sheriff here the last time I rode through. I heard he died last winter." He looked all around. "Not many takers for a sheriff's job in a town about to go under."

"To the doctor's, then?" Maria asked. Sam only nodded and turned back to the door.

Moments later, Beth Ann stood nervously at the front door when the two arrived. At the sound of the first knock, she opened the door and looked back and forth between the ranger and Maria. Behind them the big cur plopped down on the porch and sat staring, his tongue a-loll.

"Ma'am, I'm Arizona Ranger Sam Burrack," said Sam, taking off his silver-gray sombrero. "This is Maria."

"I—I know why you're here," Beth Ann replied calmly. "Please come in, and please hear what I have to tell you before you do anything to cause violence in my home."

"Yes, ma'am," Sam said, and exchanged a glance with Maria. They both looked past the young woman, their eyes scanning the room, but they kept their hands away from their guns. "But first tell us where they are, so we don't have any surprises."

"There's only one," Beth Ann said. "He's waiting in the rear of the house. He knows I'm talking to you on his behalf. When we're finished he's turning himself over to you."

"Fair enough," Sam replied calmly. "If you'll be so kind as to explain everything to Maria here?" He stepped past her and started through the house.

"But, Ranger, please!" Beth Ann called out. "Don't hurt him! He's innocent!"

"You don't have to worry about me hurting him, ma'am," said Sam, even before he'd crossed the room and started into the rear of the large house, "he's already gone."

Maria stepped forward and took Beth Ann gently yet firmly by her arm and held her back from following the ranger. "Come. You can tell me everything," she said, coaxing the young woman.

"Where is he going? Is he going after Holly?" she asked, nodding after the ranger, hearing the rear open and close behind him.

"Is that the drover's name, Holly?" Maria asked, leading her to a pair of chairs in the parlor.

"Yes, his name is Holly . . . Holly Thorpe," said Beth Ann. She cast a worried look toward the rear of the house.

"*Sí*, he will be going after him," said Maria, sitting the young woman down. "Now, you must tell me everything so I can tell him when I catch up to him on the trail. . . ."

Outside, at the rear of the house, the ranger caught sight of the drover atop his salt-and-pepper barb racing away from Creasy, disappearing into the pines lining the high trail out of town, the same trail

Mackenzie had ridden with Parks in tow two nights earlier.

Hurrying around the house to the hitch rail out front, Sam jumped into his saddle and raced away in pursuit, the big cur who had been sitting on the porch running behind him.

Once upon the trail leading up away from Creasy, the ranger put his horse into a fast but measured pace, slowing with caution at every turn, lest he find himself riding into sudden gunfire. "I'm counting on you wearing that horse out real quick, cowboy," he murmured toward the dust-looming trail ahead.

But after making a turn more than three miles up from town, Sam felt his horse's rear hoof slip. He felt the animal veer, tense up and immediately reduce its pace to a limping sidestepping walk. "Easy, Black Eye, easy," he said, slipping down from his saddle while the horse was still moving, and settling the animal quickly.

Rubbing the injured barb's side with his gloved hand, Sam walked back and raised its rear left hoof. The animal flinched, but it allowed him to work the hoof back and forth gently, enough to recognize the tightness and swelling that had already started forming along its tendons.

"All right, boy, I see what you mean," he said, answering a low pained whinny from the animal as it turned its head, facing him. "This chase is over for you." He laid the hoof back to the ground softly, seeing the animal cock it slightly off the ground.

Standing, Sam let out a breath and gazed along the trail ahead. But no sooner had he done so than his hand streaked to his Colt, drew it and cocked it. A lone rider sat slumped on his horse in the middle of the trail. "Raise your hands high where I can see them," the ranger called out, facing the rider from fifty yards away.

But the man didn't raise his hands. Instead he wobbled back and forth in his saddle, then flopped off it into the dirt.

Sam dropped the reins to his injured horse and hurried forward, his Colt raised and ready.

He stopped a few feet away and looked down at the man lying sprawled, facedown, his arms spread in the dirt. As Sam stepped even closer he saw a bullet hole in the center of a wide dark bloodstain on the back of the man's riding duster. The man raised his pale, drawn face toward Sam and said in a weak and shaky voice, "Help me. . . ."

Holstering his Colt, Swam hurried forward, stooped down and rolled the man over onto his back. The man struggled with his words but managed to say, "A—a sheriff . . . shot me."

"You hang on, mister," Sam said, "I'm going to get you to town." He made a quick glance along the trail in the direction the young man had fled. Then he put any thoughts of following the drover right then from his mind and looked down at the face of the wounded man.

As he spread open the bloody duster and shirt, the wounded man looked up at him through weak and hollow eyes and repeated in a rasping voice, "A lawman . . . did this. I saw . . . his badge."

"You keep still and save your strength, mister," said the ranger. "It was no lawman who shot you." He looked all around the trail, thinking of Stanton "Buckshot" Parks and the body of former deputy Fred Mandrin.

"He—he was . . . wearing a badge."

"I understand," said Sam, "but it was no lawman, take my word for it." He gazed again along the trail. "Not everybody wearing a badge is a lawman these days."

PART 3

Chapter 16

Davin Grissin and his new personal bodyguard, Tillman Duvall, stepped down from Grissin's private railcar and walked back to the stock car. Both men wore dapper black suits and matching riding dusters, but they differed in headwear. Grissin wore a silk-trimmed silver derby; Duvall wore a black broad-brimmed frontiersman hat, the front brim folded up, fastened to the crown with a silver scorpion stickpin.

Beneath Duvall's broad-brimmed hat, his face looked like that of a serpent's chiseled from rough faulty stone. A thick, drooping mustache hung below his chin on either side of his thin, tight lips. "There's three turds bobbing in the same chamber pot," he grumbled under his breath, staring ahead along the rail platform at Money Up Siding.

"What's that?" Davin Grissin asked, staring straight ahead.

"Nothing," said Duvall. He spit sidelong and gazed ahead with a furrowed brow.

At a stock car, Antan Fellows and Grady Black busily unloaded supplies and horses down a wooden cargo ramp. Peyton Quinn stood back observing, a thumb hooked into his gun belt, holding back the lapel of his corduroy coat. His face was covered with healing bruises and a vicious welt from a marble ashtray. His right eye was still puffy and purple-ringed. Upon seeing Grissin and Duvall, Quinn called out to Grady and Fellows through battered lips, "All right, men, *vamos*! We haven't got all day here."

Hearing Quinn, and having gotten the gist of Duvall's comment about chamber pots, Grissin said in Quinn's defense, "Peyton Quinn never let me down before."

Duvall gave a glance at Grissin's cut and battered knuckles, associating them with Quinn's face. "I say where there's a *before*, there should never be an *after*," said Duvall. He spit again. "But that's just my thinking on the matter."

"I'll take note of your having said it," Grissin replied. "I hope you and I have a good solid understanding of what I want done up here."

"I believe we do," said Duvall. "You've got a ranger you want dry-sodded for hurting your boys' feelings, and four cattle punchers you want skinned and et alive for stealing your money. I'd have to be a fool not to understand it the first time, wouldn't I?" His words came as something between a threat and a question.

"I'd never consider you a fool, Tillman Duvall,"

said Grissin, "but because I've dealt with my share of *idiots* these days, let's talk straight. To hell with *my* boys' feelings. For reasons I won't go into I don't want the ranger in our way."

"You want him killed?" Duvall asked.

"If it takes killing him to keep him from meddling, yes, that's all right by me. The most important thing is getting my money back."

As Grissin spoke, they stopped near Peyton Quinn at the cargo ramp. A tall man wearing batwing chaps, with a saddle over his shoulder and a rifle in his hand, came walking toward them from the other direction. "That's Chester Cannidy, foreman at my newly acquired Long Pines spread."

"More cowpunchers, how nice," Duvall commented skeptically. "I'm wondering if I charged you enough for this work."

Grissin gave him a sudden heated stare. "You charged as much as the market would bear, Duvall."

"If we was standing on Texas dirt, I'd oblige you to call me *Mr.* Duvall," the serpent-faced gunman said with a trace of a strange, cruel grin, letting Grissin know that heated stares didn't unsettle him in the least.

"We're not *in* Texas," said Grissin. "A day's ride and we're not even in 'Zona." His eyes narrowed, and his dark grin matched Duvall's. "See? I know where I'm at, *Duvall*," he added, leaning a little menacingly toward him.

"Meaning?" Duvall asked in a prickly tone.

"Meaning I've seen thieves and gunmen go sour

on one another when one of them becomes rich . . . the way I have," said Grissin. "They think that man turned soft for some reason." He tapped his black-gloved fingers on his gun butt. "But before you start returning me short answers and side pokes to test my bark, you'll do well to remind yourself how many men I've killed, none of them for pay, the way you have, but every damn one of them because they thought they could crowd me over matters of money."

Without taking his eyes from Grissin's, Duvall crooked his mouth sidelong and spit, then said, "I'm reminded, and you'll do well to note that I'll need no *further reminding* on the subject."

Grissin nodded slowly in agreement and turned away when Chester Cannidy stopped and dropped his saddle onto the plank platform. "Hey, cowboy," Quinn said to him straightaway, "give them a hand with these horses and supplies."

Cannidy gave him a narrowed stare.

"You heard me, *vamos*!" said Quinn in a belligerent manner, his battered face partially hidden by the shadow of his hat brim.

Vamos, your ass. . . . Ignoring him, Cannidy turned to Grissin. "Mr. Grissin, I picked up a little more news about the four drovers on my way here through Creasy."

"Good work, Cannidy, what is it?" said Grissin, giving a thin smile of satisfaction for Duvall's sake. Duvall looked away, this time toward Quinn, and spit again.

"A bartender told me two men rode into town, dressed like drovers. One of them wore spectacles and rode like he was wounded. That would be Holly Thorpe. He got himself treated by the doctor there. The ranger found him, but Thorpe got away when the ranger's horse picked up a bad bruise and a pulled tendon."

"Any word about my money?" Grissin looked at him expectantly.

"No, sir, nothing," said Cannidy. "But can I tell you what I think?"

Grissin just looked at him.

Cannidy ventured on. "I think these drovers got a hold of it by mistake and don't know how to turn it loose."

"You're telling me they're not thieves?" Grissin shrugged. "What do I care? Thieves, thugs or Methodists, it doesn't matter, they've still got my money."

"Alls I'm saying is maybe if we could let them know that all they've got to do is give it back to us," said Cannidy. He gestured a nod north toward a line of high rugged hilltops, beyond them a line of even higher, even more rugged mountains. "It would beat tracking them in this hard country."

"You're my tracker, Cannidy," Grissin said harshly. "Is this going to be too hard for you?"

"No, sir, I can track them past hell and back to Kansas," said Cannidy. "I'm just offering something for consideration, is all."

"Hmmph." Duvall looked away and spit again in disgust.

"I see." Grissin looked at him for a moment, then nodded his head. "What about this? I could get word to them, offer them a reward of some sort?"

"I hadn't gone that far, but I expect it couldn't hurt," said Cannidy.

"How much . . . ?" Grissin looked back and forth, studying the idea. "Say, five hundred, a thousand dollars maybe?"

"Well, I—" Cannidy stammered.

Grissin cut him off with a jerk of his head. "Get the hell over there and help with the horses! Track these drovers for me!" he bellowed. "Leave all the thinking to me!"

Cannidy jerked his saddle back up over his shoulder and stepped away.

Duvall looked off, muffling a laugh. A moment later, spotting a rider on a big black-and-white-speckled barb with a black mane and stocking, he asked Grissin, "Have you got any more *experts* coming to join us?"

"Yeah, I do," said Grissin, looking out across a flat stretch of land at the rider in the long tan riding duster and black suit. "This man used to be chief detective for Midwest Detective Agency."

"Used to be, huh?" said Duvall, with a sarcastic turn to his voice. He spit sidelong again, this time blowing out his jawful of tobacco and reaching for a fresh plug from the twist of Red Circle inside his duster pocket.

Grissin looked at him. "Yeah, he *used to be.* Now he's not. The ranger shot him. He lost his job over it.

Now he wants a piece of the ranger's hide. See why I hired him?" he added stiffly.

"Hell, that's Clayton Longworth," said Duvall, his attitude perking up a little. "Now you're talking. I was starting to wonder if you even *knew* any gunmen." He bit a fresh plug off the twist of Red Circle tobacco and stuck the remaining twist back into his pocket.

Grissin gave him a smoldering look, but decided not to respond. Instead, he said, "Being chief of detectives was no small job. I'm going to need a man with that kind of knowledge around me from now on." He looked at Duvall pointedly and said, "A man with knowledge might be as important as having a bodyguard."

"Not if there's somebody bent on killing you," Duvall replied without facing him. He turned sidelong and spit again.

At the wooden cargo ramp, Quinn looked at Cannidy and said dryly, "Welcome to the hunt, cowboy. Throw your saddle over something, go hitch it and get yourself back over here. We've got lots of work left to do."

"Don't call me cowboy," said Cannidy, in a prickly tone. "My name is Chester Cannidy. I'm the tracker for this party."

"I know your name, *cowboy*," said Quinn. "Mr. Grissin told us you'd be meeting us here. Now get a cayouse under your saddle and *vamos*."

Vamos *your ass*. . . . Cannidy turned away, biding his time for now. He eyed a stout-looking little red desert barb, walked over and slung his saddle up over its back.

He had a feeling that finding these drovers wouldn't be the hardest tracking he'd ever done. But like a man cornering wildcats, once he had them what was he going to do with them? He knew Mackenzie and his drovers wouldn't give up easy. He also knew that Cleland Davis had a cabin in the north of the territory. If he knew about that cabin he was sure all of the former Long Pines drovers knew about it too.

He'd learned about the cabin himself back when he'd worked as a drover for a big English cattle syndicate. Cinching the saddle, he shook it back and forth with both hands, testing it. The real question, he thought, was whether he wanted to lead Grissin and these men there and take a chance on getting Mackenzie and his pals killed. *Damn it . . .* , he said in silent reply. How'd those four manage to get into such a mess?

In Creasy, Sam and Maria had lost two days after the ranger's horse pulled a tendon while they were bringing the wounded man to town. It had not been easy to find a good replacement horse for Black Eye, but he'd finally arranged to rent a fiery-spirited roan from the town veterinarian. At the same time he'd seen to it that the young veterinarian would be keeping Black Eye quartered and well cared for while the tendon healed.

When Sam had saddled the haughty roan, he led it over to Dr. Ross' office and hitched its reins to the rail out front. As he walked up to the front door and reached for the brass doorknob, the big cur circled once, then plopped down on the porch to await his return. Walking inside, Sam found Maria sitting in a chair outside the treatment room, waiting while the doctor changed the dressing on the wounded man's chest. She set a teacup down and stood upon Sam's arrival.

"Is the rancher doing any better?" Sam asked, taking off his broad-brimmed sombrero. The wounded man, Owen Bleaker, owner of a small spread thirty miles from Creasy, had drifted in and out of consciousness ever since the ranger had brought him to Creasy. The man Parks had killed, Harold *Red* Herbert, had been Bleaker's partner.

"*Sí*, he is better." Maria nodded. "The bullet went through him clean. Dr. Ross says he will live if infection does not set in." As she spoke she reached her hand out and brushed a strand of hair from the ranger's forehead. "What about you? You look like you could use some rest."

"I could use some rest," the ranger said with a faint tried smile, "but I'll have to settle for some strong hot coffee instead. I can't stop, not as long as I know these four young men are taking the brunt of everything Buckshot Parks is doing out there."

As the two talked back and forth, the doctor stepped out of the treatment room and shut the door quietly behind himself. He looked the ranger up and down from behind a pair of spectacles perched low on his nose. As if knowing what the ranger and Maria were talking about, he said to Sam, "I sure hope you find this son of a bitch who killed Red Herbert and did this to Bleaker." Catching himself, he looked quickly at Maria and said, "Begging your pardon, ma'am."

Maria only nodded curtly, accepting his apology. "We will catch him, Dr. Ross." She paused, then asked, "Is Beth Ann going to be all right? She seemed terribly upset."

The doctor sighed. "Yes, she will be all right. Like all of us in the healing arts, she hates to think that her good works might come to a bad end."

"All the more reason for us to get under way and stop Stanton Parks from doing these fellows any more harm," Sam said.

"Yes, I understand," said the doctor. "Bleaker said to tell you the man rode away with Red Herbert's big fifty rifle. It's scoped and ready for long-range shooting."

"Obliged for the tip," said Sam.

"He would like to thank you personally before you leave," said the doctor, "but I'm afraid he is back to sleep just now." He gestured toward the front door. "So I'll tell him I thanked you for him. . . . That will have to do for now."

"Obliged again, Doctor," said Sam. "I'll come look in on him when we've finished with Parks and I return here for my horse."

"I hope that shan't be long, Ranger Burrack," said the doctor as the two turned and walked toward the door.

"So do we, Doctor," Maria said, looking back over her shoulder.

Out front at the hitch rail, the two stood for a moment while Sam produced the broken paper money band from his pocket and looked at it. "The veterinarian said there was a cowhand through here right after I brought Bleaker to town. Said the cowhand was on foot, carrying his saddle and gear. The cowboy told him he'd had to put his horse down from a snakebite."

"Oh?" said Maria, listening to see where this was going.

"Yep," Sam continued, "the horse doctor said he referred the man to the livery stable to buy himself a horse, but the man turned him down. The man asked *why would he waste his money?* There'd be a good horse waiting for him up the trail."

"Davin Grissin?" Maria said, catching on immediately.

"Could be," said Sam. "He's had time to gather support and make a move in all this. After all, it was his money stolen"—he toyed with the money band—"even though it was wrapped in these new money bands that the bank in Santa Fe had only started to use right before they were robbed."

"Are you saying you think Grissin had something to do with robbing the bank at Santa Fe?" Maria asked.

"I don't know," Sam replied. He put the paper money band away and unhitched the roan. "But Grissin is too rich to send money across this country unguarded . . . unless it was the law instead of the robbers he was worried about."

The two swung up into their saddles, turned their horses and put them toward the north trail. The big cur sprang ahead of them and ran and circled and sniffed the ground, then loped on, leading them on a hunt.

Chapter 17

Jet Mackenzie kneeled beside a cool running spring just off the high trail he'd ridden throughout the past day and night. He dipped his bandanna into the bracing water and pressed it to the fierce exit wound the bullet had left in his upper right shoulder. When he heard the breaking of brush across the narrow stream, he looked up, but was unable to draw his Colt with his right hand. By the time he'd gotten the gun up with his wet left hand, the figure across the stream revealed himself.

"Mac?" said Tad Harper, looking surprised and happy to see him. Then his eyes went to the bloody wound and stopped there.

"Yeah, Tadpole, it's me," Mackenzie said, letting out a breath of relief. He holstered the gun awkwardly and struggled to get up.

"Hold on! Let me give you a hand," said Harper, pulling his white-faced roan along by its reins across the shallow stream.

In the few seconds it took Harper to cross the water, Mackenzie made it up onto his feet. "I'm good," he said, staggering a bit, then catching himself.

"You don't look too good," said Harper.

"I'm a lot better than I was," said Mackenzie.

"How'd you get shot? Who shot you?" Harper asked, staring at the bloody wound.

"I don't know who shot me," said Mackenzie. "I had a sheriff tied down over a mule. Two riders found us and I got shot trying to get away. Leastwise the fellow over the mule said he was a sheriff. His story changed once I got the upper hand on things." He dabbed the bandanna against the wound. "It's stopped bleeding some, but my arm is stiff from it." As he spoke he turned his head quickly toward the sound of another man walking through the brush.

"It's all right," said Harper, "that's just Brewer. We met up on the trail this morning at daylight. I walked on ahead to the water just to play it safe." He looked across the water into the brush and called out quietly to Jock Brewer.

"That was good thinking, Tadpole," said Mackenzie.

"Was it?" Harper grinned. "See, I figured if one of us came ahead and got into trouble, the other would come and give him some backup—"

"I got it, Tadpole," said Mackenzie, stopping him short. He gazed into the brush as Jock Brewer walked into sight leading his brown-speckled barb.

"Dang, Mac!" said Brewer upon seeing the wound

in Mackenzie's shoulder. He hurried across the stream leading his horse, then stopped and asked, "What happened? Are you shot?"

Mackenzie drew a patient breath, hating to have to repeat himself.

"He danged sure was shot," said Harper on Mackenzie's behalf. "He had a sheriff tied over a mule, didn't you, Mac?"

"Where's Holly?" Brewer asked with a wary look, disregarding Harper.

"I had to leave him in Creasy," said Mackenzie. "But the last I saw of him he was being looked after by a pretty, young woman. . . ."

Mackenzie gave them all the details of the doctor's daughter, of being caught off-guard in the livery barn and of knocking the sheriff out and being on his way taking the man far from town when he ran into the two riders. When he finished, Harper and Brewer looked at each other in astonishment.

"That was some *time* you and Thorpe had," said Brewer, taking it all in. "I just hope ole Holly is all right there by himself."

"At least I managed to get the sheriff away from him before I took this bullet," said Mackenzie.

"You don't think this sheriff's posse might have caught Holly and taken him prisoner, do you?"

"I can't swear to it, but I don't think so," said Mackenzie. "Fact is I don't believe this sheriff had a posse—I ain't convinced he was even a real sheriff," he tacked on.

"Did you see his badge?" asked Brewer.

"Of course I saw his badge," said Mackenzie, pressing the wet bandanna to the wound.

"Then he must've been a sheriff," Harper cut in.

Mackenzie and Brewer gave each other a look. "When I left Thorpe," said Mackenzie, "he was awake and knew what was going on around him. I expect if he smelled even a whiff of trouble he skinned out of there."

"But we don't know that, do we?" Brewer asked.

"That's right, we don't," said Mackenzie. "I told him to head for the cabin up around Marble Canyon. If he doesn't show up there in a few days . . ." He let his words trail.

Brewer gave him a firm look. "Then we'll be bound to go to Creasy and start looking for him from there. Wouldn't you say?"

"That's right, we will," said Mackenzie, returning the look. "Every one of us is innocent of any wrongdoing. The only way any one of us gets freed of this is if we all get freed from it."

"That sounds right to me," said Brewer. The two nodded at each other, then turned to Harper. "What do you say, Tadpole?" Mackenzie asked.

"Right as rain," said Harper. He picked up the reins to Mackenzie's horse and handed them to him. "Are you able to make your saddle left-handed?" he asked Mackenzie with a slight grin.

"Stand back and watch me," said the tired, wounded trail boss.

"It's near a two days' ride to Clel Davis' cabin,"

said Brewer, stepping up into his saddle beside Mackenzie's horse.

"A hard ride at that," Harper added, stepping up into his saddle as well and pulling his white-faced roan back a step. "Are you going to need that shoulder looked at?"

"I've looked at it," said Mackenzie.

"Oh, are you a doctor now?" Brewer asked in a gigging manner.

"No, but I watched the doctor's daughter take care of Thorpe," said Mackenzie. "I believe I've got the hang of it."

"Mac's got the hang of taking care of bullet wounds, Tadpole," said Brewer, nudging his brown-speckled barb forward beside Mackenzie's claybank dun. "What do you think of that?"

Harper gave the young but senior trail hands the lead and nudged his horse along behind them. "Mac's the boss," he said. "Whatever he says is jake with me."

Evening had drawn long shadows across the high trails when Stanton Parks stepped down from his saddle and led his horse to the stream. Following the same hoofprints he'd trailed throughout the day, he watched a coyote raise its muzzle and slink away as he approached. At the spot where the coyote had stood, he looked down at the blackened bloodstains the coyote had been licking.

Parks grinned to himself and said under his

breath, "I hope I find you bled out and dead, you cowpoking son of a bitch."

Looking all around at the boot- and hoofprints joining Mackenzie's from across the stream, Parks rubbed his boot toe back and forth in the dirt and said, "That's good, get all of my money bunched up to where I can take it back at once."

He turned and mounted and rode on, still following the tracks that had now grown from one single wounded rider to three, two of them well armed and capable. But Parks didn't care. These were drovers, he reminded himself, not outlaws, not thieves and killers—not men like himself, he thought. Once he got them all rounded up, he would take what was his without any trouble.

True, the young trail boss had gotten the best of him back in Creasy, he thought, rubbing his battered face with a gloved hand. But that had been only a lucky fluke on the drover's part. He had to admit he'd underestimated the man's speed and cunning. But that was a lesson learned that he would not have to learn again.

"You're dead when I get my hands on you," he growled, recalling the incident as he'd slowed for a moment to look down at the three sets of tracks. Then he batted his heels sharply to his horse's sides and rode on.

As the last thin mantle of red sunlight sank below the distant horizon and darkness descended behind it, he sat his horse atop a ridge and stared down at a narrow clearing. Thirty yards below him, out in front of a small log and plank shack, a shaggy dog barked threateningly at his shadowy silhouetted presence. The animal lunged wildly on the end of a chain secured around a hitch post.

Parks stared stone-faced as a man stepped from the shack pulling his galluses up over his ragged upper long johns. "Down, Tip!" the man commanded, staring up along the cliff line toward Parks. But the big shaggy dog would have none of it. Finally, the man reached over and kicked the dog soundly with his bare foot. The dog yelped and settled a little, but still strained against the chain and kept a low growl rumbling in its chest.

"Who goes up there?" the man called out, holding up a lit lantern that gave him no assistance, yet provided Parks with a good clear shot had he wanted to take it.

Bang! Parks stared for only a moment, reminding himself how easy it would be. Then he called out, "I'm Sheriff Mandrin, from south of here."

"Oh, a sheriff . . ." The man's face look relieved in the dim lantern light. "Welcome, Sheriff, ride on down. Let my woman pour you a cup of coffee and get you a plate of grub, if you ain't et."

This was too easy. . . . Parks nudged the animal forward and down a steep cutbank, leaning far back in his saddle until the horse found level ground and walked on toward the front porch of the shack.

Seeing the badge on Parks' chest in the lantern light, the man said, "I reckon you'd be the first to chastise me, Sheriff, for stepping out unarmed in the dark of night." He swung an arm toward the front door that stood open a crack. "But the fact is, my woman stands there with a shotgun." His eyes stayed on the badge. "It would be pointed at you right now, were you not a lawman come calling."

"The hell you say," Parks grumbled, seeing the thin dark outline in the opened crack of the door. To the man he said, "That's wise thinking on your part, friend." *This damned fool. . . .* "If more folks were cautious like you, I'd spend less time burying innocent victims, and more time pursuing the lawless . . . which is what I'm now doing." He stopped his horse as the man gathered the dog's chain and held the animal near his side.

"I'm Baines Taylor," the man said. He gave the dog another poke with his bare toes to settle its menacing growl. "This is my woman, Laura Bird Taylor." The door opened a little farther and a thin woman stepped out wearing a long shapeless linen housedress. She held a shotgun out of sight behind the door. "Laura Bird can't speak a word, but she'll shoot a man in half, the least word from me."

"There's an admirable trait in a woman. Evening, the both of yas," said Parks with an air of authority, touching the brim of his hat. "I'm Sheriff Fred Mandrin." Swinging down from his saddle, a rifle in hand, he stretched and said, "As a lawman I hope I can impose on your hospitality for a night's rest in a bed. This hard ground is taking me apart."

"Evening to you as well, Sheriff Mandrin," said

Taylor. "I'll just hold ole Tip here whiles you step inside. It's not like to him to carry on in such a manner toward a stranger."

"I'm afraid it's me," said Parks, stepping onto the porch and over to the door as it swung open to accommodate him. "Dogs smell the evil that I have to handle, day in and day out. It's part of the cross I bear for upholding the law."

"Well, Sheriff Mandrin, I for one don't know what we'd do without the law," said Taylor, stepping inside the shack behind him, trimming the lantern down and handing it to the woman.

"Obliged for you saying so," said Parks, looking all around the shack. He reached a hand out to the woman and said, "Give me that shotgun, little lady. You can both relax . . . you'll be under *my* protection tonight."

The woman handed the shotgun to him with a thin hand. Parks stared into her dark eyes for a moment, then looked down at her small breasts behind the linen housedress, and down at her bare feet on the dry earth floor. "Not a word, huh?" Parks asked Baines Taylor.

"Not in the seven years she's been here with me," Taylor replied. "Although as you can see, she does have a tongue." He reached out, took the small woman by her jaws and opened her mouth with his thumb.

"That is curious," said Parks. "You said something about some grub?"

"Yes, sir, Sheriff, sure thing," said Baines. He turned to the woman and made a gesture that prompted her toward a coffeepot sitting inside a blackened open hearth.

"All right, then. . . ." Parks sat down at a rough wooden table, unloaded the shotgun and laid it broken down on the tabletop beside him.

When the woman set a cup of coffee in front of him, Parks looked around, saw Baines busily shoving wood into the hearth and roughly clamped his hand up onto the woman's warm crotch. The woman stiffened for a moment, but made no sound, no effort to remove his hand.

Drawing his hand away from her, Parks chuckled under his breath and said quietly, "I have landed softly this night."

Later, when he'd finished a plate of food, he wiped his hand on his mouth and said to Baines, "Now for some rest." He looked Baines Taylor up and down, Taylor sitting with his rough hands folded on the tabletop across from him. "Is that barn out back suitable for a man to sleep in?"

"Yes, I believe it is," said Taylor. "A circuit preacher has slept in it from time to time, and a stock dealer selling horses to the army—"

"Say no more." Parks raised a hand. "I look forward to seeing you first thing in the morning." He wiped his hands on his trousers legs and stared expectantly at Taylor. After a moment when Taylor made no move or comment, Parks said a bit impatiently, "Well? Is there anything else?"

"No." Taylor shrugged. He sat with a confused look on his bearded face.

Parks drew his Colt and let it point loosely at Taylor's blank face. "I said, 'is there anything else?'" he repeated.

A light of revelation came on in Taylor's eyes. He gave Parks a strange look and said, "Now, wait a minute, Sheriff! I won't stand for nothing like that! You're welcome to food and hospitality, but—"

"I am the law, Baines Taylor," Parks said in a fierce tone. "Are you going to argue with the law and do as you're told, or will you ignore the law and do as you damn well please?" He cocked the Colt and straightened the aim.

Taylor scooted his chair back and stood unsteadily and backed away, his hands chest high.

"Grain my horse while you're at it." Parks chuckled under his breath watching Taylor quickly gather his coat, his boots and a ragged blanket on his way out the door. As he opened the door, the dog flew into a barking frenzy. "Take that yapping dog with you," Parks said. "Don't come back until I tell you to."

Listening until Taylor and the dog moved away toward the barn, Parks gestured the woman to him. She came and stood at the table with dull resolve in her eyes. Parks reached up under her dress. "I hope you're going to cooperate with the law, little lady," he chuckled.

The woman only nodded stoically.

"Good," said Parks. "Get that dress off and go

stand by the fire till you're hot all over. Then get yourself into the bed." He sipped his coffee and grinned to himself. Hell, he thought, he would've become a lawman years ago if he'd known it was this much fun.

Chapter 18

In the silver gray before dawn, Parks stood up naked from the bed and walked across the darkened room to the front window. Laura Bird Taylor lay in the bed feigning sleep, naked and trembling beneath a coarse wool blanket. At the front window Parks stared out at the looming black outline of the barn. He gazed along the cliff line where he had sat atop his horse, and he looked away along the dark trail he'd ridden in on.

After a long moment of silence he reloaded the shotgun and walked over to the bed. He lifted the blanket off the woman with the tip of the gun barrel and tossed it aside. The woman lay in a fetal ball, quaking and sobbing the way she had done throughout the long night. "For a person who's unable to talk, you've been the noisiest woman I've ever seen," Parks said in a lowered voice. He fired a blast of buckshot down into her. The bed bounced with the impact. Blood flew.

From the barn, Baines Taylor had held a grim vigil throughout the night, staring hollow-eyed toward the shack through a crack in the barn door. When he saw the fiery streak of blue-orange flash through the dusty window, and heard the accompanying roar of the gunshot, he slammed the barn door behind him and came running barefoot to the shack.

"Did you get him, Laura Bird? Did you get him?" he called out. In the barn behind him, the big shaggy dog barked and scratched at the closed barn door.

At the shack, Taylor threw the door open wide and called out again, "Is he dead, Laura Bird? Did you kill that son of a—"

But inside in the darkness, the other hammer on the shotgun cocked and waiting, Parks said, "I told you to stay away. Now you've broken *the law*!" He pulled the trigger and watched the impact of the shot pick the man up and hurl him backward, out the open door, into the dirt.

At the hitch rail Parks' spooked horse whinnied and reared and pulled at its tied reins for a moment as the dead man landed at its hooves. Inside the barn the shaggy dog growled and barked and scraped madly at the closed door.

Stanton tossed the empty shotgun aside, picked up his rifle and walked out onto the front porch and stood naked in the cool morning air. Gazing toward the sound of the dog's scratching and barking, he raised the rifle to his shoulder and fired shot after shot through the plank barn door until the dog let out a sharp pitiful yelp, then fell silent.

He stood for a moment longer, enjoying the quiet until at length the ringing silence began to annoy him. He scratched his belly and thought about the mute woman, wishing he'd not killed her until after she'd fixed his breakfast. But it was too late now, he reminded himself. He walked inside, dressed, walked back out front, mounted his horse and rode away.

Being a lawman might be something worth doing from now on, he told himself. No wonder so many thieves and gunmen took to wearing a badge at some time or other. There was a feeling to this like nothing he'd ever known, he told himself. So long as folks respected the law, he thought, lawmen do as they damned well pleased. . . . He grinned and batted his boot heels to the horse's sides, and rode away from the pain and death he'd caused.

Nine hours later in the afternoon heat, Chester Cannidy and Clayton Longworth stopped their horses at the edge of the clearing and stepped down from their saddles. They eyed the body of Baines Taylor lying dead in the dirt. Davin Grissin and Tillman Duvall stayed atop the cliff observing from their horses. Below them, the others had spread out in a circling position within the trees and brush surrounding the shack.

"Hello, the house," Cannidy called out.

"Damn, hello the house," said Peyton Quinn,

nudging his horse forward, Antan Fellows and Grady Black riding forward flanking him. He gestured toward the body in the dirt, the day's heat already taking a toll on it. "You can see this son of a bitch is dead. Let's get on with it. We'll be pussy-footing around all day here if you have your way about it."

Cannidy started to step forward, enraged by Quinn. But Longworth stopped him with a hand on his arm. "Let this go," he said under his breath. "He's only trying to impress Grissin."

Quinn and Fellows handed Black their reins and stepped down and walked into the shack, their guns held out before them. A moment passed and the two came back out onto the porch, swapping at flies with their hats. "Whew-*iee*," said Peyton Quinn, "they left one in there curing in her own juices."

Longworth and Cannidy left their horses at the edge of the clearing, walked over and stepped up onto the porch and looked inside. Seeing the remains of Laura Bird Taylor lying dead in a bloody chewed-up ball on the bed, the two stepped back from the open door. Cannidy said, "I've got news for you, Quinn, Mackenzie and his drover pals didn't do this."

"What makes you so cocksure of yourself, *Cowboy* Cannidy?" Quinn said, knowing the new nickname *Cowboy* didn't set well with the ranch foreman.

"Because I know Jet Mackenzie," said Cannidy. "I also know Jock Brewer, and the other two. None of these boys are stage robbers, let alone cold-blooded murderers, like this." He gestured toward the body in the dirt.

"Well, somebody sure as hell killed these two," said Quinn. "It ain't very damn likely that they killed themselves."

His words brought a dark chuckle from Fellows and Black. "Yeah," said Black, "you tracked four sets of hoofprints to that ridgeline up there. If the drovers didn't leave those tracks, who did?"

"I tracked them there," said Cannidy, "but that doesn't mean they left the trail and rode down here." He looked at the dirt again, then said, "We'll never know for sure, now that you three jumped your horses out here and stirred everything up."

Quinn, Black and Fellows looked at the ground and the hoofprints. Quinn saw what a mistake he'd made riding over to the shack, but he wasn't about to admit it. Instead he said, "I'm wondering if maybe you ain't just a little too friendly with these drovers to be tracking them down for us."

"I work for Davin Grissin, Quinn," Cannidy said, bristling. "If he has any problem he'll be the one to take it up with me, not some lackey who can't keep from getting his gun taken away from him."

"You dirty cowpoke!" Quinn spun toward him, his gun hand poised and tense near the butt of his big holstered Colt. "Let me see *you* take my gun away from me!"

"Nothing would suit me better," said Cannidy. He pitched his rifle to Longworth, who caught it and stood watching as the hard-bitten ranch foreman spread his feet shoulder-width apart, facing Quinn.

But before either man could make a move, Tillman Duvall called out from the edge of the clearing, "Both of you *bad men* stand down, before I have to backhand the two of yas."

Both Quinn and Cannidy cut a glance toward Duvall as he stepped down from his saddle and led his horse forward into the clearing. As he walked he took off his black tight-fitting riding glove, pulling on it one finger at a time.

"This is none of your concern, Duvall," said Quinn, still facing Cannidy intently.

"I know that," said Tillman Duvall, "but I don't give a damn if it's any of my concern or not." He gestured toward Grissin, who sat atop his horse looking down from the cliff line. Grissin reined his horse away from the cliff's edge and headed down the trail toward them. "The boss told me to ride down here and keep things in order among you bungling idiots. So I will, even if I have to kill you to get it done." Duvall stopped walking and stared coldly at Quinn. "Now stand down or start grabbing. It offends me to have to talk to a fool like you."

Quinn boiled in rage, but he knew Duvall would kill him. He eased his hand away from his gun and said, "We work for the same boss, Duvall. I'm not out to start trouble amongst us. Getting Mr. Grissin's money back is my only concern here." He said sidelong to Black and Fellows, "You two heard me say it. I'm looking out for Mr. Grissin's best interest here, ain't I?"

"We heard you, Sheriff," said Fellows.

"Dang right," said Black.

"Well spoken," Duvall replied to Quinn with a look of disdain. He turned toward Cannidy and said, "What about you, Cowboy? Are you going to stand down like I told you to?"

"My name's not Cowboy," said Cannidy, not backing an inch. He nodded toward Quinn and said, "He's the only one who calls me that, and that's part of the reason I'm ready to take his head off at the shoulders." He shifted his gaze back to Duvall. "My name is Chester Cannidy, nothing more, nothing less."

A smile came to Duvall's face. "Duly noted, Chester Cannidy." He paused, then said, "Mr. Grissin tells me you know these drovers pretty well."

"I was their foreman what time they were at Long Pines," said Cannidy. "Most times they were on the trail, pushing a herd. But yeah, I know them well enough, I expect."

"Then what's the game here?" Duvall asked as Grissin rode up to the edge of the clearing and stopped.

"There's no game here, not as far as Mackenzie and his pals are concerned," Cannidy said to Duvall.

Peyton Quinn cut in, saying, "He says those drovers had nothing to do with any of this." He gestured toward the body in the dirt and the one inside the shack.

"Oh yeah?" said Duvall, looking at Cannidy. "Then who did?"

From the opposite edge of the clearing, the ranger called out in a firm voice, "Stanton 'Buckshot' Parks is the one who did this."

Duvall spun toward the sound of the voice, his hand going to the butt of his Colt. The other men followed suit, startled by the ranger and Maria having slipped up on them while they stood bickering among themselves. Davin Grissin shook his head and stepped his horse forward into the center of the clearing and took over, saying, "Well, well, if it's not Arizona Ranger Sam Burrack. To what do we owe such an honor?"

"I'm tracking Buckshot Parks," said Sam. Twenty feet away at the edge of the clearing, Maria stood holding a sawed-off shotgun ready and braced against her hip. "I've got a feeling he's the one who robbed the stage carrying your money, Grissin."

"My money?" Grissin tried to be evasive. "Ranger, as a part owner of the stage lines, I consider anybody's cargo on board as important as the next."

"I'm sure you do," Sam said skeptically. Then he asked pointedly, "Are you saying you personally had no money on that stage, in the hidden cargo compartment?"

"I didn't say that, Ranger," Grissin replied tight-lipped, careful of what information he let out. "But as far as Stanton Parks goes, I can't say this looks like his type of handiwork either." He gestured toward the body on the ground. "I've always known Buckshot Parks to be a robber and a rake. I've never known of him doing anything like this."

"Ordinarily he wouldn't have," said Sam, he and Maria stepping forward, their horses tagging along a few feet behind them. "But he's managed to get his hands on a sheriff's badge and it's eaten him up."

Grissin considered it and nodded. "You mean all that legal power has gone to his head?" He gave a smug half grin and a slight chuckle. "Isn't that what happens to everybody who pins on a lawman's badge? They start getting above themselves?"

"It happens to some, not all," Sam said, ignoring the insult. "In Parks' case, it only brings out the worst because the worst is all he's got. He's learning how many doors that badge will open for him. An open door for Parks just means he can get his hands on one more thing he can destroy." Sam paused and looked up at Grissin. "Things will only get worse until somebody stops him."

"Then lucky for all of us, we've got one of Arizona Territory's *finest lawmen* looking out for us, eh, Ranger Burrack?" Grissin said with a sarcastic edge. The men gave a dark, quiet chuckle.

Sam brushed it aside and said, "Here's the deal, Grissin. I want to be able to talk to those drovers and let them know they can give up the money without getting themselves shot or hanged."

"If you're asking for my help, Ranger, you're wasting your time," said Grissin, his tone turning harsh now that he saw the ranger had nothing to offer him. "I'm taking my money back from them, no ifs, ands or buts about it." He lowered his voice and added, "I can't think of a better time for me to set an example. If I let these drovers ride away with my money, every half-assed owl-hoot this side of St. Louis will figure they can do the same."

"But they didn't steal your money, they just ended up with it," Sam said.

"It makes no difference," said Grissin. "People go by what they see and hear. Word gets out that these drovers skinned me, I'll never live it down."

"So you'll let innocent men pay for what Parks and his robber pals did to you?" Sam stared at him.

"Yeah, now you're getting the picture, Ranger," said Grissin. "I didn't ask for your help and I don't want your help. You're warned as of now to stay out of my way."

"This is a legal matter, Grissin," said Sam. "I'm doing my job whether you like it or not."

"Careful where you step, Burrack," said Grissin. He nodded toward Clayton Longworth, Peyton Quinn and the other two men. "It appears everybody here has a reason to want to nail your hide to a board. I can't guarantee your safety."

Sam looked at Longworth, then at Quinn, Fellows and Black. "You don't need to guarantee my safety, Grissin. But you do need to listen to what I can tell you about Buckshot Parks—"

"I've got a good sheriff and two good deputies with me, Ranger," said Grissin, cutting him off, "so we're a lawful posse, within the law and doing our civic duty."

Sam and Maria stood staring as Grissin motioned for Duvall and the others to mount up.

"What about the two dead?" Cannidy asked, gesturing toward the shack.

"What about them?" Grissin asked stiffly.

"Are we going to bury them?" Cannidy asked.

"Naw, to hell with them, we're going to keep moving while the trail is fresh," said Grissin.

"There's something you ought to know about Buckshot Parks," Sam said, trying for the second time to tell him about Parks carrying the big rifle.

But Grissin turned his horse, looked down at Sam and said, "You want something to do, Ranger? Bury the dead before they stink up the countryside."

The men chuckled under their breath. As Tillman Duvall turned his horse, he spit down on the ground in front of the ranger's boots. "Good day to you, Ranger Burrack," he said in a mock tone. "Ma'am," he said, touching his hat brim toward Maria.

The two watched as the men rode out of sight. Finally Sam said, "I'll go find a shovel, we'll get these folks buried proper."

"You tried twice to tell him about the big rifle Parks is carrying, but he wouldn't listen," said Maria. "It serves him right."

"If they catch up to Parks they'll know about the rifle soon enough," Sam said.

At the edge of the clearing the big cur had sat

watching patiently. Now that the men were gone he loped forward and over to the barn door, where he sniffed and scratched until Sam walked over to him, opened the barn door and looked down at the dead dog lying on the dirt floor. "Don't worry, Sergeant Tom Haines, we're going to get him," Sam said, reaching down and patting the big dog as it sniffed and whined over the shaggy dog's body.

The big dog looked up and barked, and looked back down at the bloody ground.

Chapter 19

Ten miles from the Taylor shack, Cannidy and Longworth rode a hundred yards ahead of the others. Finding the tracks of four horses leading down over the edge of a trail and through a hillside strewn with cedar and pine, Cannidy raised his rifle and waved it back and forth for the riders to see.

Looking at Cannidy, Longworth said, "I don't figure you for riding with the likes of Davin Grissin."

"The likes of Davin Grissin?" Cannidy looked at him curiously. "That kind of talk could easily get you killed amongst this crowd."

"Only if you told anybody I said it," Longworth replied. He held Cannidy's gaze until the ranch foreman turned tracker shook his head and said, "You needn't worry. I won't be mentioning it to anybody. If I had this to do over I wouldn't have come along."

"Why did you?" asked Longworth.

"I figured maybe I could keep Mackenzie and his pals from getting themselves killed," said Cannidy. "Those boys got a bad deal from Grissin as it is." He stopped and studied Longworth for a moment, then asked, "What about you? What are you doing here?"

"I needed work," said Longworth. "Besides, the ranger shot me, didn't you hear? That was enough reason for Grissin to hire me." He gave a cruel smile. "Any *enemy* of the law is a *friend* of Davin Grissin."

"That's another thing," said Cannidy. "I knew Grissin used to rob trains and banks, but now I'm thinking maybe he's still got a hand in that game."

"You don't have to wonder," said Longworth, "you can take my word for it, he *does.* Grissin has turned robbery into a trade craft. He buys inside information from payroll clerks and crooked conductors, so he'll know the best time and place to make a raid. He does the same thing with banks. He's so good at it, he never even gets questioned. Most times he's a hundred miles away when the robbery happens. But it's still his handiwork, you can bet on it."

"You sure know an awful lot about it," said Cannidy, eying him closely.

"I should," said Longworth, "it was my job to know all about it."

"It's not *still* your job, is it?" Cannidy asked quietly, as if to keep anyone from hearing him as the riders drew nearer.

Longworth didn't answer. Instead he turned his horse toward the approaching riders and said, "My *job* is to help you get us on the right trail, to catch up to these drovers." He pushed his horse forward and looked back at Cannidy over his shoulder and added with a note of sarcasm, "The most important thing in the world is that we get Grissin's money back."

When Grissin and Duvall rode up to Longworth and Cannidy, the rest of the men behind them, Grissin said to Cannidy, "You better have something good for me. I'm not riding all over hell looking for these men."

"This is them all right," said Cannidy. "I can show you." He stooped down over a jumble of hoofprints.

Grissin gave Duvall a nod. "Check it out."

Duvall stepped down from his saddle and stooped down beside Cannidy. "Okay, *Chester*," he said, emphasizing Cannidy's name. "Show me what a good tracker you are."

"Here's Mackenzie and two of the other drovers, so Thorpe hasn't joined up with them yet. But he will, I figure," Cannidy said, "because these boys stick together." He pointed to another hoofprint and drew a finger around it in the dirt. "I figure this belongs to Buckshot Parks' horse."

"Oh, why's that?" Duvall asked.

"See how this one tops down over these others?" said Cannidy. This one came later, long after the dust had settled. He gave Duvall a level stare and said, "I figure Parks knows we're behind him too. He's not going to be happy, thinking we might get to the money before he does."

"Yeah, you figure, huh?" Grissin said, listening from atop his horse. "You better hope all this *figuring* gets me to my money." He nudged his horse forward and looked off across the rugged desolate land.

"You heard him, *Chester*." Duvall grinned and stood and dusted his hands together.

Cannidy stood up and did the same thing. "Mr. Grissin," he called out, "the trail's going to narrow up ahead and cut through some tight passes. I figure if Parks had a mind to slow us down some that would be—"

"Enough figuring, Cannidy," said Grissin. "Let's get moving. If I get my hands around Parks' neck, you can *figure* I'll choke his eyes out their sockets." He reached back and slapped his reins to his horse's rump.

Duvall chuckled and said, "It appears that Buckshot Parks is about to get himself between a rock and a mighty hard spot."

Buckshot Parks sat hidden from sight by the overhanging bough of a thick pine clinging to a rocky overhang. He'd spotted the riders behind him over an hour earlier and watched them through the rifle scope until he'd recognized Davin Grissin. He knew he would have to deal with Grissin sooner or later. So be it, he thought. He wasn't about to let Grissin get ahead of him and get to the drovers before he did.

While he waited, he'd cleaned and checked the big rifle and gone through the saddlebags on the horse he'd stolen from Red Herbert. He came up with over thirty cartridges for the big fifty caliber rifle—more than enough bullets to do what he needed done, he told himself, running a wadded bandanna along the brass rifle scope.

Five hundred yards away at a turning in the trail below, he watched Grady Black lead the riders into sight, riding beside Antan Fellows. "In the *name of the law* I hereby condemn all of you jakes to death . . . ," Parks whispered to himself, raising the big rifle and looking down through the scope. Behind Fellows and Black rode Davin Grissin and Tillman Duvall, followed by a sullen Peyton Quinn. Cannidy and Longworth were somewhere ahead of the others, out of sight and scouting for the drovers' tracks off the main trail.

On the trail, Grady Black said to Antan Fellows, "I don't like being put out front this way. If this is what it takes to be Quinn's deputy, I'm ready to turn the job over to you."

"I'm not so sure I'd take it," Fellows replied. "Ever since that ranger backed us down and took our guns, Quinn has got every raw deal Grissin can throw at him."

"Yeah, and he's passed it all along to us," Black said bitterly. "The trouble with all this is th—"

His words stopped short as a puff of dust sprang

from the center of his chest, followed by the sound of a distant rifle shot.

"Holy Joseph! Grady's shot!" shouted Fellows, seeing Black roll back and forth drunkenly in his saddle as a string of blood swung from his parted lips.

The commotion caused Black's horse to spook and bolt forward, sending Black falling backward to the ground. Behind Fellows and the riderless horse, Grissin and Duvall cut away quickly and took cover in the rocks along the trail. Grissin didn't realize that he'd just removed himself from the circle of the rifle scope in time to keep the next shot from clipping his head off.

"Grissin, you lucky son of a bitch . . . ," Parks growled under his breath, lifting the rifle barrel and saving his next shot for a better target. With his naked eye he watched the men and horses scramble for cover.

From behind the cover of rock and brush, Grissin and Duvall wiped Grady Black's blood from their faces and tried to get a look up into the hill line where the shot had come from. "All right, Parks, if this is how you want to play it, you two-bit thieving bastard," Grissin said to himself, levering a round into his rifle chamber, realizing he was too far away to do any good.

Seeing Grissin's move, Duvall looked surprised and said, "What are you doing? We're too far away."

"We are, but Longworth and Cannidy's a whole lot closer," said Grissin. He rose enough to get a shot up at the hill line. Then he ducked back down before Parks could get him sighted.

Farther up, off the trail, Cannidy and Longworth had both ducked down at the sound of the big fifty-caliber rifle. They'd been able to look down behind them and see Black's body lying on the trail and his horse racing away. Upon hearing Grissin return fire, Cannidy looked up along the hill line and said to Longworth, "There's our cue. Watch for the next shot. I'm moving up closer."

"I've got you covered," said Longworth. He crouched down behind the trunk of a thick pine tree and kept watch on the rocky hill line.

Above the trail, Parks levered another round into the rifle chamber and raised the scope to his eye. Slowly and carefully he scanned back and forth, seeing no one in the open. "Come on, you cowardly jakes," he grumbled, "give me something to cut into."

Growing impatient, Grissin called out to Peyton Quinn, who along with Fellows had taken cover behind a large boulder on the opposite side of the trail, "Quinn, get over here, pronto. Bring Duvall and me some ammunition. We've got none in our saddlebags."

Quinn and Fellows looked at each other. "Jesus," said Quinn. He looked up at their two horses, knowing there was spare ammunition in their saddlebags. After a pause he swallowed a lump in his throat and said to Fellows, "Antan, get on over there. Take some of our ammunition to them."

"Are you loco?" said Fellows, keeping his voice down just between the two of them. "He doesn't want ammunition, he wants us to draw some fire, so Cannidy and Longworth will see who to shoot at!"

"It makes no difference why he wants it done," said Quinn. "He's the boss. Now do it."

"Huh-uh, you do it," said Fellows. "You're his sheriff. I'm just a hired gun."

"That's right, half-breed," said Quinn, "a hired gun is all your are." He cocked his Colt quickly and aimed it at Fellows' belly. "You can do as you're told, or you stay right here beside Grady Black until the buzzards come looking for you."

"Don't shoot, I'm going," said Fellows. He stood up in a crouch, stepped over and rummaged through his saddlebags until he pulled out a cartridge belt full of bullets. Gazing out toward Black's body with a grimace, he said, "I hope he's not out to get all three of us killed."

"Stop carping about it and get the ammunition over to them," said Quinn.

"Here goes," said Fellows, ammunition belt in one hand, his rifle in the other.

From across the trail, Grissin and Duvall watched the gunman race from behind the rock. "Watch the hills, here he comes," Grissin said to Duvall. He gave a slight grin at the sight of Fellows racing along, zigzagging back and forth. "That is one *fast* injun," he said with a dark chuckle.

High up the rocky hill line, Parks caught sight of Fellows running across the open width of the trail.

But by the time he got the big rifle raised and readied, Fellows had dropped out of sight. "Damn it!" Parks growled to himself. "I dare yas to try that again. . . ."

Behind the cover of rock, Fellows lay panting on the ground, more out of breath from fear than from the run itself. He slung the loaded ammunition belt to Duvall. "There," he said. "That ought to be enough to take care of you."

Grissin ignored him, gazing intently up at the hill line. Disappointed that Parks had not fired a shot and revealed his location, he called out to Quinn, "Okay, Sheriff, now your turn."

"My turn?" said Quinn in an unsteady voice.

"You heard him, damn it," said Duvall. "Get yourself over here where you're most needed." He chuckled under his breath and watched the upper hill line. "Don't worry, we've got you covered."

"You can't have me covered," said Quinn, "he's too far out of range."

"How about showing a little faith?" Duvall said in a scoffing tone.

"Sons a' bitches," Quinn growled to himself. He stood, crouched and raced out across the open trail.

This time Parks was ready, the scope already up to his eye as he'd sat scanning and waiting.

"Run, Peyton, run!" Fellows shouted, catching a harsh flash of sunlight off the brass scope high up in rocky terrain. Instead of hastening Quinn, the sound of Fellows' voice caused him to turn and look up as he raced along. Quinn's quick glance cost him a split second, but in that split second a silent bullet zipped by and took his right ear off in a spray of meat and blood. He bellowed and ran harder, his voice drowned out by the following rifle explosion.

Quinn hit the ground at Fellows' feet, rolling and cursing and crying out in pain. "My ear! It's gone. He shot my ear off!" Quinn bellowed in pain, his hand cupping the small mangled remains of his earlobe.

"There he is!" said Grissin, staring up at the hill line, paying no attention to Quinn. He raised his rifle and began firing toward the sound of the rifle shot, giving Cannidy and Longworth direction.

From their spot in the trees and brush higher up, Cannidy and Longworth both homed their fire in on Parks' position, forcing Parks to pull back and abandon his spot and hurry up to where he'd left his horse.

Once atop his horse, Parks batted his boot heels hard to the animal's sides, sending it racing away along the trail, leaving nothing for Grissin and his men to shoot at but a rise of brown dust. That was good enough, Parks told himself. He'd killed one of them, maybe wounded another, he thought. He'd slowed them down; he'd kept them from getting around him and closer to *his* money.

Three miles back along the trail, on the other side of the steep hill line, Sam and Maria had heard the gunfire as they rode on, having buried the Taylors and their dog. Slowing for a moment, the two looked at each other. "It sounds as if Grissin and his men have learned that Parks has a long-range rifle," Maria said.

"Yep, I'd say so," Sam replied. "As bad as I want Parks, I hope him and Grissin will keep each other busy while we circle around and get between them and the drovers." He nudged his horse on along a stretch of grassy meadow land, just off the trail.

"Si," said Maria with a trace of a smile, "that would be most obliging of them." She nudged her horse along beside the ranger as the gunfire fell silent in the rugged hills above them.

Chapter 20

Jet Mackenzie, Jock Brewer and Tad Harper stopped and looked at the sun-bleached wooden sign standing at the fork in a trail. Harper read aloud, "Welcome to Paí—Paí—Duro."

"Welcome to País Duro," Brewer said, finishing his struggling words for him.

Harper stared studiously at the sign, then asked the other two, "What does *País Duro* mean?"

"It means *hard country,* Tadpole," Brewer said, crossing his wrists on his saddle horn and looking around at the jagged rocky hills surrounding them.

"Welcome to *hard country,*" Harper repeated with a crooked grin. "How are we supposed to tell the difference?"

The three shared a short laugh and nudged their horses on toward the small ghost of a town lying in a rocky valley southeast of Marble Canyon. Mackenzie rode a bit low in his saddle, his shoulder wound healing slowly beneath a bandage made of strips of an old linsey-woolsey shirt he'd rummaged from the bottom of his saddlebags. Earlier in the day they had heard the sound of distant rifle fire in the hills and canyons behind them. The gunfire had served them as a reminder to keep moving.

"There's Holly's cayouse," said Harper before they'd gone fifty yards along the town's dusty street. He nodded ahead at the salt-and-pepper barb standing at a pitted iron hitch rail. As they rode onto the dusty street of País Duro, they saw Holly Thorpe step out of a low-roofed adobe cantina. He gave a short wave and limped over beside his horse and awaited them.

"It's about time you all got here," Thorpe said. "I was starting to get concerned."

"You needn't," said Brewer. "We had an easy ride, except for boss here taking a bullet and me and Tadpole dodging every rider we come upon along the trail."

"Mac's *shot*?" Thorpe gave Mackenzie a troubled look up and down as the three stopped their horses at the iron rail.

"Not so's you'd notice," Mackenzie said. "Anyway, I learned enough watching the young woman treat you that I knew what to do."

"Who shot you?" Thorpe asked.

"Some riders I ran into while I was taking that sheriff away from Creasy," said Mackenzie. He stepped down from his saddle and let Thorpe have his reins instead of using his weakened right hand.

"Dang, I feel bad about this," Thorpe said.

"Well, don't," Mackenzie said sternly. "You had nothing to do with it."

"But dang it, you got shot trying to get the law away from me," said Thorpe.

"I got shot trying to do what was needed for all of us," said Mackenzie, "the same as you would had it been the other way around. So make nothing of it." He looked at Thorpe closely and said, "Anyway, I'm fine as can be now. How're you making out?" He gestured toward Thorpe's wounded side, noting the way he had limped out to the iron hitch rail.

"I'm good," said Thorpe. "I had to back-door out of Creasy when Arizona Ranger Sam Burrack and his woman rode into town."

"Sam Burrack?" said Brewer. "Is he after us now?" The four gave one another a troubled look.

Mackenzie said, "I expect he was after us all along if he thinks we stole that money." He glanced around and said under his breath, "We ought not be talking about this out here, in the open."

"How much farther is it to Clel Davis' cabin?" Harper asked, gazing off along the distant rugged hills between the town and the Marble Canyon area.

"Not much farther," said Mackenzie, "less than half a day's ride. Let's water our horses, take on some supplies and get going. The quicker we're out of sight, the better I'm going to like it."

"How are we going to pay for supplies?" Harper asked with a blank expression.

"Dang it, Tadpole!" said Brewer. "Use your head." He reached over with his battered hat and slapped Harper jokingly on his dusty shoulder. "We're every one of us sitting atop more money than we've ever seen in our lives."

"But like Mac said when we started, that ain't our money we're carrying, right, Mac?" said Harper.

"That's right, Tadpole," said Mackenzie. He frowned at the thought of using any of the money they had in their saddlebags.

"I agree with you," Jock Brewer said. "But it ain't like we're stealing the money. We're just talking about using some, enough to feed ourselves until we find a way to turn it in." He grinned, trying to make a joke of it. "I feel foolish living on lizard and jack-rabbit up there while my saddlebags are busting with money."

"I like lizard and jackrabbit," Mackenzie said stubbornly.

"I know you do," said Brewer, "about as much as we all do." He paused, then said, "You're the trail boss, Mac, and I'll go along with whatever you say. But dang it. Look at us. You're shot . . . Thorpe is shot. We ain't none of us tried to do a thing but what is right. We didn't bring any of this on our-selves. We ought to at least be able to get some good from it."

"Why?" Mackenzie said sharply. "What makes us so special? Because we're trying to do right?"

"Yeah, sort of," Brewer said, spreading his hands out. "We didn't have to do what was right. We could have all run high, wide and away with all this money—"

"Doing right doesn't expect to get rewarded," Mackenzie cut in. "Doing right *is* the reward. We did right because, dang it, that's how things are supposed to be."

"You think?" Brewer said firmly.

"I think," Mackenzie resolved.

Brewer blew out a breath. "I need convincing."

"I've got nothing for you," said Mackenzie. He looked from one to the other. "I was ramrod for this bunch on some trail drives. My job was to look out for you and tell you what to do and what not to. But that's all done. If you need me to *convince you* to do right after all this time, then I wasn't much of a boss to begin with."

"He didn't mean nothing, Mac," said Harper.

But Mackenzie continued, saying, "Davin Grissin owes us money. We've got every reason to take what's ours out of his money. But we won't, not if it's my call." He looked around. "The money is all split up between us. I won't judge any of you if you want to hightail out of here and keep what's in your saddlebags."

"But count you out," said Thorpe, adjusting his wire rims on his nose.

"That's right, Holly, count me out," Mackenzie said flatly. "I didn't earn that money with my own sweat, it's not mine to spend."

The four remained silent for a long moment. Finally, Brewer said, "All right, pards, I'm taking the money and hightailing to old Mex. If you ever come to see me I'll be twirling some dark senorita with a red rose clamped between her teeth." He grinned and twirled in the dirt on his boot heels. "I'll swear I never seen any of you saddle tramps before in my life!"

"Whoo-ieee!" said Harper. "Can I come with you? I've got money too!"

"You two go to old Mex," said Thorpe. "I'm taking my loot and heading for Spain—get me a big ship and go discovering, the same way Columbus did."

Shaking his head, Mackenzie gave in a little. He let out a breath and said to the three of them, "All right . . . if we keep tabs on what we spend—just for supplies, no foolishness. . . . I suppose we'd still be doing right."

"Are you sure, boss?" Brewer gave him a dubious look and said, "I've kind of got my heart set on old Mex."

"A bottle of rye whiskey too," said Mackenzie, giving in. "And some clean dressing and salve for our wounds, all right?"

"Whatever you say, boss," said Brewer. All three of them nodded in unison.

In the late afternoon, long after the four drovers had left on the last stretch of their journey, Stanton Parks followed the three sets of hoofprints into País Duro. He stepped down from his saddle at the same pitted iron hitch rail out in front of the cantina.

Looking all around, he slapped dust from his shirt and his badge and walked inside, the big long-range rifle in hand.

Behind a low bar made of planks laid between three rain barrels and covered with ragged blankets, an elderly Mexican squinted at the badge in the dim light and said, "*Alguacil, acepta. Hombre de la ley son aceptan siempre aquí—*"

"Speak English, you heathen," Parks said, cutting him short with a raised hand.

"Of course," said the cantina owner. "I said welcome, Sheriff. Lawmen are always welcome here—"

"I heard what you said," Parks replied gruffly, cutting him off again. "I just don't like foreign tongue spoke at me." He laid the big rifle up onto the plank bar top. "Do you have anything here fit for a white man to drink—something that has no dead critters in it?"

"I have some good rye whiskey, Sheriff," said the cantina owner. He hurriedly set a fresh bottle and shot glass on the bar in front of Parks. As he opened the bottle he said, "I am Ramon Ortiz, and I too am a citizen *americano*, just like you."

"Yeah, you look it," Parks said skeptically, watching the man fill the shot glass.

"It is true," said the cantina owner, pushing a point that he should have left alone. "My family was in this territory long before the French fur traders came down from the—"

"I don't give a damn," Parks said, swiping the shot glass from the bar and tossing back the fiery rye. He made a hiss and set the glass down loudly. "Since you are such a proud *ciudadano americano*, you can help me uphold the law. I'm looking for three drovers who rode in here earlier today. From the looks of the tracks out front they might have met up with a fourth man and rode out together. Is that *correcto*?" he asked sarcastically.

"*Sí*—I mean, yes, that is correct, Sheriff," said Ortiz. "So few have come and gone lately, it is easy to remember." He grinned and tapped his forehead. "Even for a fool like me, eh?"

"You said it, I didn't," Parks grumbled, bumping his shot glass on the bar top for another drink. "What did they take with them?"

"Take with them?" Ortiz looked bewildered.

"Come on, Mex," said Parks, "don't make me have to jog your mind. What did they take? Supplies? Lots of supplies? A few supplies?"

"Oh, supplies." Ortiz nodded briskly. "They took plenty of supplies . . . and some bandages and some rye whiskey too, for medicine, I think."

"Yeah, for medicine," Parks said in the same skeptical tone, "that's why most drovers are carrying whiskey." He threw back his shot and bumped the bar top for a refill. This time he swiped the bottle from Ortiz's hand and carried it as he walked over to a small open window and looked out toward a rugged hill range.

"These men, they have broken the law, Sheriff?" Ortiz asked.

"Oh yes, in the worst sort of way," Parks said

over his shoulder. He tossed back the shot and pitched the glass to the dirt floor. He took a long swig from the bottle and wiped his hand across his wet mouth.

"Are these men murderers? Did they kill many peoples?" Ortiz asked solemnly.

"Murderers, yes," said Parks. "How many *peoples* did they kill?" he mimicked. "I expect we'll never know just how many. But a hell of a lot." He took another swig and gazed off toward the hill line, the whiskey beginning to boil in his brain. "They stole money that was rightfully mine." Without turning to face the cantina owner, he said, "Do you have any notion how serious that is, stealing money from a *real, honest-to-God* sheriff? A man of the law?"

"It is *most* serious, I think?" the Mexican ventured warily, not sure what his words might evoke.

"Most serious, you're damned right," said Parks. He took another swig, then shook the bottle. Whiskey sloshed over the tip. "Whatever money they spent here was *my* money. So consider yourself paid." He raised the bottle as if in a toast, then took another swig.

The cantina owner remained quiet, deciding it best not to raise a disagreement with this man.

"Where did they get their supplies?" Parks asked, his voice starting to take on a whiskey slur.

"At Widow Bertrim's Mercantile up the street," said the cantina owner.

"At Widow Bertrim's Mercantile up the street," Parks repeated under his breath. He walked over, snatched the big rifle from the bar, walked outside, grabbed the horse's reins and stomped away along the empty street.

Inside the mercantile, the tall, robust widow stood using a feather duster, dusting the same cans of airtights she'd dusted for weeks. When Parks barged in through the open door and stood staggering a bit in place, she looked him up and down, noting the badge on his chest.

"Good evening, Sheriff, and welcome to País Duro," she said. "What can I do for you?"

"You can do whatever I damned well tell you," said Parks. "First, rustle me up some supplies, the same as you did for those drovers I'm hunting."

The woman looked shocked, both at Parks' manner and at the four young men being wanted by the law. "Those well-behaved young men are criminals? My goodness!"

"Do like I told you, woman, before I put a boot in your ass," Parks said drunkenly.

"Sheriff," she gasped, "there's no call for that kind of language." Even as she protested, she began grabbing supplies and stuffing them into a feed sack.

"As soon as you're finished, you climb right out of that dress," said Parks. "I want to see what you've got under there. I might want some of it right there on the counter."

But the widow stopped cold, bristling, and said in a harsh tone, "The hell you say."

Seeing her take a stand, Parks leveled the big rifle

at her. "Oh, you want to argue with the law?" he said.

"The law doesn't act this way, Sheriff," said the tall sturdy-looking widow. "If you think you're getting inside my dress, you've got another think coming."

"Suit yourself," said Parks. "I'll burn this place to the ground."

The woman looked even more shocked, as if this were all some terrible dream. "Sheriff, you're drunk. I don't think you know what you're doing!"

"Drunk or sober, I am *the law*, woman," said Parks. "Get my supplies and get out of that dress. You can hang for refusing to obey a sheriff! Do you realize that?"

The widow doubled her fists, took a firmer stance and said, "Get your rope, you son of a bitch."

From the cantina, the only other business open in País Duro, Ramon Ortiz heard the commotion and ran out front for a look. Through screams, gasps and curses, he saw both jars and cans of airtights fly out the broken window into the dirt street. *Uh-oh. . . .* He ran back inside his cantina, found his old eight-gauge shotgun and loaded it nervously.

But by the time he ran back out into the street and started toward the mercantile store, shotgun in hand, he saw Parks stagger out with the big rifle clamped under his arm. Shoving the rifle into its boot, Parks stepped up into his saddle with a feed sack of supplies slung over his shoulder. His hat was missing. Blood trickled from his right eye where the edge of a tin can had clipped him.

From the broken mercantile window a stream of black smoke began to roll out and rise up the front of the building. "What have you done?" Ortiz shouted, running forward, catching a glimpse of Widow Bertrim run half naked from the mercantile with an empty bucket in her hand.

From his saddle, Parks turned, raised his Colt and fired three wild shots at Ortiz before turning and racing away across the barren rock land northwest of town. Ortiz stopped long enough to shake his fist and bellow out loudly, "What kind of lawman are you? You son of a filthy pig!" Then he dropped the shotgun to the dirt and hurried to the water trough where the widow Bertrim had filled her bucket and ran back with it toward the burning store.

Chapter 21

The ranger and Maria had ridden wide of the gunfire and managed to circle around both Parks and Davin Grissin and his men as the two sides shot it out on the main trail. Once around them, Sam picked up the hoofprints of the drovers' horses northwest of País Duro and followed them on toward Marble Canyon. The ranger had no fear of losing Stanton Parks, knowing that wherever the drovers were, Parks would be close behind.

Camped deep inside a hillside thicket of pine, the two had watched a spiral of smoke rise from the direction of País Duro. But they looked at each other in relief when they saw the smoke dissipate almost as quickly as it had sprung up. They drank their evening coffee without discussing the fire or what possible role Parks might have played in causing it.

On the ground between them, Sergeant Tom

Haines lay sprawled, watching the low flames, his muzzle resting on his forepaws. "I've given it some thought," Sam said after a moment, taking out the broken money band and examining it as he had numerous times before. "These money bands don't prove a thing. I won't be able to connect Davin Grissin to the bank robbery in Santa Fe—not if I want to rely on good solid proof." He folded the money band and put it back inside his shirt pocket.

"Then Davin Grissin will get his money back?" Maria asked. "That hardly seems fair, when you know he is responsible for so much robbery that goes on."

"It's not fair, but it's the rules of the game," Sam said. "I know the rules. I've got to play by them."

"But . . . ?" Maria said, as if expecting more on the matter.

"But nothing," Sam said with a tired smile. "If I get Stanton Parks, and I keep him and Grissin from killing these drovers . . ." He let his words trail.

"Saving innocent lives is no small matter," Maria offered quietly.

"I know," said the ranger. "I didn't mean to sound like it is. If these cowhands get out of this with their skin still on, I'm satisfied. I'll get Parks. Grissin won't get away with his crimes forever. He'll slip up somewhere along the way. Maybe I'll be there when he does." As he spoke he once again took out the money band from his shirt pocket and toyed with it restlessly, as if something about it was still unsettled in his mind.

"You say all these things," Maria offered, "and yet you still search for an answer in this scrap of broken paper."

"I know," Sam said, closing his fist around the broken money band. "Sometimes it's the smallest piece of evidence that bags the biggest thief." He opened his fist and stared at the money band again. "Davin Grissin knows that as well as I do. He's no ignorant horseback thief. He's gone far beyond that." He fell silent for a moment, studying the scrap of paper closely. "Every time I look at this, something tells me it's the evidence that will bring him down. I just haven't figured out how. . . ."

Maria didn't reply; she knew a response was expected. Instead she drank her coffee in silence. He would work it out, she told herself, he always did. Yet when she lay down in her bedroll moments later, the ranger still sat in the glow of the small fire, staring at the scrap of paper, the big cur asleep on the ground at his side.

The next morning, the ranger and Sergeant Tom Haines were already up. Sam had boiled fresh coffee and started warming jerked elk meat and cooking a pan of biscuits before she'd awakened. The dog sat watching intently, his nostrils piqued at the scent of warm food.

After a hot breakfast, the three set out while the

sun still lay in a thin purple mantle on the horizon. By midmorning they had picked up the drovers' trail and followed it into a canyon that grew more narrow, rocky and tree-studded as they went. When they had veered off the trail in order to follow the hoofprints, Sam stopped suddenly and held up a hand. Ahead of them the dog had also stopped. He looked back at the ranger and Maria as if seeking their permission to continue on.

But the ranger gave him no such permission. Instead, he and Maria stepped down from their saddles and led their horses forward quietly. Touching the dog on its head as a form of reward, Sam ventured to the edge of a steep cliff overlooking a wide stream and a clearing below. On the far side of the stream stood a cabin, half of its roof missing and collapsed. Behind the cabin stood a barn constructed of pine logs and rocks from the streambed.

Beside the ranger, the dog watched quietly as a young drover walked from the barn back to the cabin. Through the half-open roof, Sam watched another drover stoke logs in the open stone hearth. As Maria slipped in beside him and looked down, Sam said, "Looks like we got here before anybody else. Now let's see if we can ease down there quiet-like and manage to do some good." He gestured a nod toward a narrow path that wended down steeply and came out at the edge of the braiding stream. . . .

Inside the cabin, Harper walked over to where Jock Brewer stood pouring a cup of coffee from a battered tin pot they'd rummaged out of the debris left after a storm had destroyed the roof. A few feet away, Mackenzie sat tending his wound, having first changed the bandage on Thorpe's side.

"The horses are grained and watered," said Harper. "But they could stand some grazing in the sweet grass we passed alongside the water on our way in."

"Maybe later," said Brewer, pitching another short log into the open hearth. "Mac wants one of us to go stand lookout from atop the hill, make sure nobody rides in off the main trail without us knowing about it."

"I'll go," Harper said.

"Hold up, Tadpole," said Mackenzie, rising, directing his attention toward the stream and the hillside beyond the cabin walls. "I heard something out there."

"You must have awfully good ears," said Harper.

But almost before he'd finished his words, the four turned toward the sound of the ranger calling out, "Hello the cabin." The drovers' hands went instinctively to their guns.

"Hello the cabin," Sam called out again. "This is Arizona Ranger Sam Burrack. Don't shoot, I'm here to talk to you."

Before the drovers responded, they spread out along the thick cabin wall and took positions.

Mackenzie looked back and forth, made sure each man had well covered himself, then called out, "We haven't had much luck talking to the law, Ranger Burrack. Why should we think talking to you is going to be any different?"

"I know about the money. I think I know how you come upon it," Sam yelled back.

Mackenzie looked at the faces of the other three as if for approval. "We're listening."

"I know you didn't rob the stage," Sam said. "I'm after the last of the men who did rob it. His name is Stanton 'Buckshot' Parks, but he is carrying a badge and impersonating a sheriff. He's trailing the four of you. Things are not going to get any better until you're rid of him."

Mackenzie ran things through his mind. "Do you know a sheriff by the name of Fred Mandrin, Ranger?"

"Not anymore, I don't, he's dead," said the ranger. "Buckshot Parks killed him. He left blame for Mandrin's killing on you four. Mandrin was a former deputy who stole a sheriff's badge. That's the badge Parks is using to impersonate a sheriff."

Mackenzie let out a breath.

Sam paused for a moment, then called out, "How do you like our conversation so far?"

Mackenzie looked from one drover to the next. "Who's out there with you, Ranger?"

"Just me, my partner Maria and a dog that belonged to the colonel, who was on the stage you found."

"The colonel's dog?" Mackenzie said. He stepped out and saw the dog on the other side of the stream. "I saw him lying beside the wrecked stage. I thought he was dead."

"He nearly was," said Sam. "But he pulled through it. Do you want to invite us in, or do you want to come out here and talk to us?"

"What if we don't want to talk to you?" Mackenzie asked.

"I know you didn't break any laws," Sam said. "You just happened to be in a bad place at the wrong time. If you won't talk to me, I'll have to back away and leave you alone. But if I were you I wouldn't do that. I'm the only lawman involved here. Everybody else is out to nail your hides to the wall."

"Let them try," Mackenzie said, "we know how to look out for one another."

"I know you do," said Sam, "I've seen that. But the fact is, I could use some help taking down Stanton Parks and Davin Grissin. I was hoping I could count on you fellows."

A tense silence passed as Sam turned around and looked at Maria and the dog. The two stood waiting on the other side of the stream. Finally Mackenzie said, "All right, Ranger. We're coming out. We've all heard good things about you. Don't let us down."

Sam and Maria stood back and waited. The dog

circled slowly and dropped out of sight on the rocky hillside.

When the four drovers stood facing the ranger out in front of the cabin, Mackenzie held two stacks of the stolen money in his left hand. Pitching them one at a time to the ranger, he said, "Just so you know, we never had any notion of keeping this money, even though Davin Grissin owes us all wages."

Sam caught the two stacks and looked at them, seeing the same kind of money bands he had in his pocket. "I understand," he said. "Is the rest of it close by?"

"It's inside," said Mackenzie, nodding toward the cabin. "We carried it separately for a while to make it easier to handle, but it's now back in the same bag we found it in."

"Good thinking," said Sam, inspecting the two stacks of money as he spoke. He looked up at Mackenzie and said quietly, "I'll be taking the money for safekeeping from here."

"I say good riddance to it," said Mackenzie. "You're welcome to every dollar. It's all there, except for a few dollars we kept for supplies and such. I've writ down how much and what we bought."

Harper cut in and asked, "How do we know we can trust him with this much money?"

But Mackenzie silenced him with a stare. "You'll have to excuse Tadpole, Ranger," he said. "We've seen our share of distrust since we found that stage wreck."

"I understand," said Sam. He looked at Harper and asked, "Tadpole, is it?"

"Yes, sir, to my pals," said Harper, courteous but not overly friendly.

"I hope you'll excuse our rudeness, Ranger," said Mackenzie. "We haven't been on our best manners of late. This is Jock Brewer, Holly Thorpe and Tadpole Harper"—he emphasized *Tadpole*—"who you just met."

Sam nodded, looking from one face to next. "Pleased," he said. "This is Maria, my—"

Before he could finish speaking, a bullet reached down from high atop the rocky hillside, hit Harper in his chest and slammed him back against the front of the cabin. "Get down!" Mackenzie shouted at the others. He made a dive for Harper, grabbed him and dragged him inside the cabin as another bullet thumped into the dirt at the ranger's feet.

"I'm taking my money!" Parks shouted from a cliff above the hillside.

Jock Brewer had jumped for cover, but upon hearing the rifle shots and Parks' voice, he made a run for a better position, his rifle in hand. But the next shot from high up the hillside grazed across his thigh and sent him sprawling into a loose stack of firewood. As he struggled to right himself, the ranger rose from behind a low stack of firewood and fired shot after shot toward the sound of Parks' rifle.

Sam knew his pistol was too far out of range,

but it gave Brewer some protection until he had hurriedly crawled behind the loose wood and taken cover. "Maria, are you all right?" Sam called out.

"I'm all right," Maria replied from behind a three-foot-tall rock alongside the stream. "But Sergeant Tom Haines is gone!"

With no time to consider the dog, Sam watched as Thorpe looped Brewer's arm across his shoulder, ran from cover and ducked inside the open doorway. As soon as the two were safely indoors, Sam raced across the open yard and dived in behind the rock where Maria sat hunkered down. A bullet kicked up dirt right behind him. Grabbing his shoulder, Maria said, "Sam, are you hit? Are you all right?"

"I'm good," Sam said. "I never expected Parks to get here so soon. Him and Grissin finished up their fight awfully quick."

"Money has a way of making men like Parks and Grissin do the impossible," Maria commented.

Sam didn't reply. He looked upward, past the spot where they had left their horses hidden in the trees and brush on the hillside. "I've got to get up there and stop him."

"I can offer you no cover with this," Maria said, nodding at the shotgun in her hands.

"I know," said Sam. "He's too far away for anything but a long-range rifle to do us any good. We're going to make a run for the hillside. Once you get to the horses, I want you to wait there for me. Grissin and his men could be showing up any time now, if there's anything left of them."

"I have a feeling there are plenty of them left," said Maria. She gazed up along the hillside of broken rock and trees and brush. "I am ready when you are," she said quietly.

Chapter 22

Inside the cabin, kneeling over Harper, Mackenzie hurriedly opened his shirt. But beneath the fierce bullet hole in the center of the shirt, the young trail boss saw no blood, no gaping wound. Pulling the shirt open wider, he stared at the red welt left from the bullet striking one of the stacks of money Harper had stuck inside his shirt.

"Don't—don't be mad at me, Mac," Harper said, still struggling to regain his breath. "I know I let you down."

The lopsided bullet fell out of the stack of money and landed on the dirt floor. Mackenzie picked it up and looked at it. "Dang it, Tadpole," he said in exasperation. "I don't know if I should be cussing you for not doing what you was told, or just glad you did what you did and it kept you alive."

Thorpe and Brewer saw what had happened. They'd circled around Harper, both of them looking relieved even as another shot from high up the hillside thumped against the front of the cabin. Seeing the young drover was all right, Brewer tightened a bandanna around his own leg wound and said, "You can't be mad at him. He's just a worthless tadpole. I told you he'd never 'mount to nothing."

Harper said, "Believe it or not, I was keeping this money for all of us. In case things didn't go our way, I'd pull it out and say, 'Look, pards, we've still come out all right.'"

"Yeah? When was you going to say that," said Thorpe, a hand pressed to his healing side wound, "right after they tightened the rope around our necks and got ready to pull the lever?"

Seeing their teasing attitude toward him, Harper coughed and caught his breath and said with a devilish grin, "Better late than never, I say."

As another shot exploded, Mackenzie flinched and said in reflection, "I expect if I had it to do over again, maybe we would have just lit out to old Mex. At least we'd all had something to show for it." He felt the pain in his own throbbing shoulder. He looked at Thorpe's wounded side, Brewer tightening a bandanna around his leg and at the large welt on Harper's chest. He realized how close the young man had come to getting killed, and how he would have been killed had he followed Mackenzie's orders.

"Aw, come on, boss," said Brewer, giving Mackenzie a little shove with his bloodstained hand, "you're just wanting somebody to brag on you, and say that you did a good job."

Another shot thumped into the cabin.

"No, I'm not," said Mackenzie. He shook his bowed head. "I know I didn't handle this as well as I should have."

"I can't speak for these two," said Brewer in a sincere tone, despite the grin he gave to Harper and Brewer, "but as far as I'm concerned, you *sure did* let us all down." He said to Thorpe, "What about you, Holly?"

In the same sincere tone, Thorpe said, "I've never been so disappointed in a person in my life. I'm ashamed to say we was ever friends."

"Count me in on that," said Harper, picking up on the running joke.

"All right, that's enough out of yas," Mackenzie said, looking up with a slight frown. "I didn't even have to take charge. I wasn't even the trail boss anymore. I could've let everybody scratch for themselves."

"Oh, you were still the trail boss all right," said Thorpe, straightening his spectacles. "You'd have never let us hear the end of it if things went wrong on us because we didn't listen to you."

"That's right," said Brewer, "you were born being a trail boss, and you still are. You're never going to be otherwise." As he spoke he finished with his leg wound, lifted his Colt from his holster and checked it.

"Well," said Mackenzie, "boss or no boss, we're in a place here." He also checked his Colt. "If the ranger had come along sooner, maybe things would have gone better. As it is, nobody is going to get us off the spot here but ourselves."

"I agree," said Thorpe. He reached down to Mackenzie's saddle on the dirt floor, slid his rifle from its boot and pitched it to him. "It looked like the ranger cut up the hillside. But we can't count on him killing that murdering Stanton Parks for us." He reached down to Brewer's saddle, slid his rifle out and pitched it to him. Then he slid Harper's rifle up, reached it out to him and said, "Here, Tadpole, don't shoot your foot off."

Harper scooted upright and took the stacks of cash from inside his open shirt. "What about this money now? Are we taking it with us?"

"No," said Mackenzie. "However this turns out with Parks and the ranger, the money stays behind. I never knew money was such a dang pain in the neck."

Brewer stared wistfully at the stacks of cash and said, "Well, one thing for sure, it ain't likely any of us will ever be troubled by this much money again."

"Lucky us," said Harper, giving Brewer an understanding look.

"Yeah, lucky us," said Brewer. He took his eyes away from the money as if clearing his mind of it for the last time. Levering a round into his rifle chamber he turned to Mackenzie. "Tell us what you want us to do, boss," he said with resolve.

At the horses, the ranger pulled his long-range Swiss rifle from under his blanket roll and assembled it quickly. He looked all around and said, "I'd feel better knowing that Sergeant Tom is all right."

"He looks out well for himself," Maria said. Seeing the four rounds of ammunition in his hand, she asked with a concerned look, "Four bullets? Is that all the ammunition you have?"

"These four will get me up the hill," Sam replied. "If I can't draw a good bead on him, at least I'll force him to keep his head down—it'll keep some fire off of you and the drovers." He turned and gave her a look and a gentle squeeze on her shoulder. "Keep our horses out of sight," he said. Then he turned and slipped away, deeper into the brush, Swiss rifle in hand.

Atop the steep rocky hillside, high up on a double limb of a tall pine, Stanton Parks sat swaying back and forth on a passing breeze. He saw no movement in the yard of the cabin below. Yet, studying the small clearing, he knew at any moment the four might make a dash toward the barn, get their horses and attempt to make a getaway.

"You can't outrun the law . . . ," he said to himself as if speaking to the four drovers, "and *I am* the law."

Parks raised the rifle butt to his shoulder and scanned back and forth with the brass scope, catching only a glimpse of one of the drovers' hats through the collapsed roof. "One short little step is all you need to take," he murmured down his rifle barrel, "and I will take off the top of your cowpoking head." He eased his thumb over the rifle hammer and prepared to cock it and fire.

But something powerful thumped against the limb only an inch from his shin. As he jerked his leg instinctively, he heard the telltale sound of the rifle shot resound up the hillside. "What the—?" He looked down at the big bullet hole next to his leg. "Whoa, now!" Without a second thought on the matter, he turned and hurriedly climbed down the tree to another, better-hidden limb ten feet below.

Down the rocky hillside, Sam watched, not seeing Parks, but rather seeing the motion of limbs bouncing and bobbing as the gunman retreated downward. Drawing aim on the spot where the limbs had settled, Sam cocked the big Swiss rifle and prepared to fire again.

Hugging the pine tree, using the trunk for cover, Parks peeped around and saw a glint of sunlight on the gun barrel. All right, he knew where the shooter was, he told himself. Now he had to get settled and get an aim before he could do anything to defend himself. He stretched a foot toward a limb below. No sooner had he begun to transfer his weight to the new position than another shot thumped into the tree. This shot hit so close to his boot, he felt the impact through the leather, and lost his balance.

Down the hillside, Sam watched the limbs begin to bob again, this time violently, as Parks slid and bounced and tumbled down, until he caught on to a limb fifteen feet from the ground.

Instead of taking another aim on the gunman's

position, Sam took the lull in fire as an opportunity to hurry farther up the hillside. He raced along from tree to tree until he reached a tall land-stuck boulder, where he stopped and dropped to the ground for a moment. As he waited he heard Parks call out, still a hundred and fifty yards above him.

"Ranger, I saw it's you," said Parks. "I knew you'd be sticking your nose in where it doesn't belong!" He paused, waiting for a reply. When no response came he called out, "I will not leave until I have all my damned money!"

"It's not your money, Parks, it never was," Sam called out. Even though talking gave away his position, Sam took this for what might be his only chance to get Parks to admit to anything. "You and two other thieves robbed the stage and killed innocent people. But you didn't find the money in the hidden compartment, did you? A big bold gunman like you, how'd you miss all that money?"

"I missed it because I didn't know Grissin had any money riding the stage that day. Had I known it I wouldn't have robbed the stage. I'm no fool, me and my pards have made a killing robbing banks and trains that Grissin set up for us. I wouldn't bite the hand that feeds me. But since the money was there, I wasn't about to let some damned *cowpokers* have it."

There it was, Sam told himself. That was as much of a confession as anybody would ever likely hear Stanton Parks make. But if nobody but him ever heard Parks say it, the information was useless. He needed to take Parks in alive, he told himself. He knew how unlikely that would be, yet he knew he had to try. "You need to give up your gun, Parks," he called out.

"No," Parks said gruffly, "you need to come try and take it."

"I need to take you in alive, Parks," said Sam, leveling with him. "I need for somebody beside me to hear you say what you said about Davin Grissin."

"It ain't going to happen for you, Ranger," said Parks. "I'm one of the last of the die-hard outlaws. I tell nobody nothing. I live and die the way I am."

As Parks spoke, Sam eased his way upward a foot at a time, ever closer, hoping against hope that he might get a chance to rush him, overpower him and take him back alive.

While talking to the ranger down the slope in front of him, Parks heard the breaking of brush on the rough terrain behind him. Turning quickly, rifle in hand, he saw the big dog standing just inside the clearing. He fumbled quickly with the rifle, trying to get a fresh round into the chamber. But in his haste, he dropped the rifle and when he started to stoop down the retrieve it, a fierce growl from the dog stopped him cold.

"Easy now, doggie," Parks said, easing his hand down around the butt of his Colt, "you and me ain't never been enemies."

But the look in the big dog's eyes said something different. There was a dark, smoldering memory there, Parks decided. He could almost hear the big dumb animal say with satisfaction that now it was only the two of them . . . that now there would be no one to stop them . . . no one to question why.

"I'm a lawman, damn it!" Parks said, trying to sound forceful, on the outside chance that his words might stop the big raging beast. His hand jerked the gun from its holster. "I demand that you *stop in the name of the law*!"

But the dog would have none of it. Seeing Parks' hand come up with the big Colt, the dog shot forward. Parks could have sworn he heard the animal curse him out loud, the booming, growling voice of some angry soldier seeking revenge for the loss of someone near to him. The Colt bucked once in Parks' hand, but the dog had cut away quickly, as if knowing what to do, like some old hand at ducking bullets. By the time Parks' Colt was recocked, Sergeant Tom Haines was upon him.

Down the hillside, Sam heard the shot, the muffled scream cut short and the snarling rage of an animal given a free hand to do its worst. Hurrying, he scrambled hand over hand up the last thirty steep, treacherous yards toward the top of the hillside. But before he reached the top, the sudden fall of silence above him told him that there was no longer any urgency in his arrival.

Sam pushed himself up over a lip of stone and looked over to where the big dog sat licking its forepaw. On the ground beneath the tall pine lay the long-range rifle. A few yards away lay Parks' Colt. A few yards farther lay a bloody part of Parks himself. The ranger only glanced at the gore for a second, then looked away, back at the dog.

"Sergeant Tom Haines, look at you," Sam said with a deep sense of regret.

The big dog perked its ears at the sound of its name, and looked up from licking its paw. He stared at the ranger with a look of innocence, fresh blood circling his powerful flews.

Chapter 23

With the long-range rifle fire silenced, Mackenzie looked up from the large canvas bag of money lying on the dirt floor. "Let's go," he said to the other three. He stooped, picked up his saddle with his left hand and hoisted it stiffly atop his good shoulder.

"You heard him," said Brewer, "*vamos*, unless you still haven't yet gotten a bellyful of this place." With his leg bandaged, he leaned on his rifle for support.

"I'm sure going to miss it," Thorpe said dryly, hefting his saddle onto his shoulder in spite of his side wound. He adjusted his wire rims and followed Mackenzie out the open door.

"That goes for me too," said Harper, the welt of the rifle slug still throbbing in his chest.

"Get straight to the barn, get your horse and get out," Mackenzie cautioned them over his shoulder as he walked out from behind the protection of the thick pine log walls. "Don't stop to fool around. We don't know what happened up there." He started to nod upward along the steep hillside. But he stopped cold as he saw Davin Grissin and his men, mounted, in a half circle, facing him from fifty feet away.

"That's good advice, trail boss," Grissin said, staring with his wrists crossed on his saddle horn, a big Remington revolver hanging from his gloved hand. "Judging from all the gunfire we heard riding here, this place can get awfully dangerous."

Mackenzie and the other three stopped cold out in front of the cabin. Thorpe let his saddle fall to the ground, as did Brewer and Harper.

"I see the ranger and his lovely companion aren't here." Grissin looked all around.

Not wanting to jeopardize the ranger and Maria should the two come down the hillside, Mackenzie passed over answering him and said, "We've been expecting you most any time, Mr. Grissin." He showed no favor to his wounded right shoulder or his stiff weakened right hand as he eased his saddle down to the dirt and poised his hand near the butt of his range Colt.

"I'll bet you have," said Grissin, in no hurry, knowing he was in charge. "I would have been here sooner had it not been for Buckshot Parks ambushing us. It seems everybody is after my hard-earned money." Cocking an eye in recognition, he said, "You four are the cowpokers I cut loose when I bought Davis' Long Pines spread, eh?"

"Yep, that's us," said Mackenzie, seeing that Grissin was only dragging things out to suit himself.

"But we don't go by the name *cowpokers*," Harper cut in. "If you knew a hill of beans about ranching, you'd know that."

"That's enough, Tadpole," Mackenzie cautioned him over his shoulder in a lowered tone.

"No, let him speak." Grissin gave Harper an unfriendly grin. "Tadpole, huh?"

"To my pals," said Harper, with no grin, just a flat stare.

"To your pals . . ." Grissin nodded and added, "I see. So tell me, *Tadpole*." He continued in a sarcastic tone, "What is it you fellows prefer to be called?"

Harper stared to reply, but Mackenzie took over for him. "We drive cattle," he said. "We call ourselves drovers." He paused for only a second, then said with resolve, "But you *do* already know that."

"Yeah, I knew that . . . ," said Grissin. As if dismissing things for a moment, he straightened in his saddle, took out a fresh cigar from inside his coat and looked all around the clearing. "I wonder if the rights to this place came along with the deed to Long Pines?" he asked, not directing the question to anyone in particular.

"You ought to check it all out with your land attorney," said Tillman Duvall, seated atop his horse beside him.

"Clel Davis built this place on open land," offered Harper. "Nobody owns it . . . it's *open land* forever."

"Forever is a long, long time," Grissin mused, "just ask anybody who's dead." He bit the end off his cigar, spit it away and stuck the cigar into his teeth. On his other side stood Sheriff Peyton Quinn. He wore a bloody bandage on the spot where his ear had been, a bandanna tied around his head to keep the bandage in place. He stepped his horse forward, struck a long sulfur match and reached it over to the tip of the expectant cigar.

"Keep quiet, Tadpole," Mackenzie said to Harper under his breath.

Grissin puffed on the cigar and blew out a long stream of smoke. "Thank you, Sheriff," he said, staring more harshly at Mackenzie as he spoke. "Do you *drovers* realize all the trouble you've put me through?"

"I'm all broken up over that, Mr. Grissin," said Mackenzie, realizing how wounded and worn out he and his pals were, "but the fact is, all the trouble we've had has been because of us trying to return the money to its rightful owner."

Grissin ignored his words. "Well, now it appears you've done it," he said. His gaze narrowed. "Where is my money?"

Mackenzie gestured a nod over his shoulder toward the cabin door. "It's inside, on the floor, right where we intended to leave it."

"Go fetch it, Fellows," Grissin said to the half-breed.

Antan Fellows swung down from his saddle and walked straight into the cabin. The drovers took a step away and made room for him.

In seconds the tall half-breed stepped back

through the open door, stood in front of Grissin and hefted the bag as if to toss it up to him.

But Grissin made no motion of wanting to catch the bag. "I'll be damned, there it is," he said, sounding a little surprised. "It even looks like it's all still there."

"It's heavy enough, I expect it is," Antan said with a trace of a grin, not knowing how much money had been inside the bag in the first place. He stepped over beside his horse, the heavy money bag in hand.

"No, it's not all there," said Mackenzie. "We took a few dollars out for some supplies we needed to treat our wounds and get us up here to the cabin."

"Why would you tell me a thing like that?" Grissin asked, staring at him curiously. He shrugged and shook his head. "I would have left here not knowing."

"Because it's the truth," Mackenzie said flatly.

"Oh, the *truth*. Now I understand," said Grissin. He shook his head again. "You were going to walk away, just leave all that money lying in the dirt?" he asked, looking both puzzled and agitated by the thought of them doing such a thing. "That's damned hard for me to believe," he added bluntly.

"You don't have to believe us. Five minutes longer, you would have seen for yourself," Mackenzie said.

"We're not liars, mister," said Harper, unable to let the remark pass in spite of Mackenzie having told him to keep quiet.

"Maybe you're not liars," Quinn said with a dark scowl, testy and cross in his pain. "But you damned sure are fools."

Neither Grissin nor Duvall seemed to notice the offense the drovers had taken at Quinn's insult. But a few feet away, Chester Cannidy had seen it. In his lap his hand tightened on his rifle stock. Beside Cannidy, Clayton Longworth had not seen the tracker clutch his rifle, but he'd felt a tension seem to close in and tighten around them. He glanced back and forth, his hand also on the rifle lying across his lap.

"We're neither liars nor fools," Mackenzie replied tight-jawed. "We're just four working drovers trying to get by."

"Who lost our jobs because the spread we worked for got bought out from under us," Brewer tacked on. He looked toward Cannidy, who looked away, not liking where he knew this was headed if Grissin didn't show some good sense and manners and let them pass unharmed.

"Yeah . . ." Holly Thorpe took a step closer to Jock Brewer and threw in, "And who got gypped out of our last month's pay."

Grissin stared at the four for a tense moment, then said to Cannidy, "Foreman, did you know anything about these drovers not getting their pay?"

Cannidy had heard Grissin tell the bookkeeper to get rid of them without their pay, but Cannidy knew better than to say so here and now. Instead he ducked the issue and said, "It was that new bookkeeper, Clifford Moorland, boss. I was standing there when he told Mackenzie here that they wouldn't get paid."

Grissin gave a one-shoulder shrug toward Mackenzie and said, "There, you see, trail boss? I had no knowledge of the matter. If I had it would never have happened."

"I expect it doesn't matter now anyway," Mackenzie said.

"It still matters to me," Grissin said. "Before I leave, I want to make sure everybody here gets what's coming to them." As he spoke he nudged his horse around to where Antan Fellows stood holding the big money bag. Reaching down to him with his black-gloved hand, Grissin hefted the canvas bag up and laid it on his lap. "Kill them!" he ordered. Then he quickly nailed his boot heels to his horse's sides.

From up on the steep rocky hillside Maria watched Grissin give the order and try to ride away. She had been staying down out of sight keeping watch on the horses. But as she saw the fighting commence, she grabbed both her shotgun and her rifle and came running down across the stream to the drovers' aid.

Thorpe had kept a close watch on Grissin, expecting some sort of treachery from the former outlaw turned businessman. Before Grissin had gotten the words out of his mouth, Thorpe had raised his battered range Colt from his holster and fired. His shot sliced across Grissin's upper arm and caused him to drop the heavy canvas bag as he struggled to quickly right himself and his spooked horse.

Tillman Duvall, the fastest of the gunmen, jumped his horse between Grissin and Thorpe. He drew his big revolver quickly and shot Thorpe squarely in the head—or so he thought. Without hesitating a second to see what damage his shot had done, he spun his horse immediately and fired at Mackenzie. He didn't see Thorpe's hat fly from his head as Thorpe fell backward with a long streaking graze down the middle of his forehead.

"Look out, Mac!" Harper shouted, seeing Duvall throw down in the trail boss's direction. As he shouted, Harper spun on his heel and fired his rifle. His shot clipped off Duvall's saddle horn. Catching the impact of the flying saddle horn in his crotch, Duvall jackknifed in his saddle and toppled to the ground as his frightened horse reared high and bolted away.

"Wait! Don't shoot!" shouted Cannidy, raising a hand toward Mackenzie as if a raised hand was all it would take to stop the bloodshed.

But Mackenzie had no time to hear Cannidy's plea. He had felt a bullet from Duvall's revolver slice through the air an inch from his head.

"You led them to us!" Brewer shouted at Cannidy as he fired. His shot picked Cannidy up from his saddle and hurled him backward to the ground. Antan Fellows, who had not yet mounted after handing Grissin the money bag, ducked down under the raging gunfire and ran for cover. He dived and rolled behind a water trough and lay flat in the dirt just as a bullet from Harper's rifle whistled across his back.

Watching the bag of money, Clayton Longworth managed to avoid any gunfire. He booted his horse toward the big canvas bag lying on the ground where Grissin had dropped it. But before he got to it, he saw Grissin drop from his saddle and run over and pick it up.

"Hold it, Grissin!" said Maria, running in from across the stream and holding the big shotgun pointed in Grissin's face at close range. Longworth, seeing the big shotgun come into play, slid his horse to a dust-raising halt. "Call off your men!" Maria demanded of Grissin.

Grissin stared wide-eyed down the black open bores of the shotgun barrels. "Everybody! Stop!" he shouted, holding the bag of money against his chest, waving his other hand back and forth toward his men.

"You too!" Maria called over to Mackenzie and Harper, who stood with their guns smoking in their hands.

Mackenzie looked around quickly, seeing Thorpe rise from the dirt with a bloody bullet graze on his bare head. Brewer stood with his Colt in one hand, his rifle in his other, smoke curling from the barrels of both guns.

As he stared at Maria, something in Grissin's demeanor changed. He glanced past her, gave a slight grin and jiggled the money bag. "You have no business here, little lady, this is a private matter."

"I said *hold it*!" Maria warned him, seeing he was about to walk forward toward her.

"No, you hold it," Sheriff Peyton Quinn growled, stepping in behind her as if from out of nowhere. His forearm swung around her neck so quickly and drew her so close to him that Mackenzie and the drovers dared not risk a shot for fear of hitting her. Jerking the shotgun from her hands, he hurled it away and said, "Like Mr. Grissin told you, 'this is a private matter.' "

Chapter 24

Mackenzie stood frozen, as did Tad Harper, Jock Brewer and Holly Thorpe. Standing nearest to their former trail boss, Brewer whispered under his breath, "What now, Mac? We've got a standoff situation."

Mackenzie didn't answer; he knew he didn't have to. Brewer wasn't asking a question. It was just his way of reassuring Mackenzie that his back was covered. Mackenzie trusted the three men standing with him well enough to know that whatever move he made they were behind him to their death if need be. "Make him turn her lose, Grissin," he called out, "before you lose what little you think you've gained here."

Grissin had taken a step forward and jerked the rifle from Maria's hands. He turned slowly and gave Mackenzie a bemused look. "What little I think I have gained?" He jiggled the bag of money. "You still don't seem to understand . . . I'm the one holding all the cards here."

"All you're holding is a bag of paper and ink," said Mackenzie. "You should've left well enough alone. You had the money. All we wanted to do was leave."

"Oh? Hear that, Mr. Duvall?" Grissin mused. "All I have is a bag of paper and ink."

"I heard it," said Duvall. He stepped over in front of Quinn and Maria. He reached down and took Maria's Colt from her holster and pitched it away. "All you've got is paper and ink and all the sheriff's got here is an armful of wildcat." He grinned, cocked his gun and shoved the tip of the barrel up under Maria's chin, tipping her head upward. "But whatever we've got, it sure has gotten us everybody's attention."

"I've got her, Duvall," Quinn said, not liking the way the gunman had stepped in and begun to take things over from him. "Tell him I've got her, Mr. Grissin," the one-eared sheriff called out. "I'm the one who slipped in and caught her by surprise!"

But Grissin didn't answer the angry sheriff. Instead he spun his attention to the sound of the big dog walking down off the hillside and stopping on the other side of the stream. "The colonel's dog," Grissin said, watching the big bloody-mouthed cur sit down and stare at him intently. "I knew the ranger had to be around here somewhere." His voice dropped to a low whisper as he searched the rocky, brushy hillside.

Quinn also turned toward the hillside, Maria in front of him. His face took on a fearful look. Seeing it, Duvall gave a dark chuckle and said, "Are you sure you still want to hold on to her?" As he asked, he reached out to take Maria from him. Quinn didn't protest. He turned Maria over to Duvall and took a step back, his gun still up and cocked.

As Duvall took Maria from him, she called out to the hillside, "Sam, look out! Don't come down here!"

Duvall cut off her words with a gloved hand over her mouth.

The four drovers looked at one another, their guns still in hand.

Longworth took a cautious step backward, recalling the bullet he'd taken the last time the ranger had questioned his intentions in a gunfight. Antan Fellows stood watching the drovers, ready for them to make a move. On the ground, Cannidy struggled up onto his knees, a wide ribbon of blood reaching down the center of his chest.

Grissin stood tensed for a moment, searching the hillside, ready for whatever response Maria's words would bring. Finally he let out a breath and let the bag and his gun slump a bit. "Well, maybe even the bold Ranger Sam Burrack knows when the odds are too greatly stacked against him."

But Longworth was buying none of it. He backed away a step farther and stood in silence. His eyes moved back and forth slowly from the bag of money to the steep hillside, as if weighing his chances at some risky game.

"What do I do with her now, let her go?" Duvall

asked, starting to wonder himself just what might be at work.

"No, don't let her go," said Grissin. He raised his voice toward the hillside. "She stays with us until the ranger decides to *butt out of my business.*" His voice grew louder as he spoke.

"What about breaking the law?" Quinn cut in. "You're the one always wanting to stay clean."

"Oh, we're within the law," said Grissin. "My attorneys will see to that." He dropped the heavy bag of money in the dirt by his feet for a moment and rubbed his palm on his trouser leg. "Let's look at what has happened here," he said. "This woman comes out of nowhere, wielding a shotgun while all we're trying to do is get back what's rightfully mine." He gave Maria a grin. "My lawyers will eat this up."

"Where's your guts, Sheriff?" Duvall asked Quinn with contempt, still holding his gloved hand over Maria's mouth, his gun barrel still beneath her chin. "No wonder this pretty woman rebuked you the last time you met." He leaned his lips near Maria's ear. "I bet she wouldn't treat me that way. Would you, darling?"

"Do you hear this, Ranger?" Grissin called out to the hillside. "If you want to see this beautiful woman unharmed . . . back away."

"No hurry, Ranger," Duvall called out with a dark chuckle.

"We'll let her go farther down the hill trail," said Grissin, giving Duvall an unpleasant look.

"You'll let her go now, Grissin," said the ranger from the opposite side of the clearing, "or you'll die where you're standing."

Grissin and his men turned quickly, caught off-guard, more than just a little surprised by the ranger's having circled the clearing and slipped in behind them unnoticed. The drovers gave only a glance over their shoulders toward the sound of the ranger's voice. But they kept their attention on Grissin and his men. "Ranger Burrack, you say the word, we've all four got you covered," Mackenzie said quietly.

"Obliged," Sam replied, staring straight ahead. He stepped forward, his big Colt out and cocked, the big Swiss rifle in his other hand.

"Whoa, now, Ranger," said Grissin. "You must've heard what I just said."

"I heard," Sam said flatly.

"Then you realize that I've broken no law here," said Grissin. "I made my intention clear to you the last time we met." He tapped his foot sidelong against the canvas money bag. "I came for my money and I had every right to get it back, whatever it took to do so."

"Turn her loose," Sam repeated, the iron in his voice letting Grissin and his men know that he would not be asking again.

"All right, he's turning her loose," Grissin said, trying to appear calm and in control. With a nod from Grissin, Duvall took his forearm from around Maria's throat and stepped away from her. He kept his gun up, cocked and ready, not trusting the cold killing look on the ranger's face. "There she is, Ranger," said Duvall, "no harm done, eh?"

Maria stepped over, stooped down and picked up her Colt from the dirt and shook it off. She turned, facing Duvall with a cold stare.

"Just so long as we understand each other, Ranger," said Grissin. "I take the money and we ride away from here. We'll call all this just one big unfortunate misunderstanding." He gave an insincere grin. "Hell, I'm not even mad at these cowpoke—*drovers*, that is," he said, correcting himself.

Mackenzie only stared, his range Colt still cocked, ready, willing.

"I'll even pay them what they're owed, if it will settle the stew any," Grissin offered.

Harper spit on the ground, letting Grissin know that his money was no good.

"You meant to kill us and ride away without a thought," said Thorpe, blood running down from the graze on his head.

"If I'd meant to kill you, you'd all be dead. What the hell?" Grissin chuckled. "It was all in the heat of the situation." He turned toward the ranger and said, "No jury would ever convict me for anything that's happened here today. Tell them, Ranger."

"Are you all right?" Sam asked Maria without taking his eyes off Grissin and Duvall, knowing the drovers had the other gunmen covered.

"*Si*, I'm all right," Maria replied quietly. She

rubbed her throat where the gunman's forearm had been clamped tightly.

"I don't like to say it," the ranger called out to the drovers, "but what he's telling us is true. There's nothing he's done here that a good attorney can't smooth over for him."

"That figures," Harper said.

"Keep quiet, Tadpole," said Mackenzie.

"At least we did the right thing," Harper said grudgingly in a lowered tone.

"The right thing. That's funny," said Grissin. He laughed. Duvall laughed with him. Quinn and Fellows joined in, both of them relieved that it was nearly over. Only Longworth didn't laugh. He stood watching in silence. Cannidy still kneeled on the ground, his hands clasped to his bloody chest.

"Somebody needs to smarten you fools up a little," Grissin said. "Doing the right thing never got anybody anywhere." He gave them a look of contempt, then said to the ranger, "I'm picking up my money and leaving now, Ranger, unless you think you've got some reason to stop me."

Sam looked at the drovers, seeing all the wounds they'd taken for trying to do right. He knew that he had nothing to charge Grissin with. Grissin was smart. He knew the law and he knew how to play it to suit himself. The thought of Grissin walking away free left a bitter taste in his mouth. But he had no choice. "Yeah, you can go, Grissin," he said. But then, surprising even himself, he said, "I've got the broken money band. That should be enough for me to prove where the money came from."

Grissin started to pick up the bag and leave, but he stopped and gave the ranger a curious look. "You've got what?"

"The money bands, Grissin," Sam said, bluffing. "The bands on the stacks of money in that bag are going to prove that the cash came from the Bank of Santa Fe."

Grissin continued staring at him. "So what if it came from the Bank of Santa Fe?" He offered a feigned grin and added, "All money goes through a bank at some time or other."

"That's right," said Sam, "but the Bank of Santa Fe only started using those new paper money bands the day the bank was robbed. They hadn't used them before, they haven't used them since." He paused for a moment, then said, "But if you're innocent, none of that makes any difference, does it?"

"That's right, it doesn't," Grissin said defiantly.

"Your attorney will be able to explain why you have the only batch of money bands made, that were stolen in a bank robbery," Sam said. He stared at him, unwavering, and said, "Take your money and go. We'll work this out later, let the Bank of Santa Fe decide whether or not to charge you with robbery."

Grissin considered it for a moment, then laughed out loud and said, "Whew, you had me going there, Ranger." He stooped to pick up the bag of money. But then he looked all around and said to the ranger,

"Are you the only lawman one who knows about this—the money bands, that is?"

Sam gave a thin, crafty trace of a smile. "What does it matter? You've got nothing to worry about, being innocent."

"I don't believe you, Ranger," he said. Again he started to raise the bag; again he stopped. He kept his hand off the handle as if denying it belonged to him for a moment. He looked over at Clayton Longworth. "Hey, you ought to know about this, *Detective Chief* Longworth. Tell me something to earn your pay. Is any of this true?"

Longworth looked at Sam closely, their eyes meeting with some secret understanding between the two of them. Sam waited, neither his eyes nor his countenance wavering. "Yes, it's true," Longworth said at length.

Grissin flared. "Damn it, man, why didn't you tell me about this before now?"

"I figured you already knew it," said Longworth. "I haven't seen the money, I never figured anybody to be fool enough to ship stolen stacks of dollars with identifiable bands still around them."

"It appears some fool would . . . ," Duvall whispered to himself, a look of disgust coming to his hard, chiseled face.

Grissin stood opening and closing his fists, considering what to do. As long as the ranger held those bands as evidence, he knew he would be on the hook for the Santa Fe bank robbery. He looked at Sam, seeing in his eyes that both of their thoughts were the same. If he killed the ranger right here, right now, this would never go any further.

"Easy . . . ," Duvall purred in a gravelly voice, as if reading Grissin's deadly thoughts. "Take the money and walk away," he cautioned him. "Do that and you're the winner here."

Grissin had to shake his head a bit to jar his mind away from killing. "You're right," he said to Duvall, "I'm walking away." He stooped enough to pick up the money bag, turned and took a step toward his horse.

"See you in court," the ranger said quietly.

Grissin stopped cold. The bag hit the ground at his feet. "Damn you to hell, Burrack!" he bellowed, coming around fast, his Remington rising, cocking on the upswing.

Chapter 25

Maria saw Grissin coming around toward Sam. She had her Colt out and ready. But she knew Sam didn't want her help, only her backup. This was between him and Davin Grissin, nobody else. In a split second it came to her what the ranger had done. He had become lawman, judge and jury at a point in time where he'd seen that his was the only justice to be had. He had allowed Grissin to try himself in his own mind, and in doing so, Grissin had declared himself guilty.

The drovers had seen Grissin's move coming too, and like Maria they stood prepared, ready if the ranger needed them. Yet they all four knew without saying, without being told that this was no longer their fight; it had stopped being that once the ranger had walked into the clearing.

When Grissin had made a full turn, facing the ranger, his Remington up and aimed, Sam let the hammer fall on his big Colt with sudden finality.

The shot roared up against the rocky hillside and rolled off like a hard clap of thunder. Grissin flew backward. He bounced off the canvas money bag and landed on the rocky ground, before the last of the gunshot had swept itself away over the rugged terrain.

Sam turned the Colt quickly and fired again, seeing Tillman Duvall make a move for his revolver. His second shot nailed the bodyguard in his chest and sent him flying backward. Duvall landed with a hard jolt beside his downed employer.

"Get him!" Quinn shouted at Fellows and Longworth, realizing this might be his only chance to ever get even with the ranger for what had happened between them. But as Quinn's gun came up, Fellows threw his hands in the air and hurried backward.

"Don't shoot!" Fellows shouted.

Sam didn't even get a chance to turn toward Quinn. As Quinn swung his gun up toward Sam, Longworth's Colt streaked up from ten feet away and shot the corrupt sheriff square in his forehead. Quinn hit the ground beneath a red mist of blood. "He's down," Longworth called out to Sam, spinning his Colt down into his holster, letting Sam see that his hand was empty.

Sam took a breath of relief. Maria and the drovers stood looking stunned at Clayton Longworth. "I hope you've got yourself some paperwork, Chief," Sam called out to him.

Longworth stepped forward. "I certainly do," he

said, reaching inside his lapel and coming out with a folded document. "It explains what I'm doing here . . . legally signed by the president of Midwest Detective Agency himself."

As he walked over to the ranger and Maria with the folded paper in hand, Sam stepped over to where Davin Grissin lay dying in the dirt, a trickle of blood running down from the corner of his mouth. With a weak dark chuckle, Grissin said, "You . . . tricked me . . . Ranger."

"I didn't trick you, Grissin," Sam said quietly. "I laid out two choices for you. If the money wasn't stolen, an innocent man would have walked away. If the money was stolen, you knew you had to kill me." As he spoke he took out the broken paper money band and let it fall from his fingertips.

"Sounds . . . like a trick . . . to me," Grissin said in a struggling voice. He watched the four drovers move in and stand around him in a half circle. In an act of contrition he looked at the bloody money bag and said to Sam, "Give . . . these drovers what I . . . owe them."

"We can't take it," Mackenzie cut in firmly.

"Why—why not?" Grissin asked, his eyes fading, his voice growing more and more shallow and blank.

"You still don't get it, do you, Grissin?" the ranger said quietly.

Grissin only stared, unable to comprehend it.

"Tell him, trail boss," Sam said to Mackenzie.

Mackenzie took off his hat out of respect for a dying man in spite of all the trouble that dying man had caused him and his pals. "We can't take the money," he said in a humble tone, "it's not *ours* to take . . . it's not *yours* to give."

Grissin stared at the drovers in disbelief. "Damn . . . fool cowpokes . . . ," he said. "No wonder . . . none of you are worth anything. . . ." His words became a whisper that trailed and died on his lips.

Mackenzie stooped down and closed Grissin's eyes. Sam glanced at Clayton Longworth, then looked down at the letter Longworth had placed in his hand. He read through it and passed it back to Longworth. "I expect I'm not too surprised. I never figured you for riding with the likes of Davin Grissin and this bunch anyway."

"I'm obliged to hear you say it, Ranger," said Longworth. "I used you shooting me as a good way to get in with him. He thought I had some vendetta to settle with you. So my agency agreed that I should play up the idea of being a detective who was tired of always chasing the money, and ready to get out on the other side of the law and make myself some for a change."

"You don't look like a thief," said Sam, appraising the young detective. "But then, neither did he." He nodded down at Grissin.

"Thanks," said Longworth. "It was working. But I don't know what would have happened if you hadn't played a bluff on him. He was as cool as they come—a hard man to pin anything on. When you came up with that part about the money bands, I saw a chance to nail him, and I jumped on it with you."

"I'm glad to hear you're still on this side of the law," Sam replied.

"There's only one side of the law for me," said the detective. "I'm old-fashioned. I still believe a man is only what he holds himself to be."

Sam nodded, liking what he heard. He looked over to where Chester Cannidy had worked himself up onto his feet and stood wobbling in place. In the distance, Antan Fellows rode away fast at the head of a long stream of dust. "Help me . . . please," Cannidy pleaded, clutching his bloody chest with both hands. "I'm shot . . . I need some water. . . ."

Sam, Maria and Longworth watched the wounded drovers walk over to the wounded ranch foreman and sit him down carefully out of the sun against the front of the cabin.

"Let me look at that wound, Chester," Brewer said, opening the wounded man's shirt. To Harper he said, "Tadpole, go get a canteen and a bandanna. Give him some water . . . I'll clean this bullet hole up some and see what it looks like."

"Look at them," Maria said softly. "They let their own wounds go, yet they help the man who led trouble to their door."

"What can you say?" Sam replied.

"It looks like the good guys won," Longworth commented, watching the drovers take care of Chester Cannidy.

"The good guys will always win if I can have my say in it," Sam said. He dropped his gloved hand to the dog's head as the big cur loped over and sat down beside him. The dog had quickly made his rounds, sniffed and examined and probed until he found the area to his satisfaction.

"Yeah, me too," said Longworth.

The two lawmen watched Maria walk over to the drovers and bend down to help them attend to Cannidy. She took the canteen from Harper's hands and lifted it to the wounded ranch foreman's bloody lips.

"I owe you an apology for shooting you, Longworth," Sam said between the two of them. "I saw no other way to go at the time."

Longworth didn't look at him. Instead he watched Maria closely for a moment. Finally he let out a breath and said, "I understand, Ranger. I would have done the same."

Gritty historical action from

USA Today bestselling author

RALPH COTTON

Gunfight at Cold Devil

Fast Guns Out of Texas

Guns On the Border

Killing Texas Bob

Nightfall at Little Aces

Ambush at Shadow Valley

Ride to Hell's Gate

Gunmen of the Desert Sands

“A writer in the tradition of Louis L’Amour and Zane Grey!”

—*Huntsville Times*

National Bestselling Author

RALPH COMPTON

NOWHERE, TEXAS
AUTUMN OF THE GUN
THE KILLING SEASON
THE DAWN OF FURY
BULLET CREEK
FOR THE BRAND
GUNS OF THE CANYONLANDS
RIO LARGO
DEADWOOD GULCH
A WOLF IN THE FOLD
TRAIL TO COTTONWOOD FALLS
BLUFF CITY
THE BLOODY TRAIL
WEST OF THE LAW
BLOOD DUEL
SHADOW OF THE GUN
DEATH OF A BAD MAN
RIDE THE HARD TRAIL
BLOOD ON THE GALLOWS
BULLET FOR A BAD MAN
THE CONVICT TRAIL
RAWHIDE FLAT
OUTLAW’S RECKONING

From

Frank Leslie

THE WILD BREED

Yakima Henry ventures south of the border to save an old flame's brother from a Mexican prison—only to incur the wrath of deadly Apaches, scalp-hunting Rurales, and zealous revolutionaries.

THE KILLING BREED

Yakima Henry has been dealt more than his share of trouble—even for a half-white, half-Indian in the west. Now he's running a small Arizona horse ranch with his longtime love, Faith, and thinks he may have finally found his share of peace and prosperity. But a man from both their pasts is coming—with vengeance on his mind...

THE THUNDER RIDERS

Yakima Henry left his ranch in the White Mountains for supplies, and rode right into a bloody shootout between Saber Creek townsfolk and a gang of banditos who just robbed a stagecoach. But what really riles Yakima is the banditos making off with his prized stallion, Wolf, and a pretty saloon girl.

Available wherever books are sold or at penguin.com